UNTIL PROVEN INNOCENT

UNTIL PROVEN
INNOCENT

SUSAN KELLY

 Villard Books · New York · 1990

M
Kelly

Villard Books is a registered trademark of Random House, Inc.

Library of Congress Cataloging-in-Publication Data

Kelly, Susan.
Until proven innocent / Susan Kelly.
p. cm.
ISBN 0-394-58414-7
I. Title.
PS3561.E39715U68   1990
813'.54—dc20
89-43473

98765432

First Edition

UNTIL PROVEN INNOCENT

1

I'VE HEARD that free-lance writing is one of the worst ways to try to make a living, which just goes to show you shouldn't believe everything you hear. I'm a free-lance writer, formerly a college English teacher. I've been writing full-time for several years now. I make enough money to pay the bills, with something left over that I can either save or spend on my idea of fun. I don't have any vast material ambitions, so it's okay by me that I'm not rich, nor ever likely to be. I have the freedom to do what I want when I feel like it, and, more importantly, the freedom to do what I have to when it's necessary. Whatever else comes along is gravy. My name is Elizabeth Connors.

I write, mostly, about crime. True crime, not detective fiction. I do articles for magazines and newspapers on famous unsolved murders, missing persons, political corruption, the mob, police procedure—that sort of stuff. There's nothing else I'd rather be doing.

This only makes my present situation all the more ironic. What I'm about to put down here is another true-crime story. But it's not going to be fun to tell. I lived through the whole thing, side by side with the principal victim. The victim was someone I care for very much. I always will.

I learned early that you're lucky if you can predict with some assurance the continued existence of just one verity in your life. Perhaps I'm lucky, because I have two—my writing and Jack.

Jack is the victim in this true crime story. And that may be the biggest irony of all. Jack is a cop.

He's a detective-lieutenant in the Cambridge Police Department. He and I have been together for a bit over five years—not married, but the closest thing to it. He's forty-five; I'm thirty-seven.

We met when I was just starting out as a writer. One of the local magazines had asked me to do an article on missing persons. I went to the Cambridge Police Department to do some of the research. After the captain of detectives had established that I wasn't just another weirdo who wandered in off the streets (cops tend to be suspicious of journalists they don't know, and even more of some they *do* know), he directed me to Jack. But Jack had been too busy that day to give me any time, and I'd been dismissed with cool politesse. I was not to be put off, however, so I hit him up again the following day. That second time I caught him in a better mood; he answered all my questions patiently and thoroughly. And after that, he asked me out for a drink.

Jack's wife had died three years before we met. I think I was the first woman he'd been seriously interested in since. I suppose I was in the right place at the right time. You can plan your life with as much attention to detail as if you were charting the course of the space program for the next fifty years, but most of the important stuff in it still seems to happen by accident. That's true of my life, anyway.

The Sunday before the roof fell in, or at least began to sag, stands out in my mind as having been a good one. Even the weather was gorgeous: cool, crisp, and sunny. Maybe I should have knocked on wood, although at the time it never occurred to me to do so. We were going to dinner at a new Portuguese restaurant that night. We spent the afternoon in my living room—Jack watching a football game on TV and me thrashing through the Sunday papers. I was finishing a *Boston Globe Sunday Magazine* article about the New England Mafia when the Patriots lost to the Jets. Badly.

Jack rose from the couch and turned off the television. "You have to be an animal to survive as a quarterback now," he remarked, shaking his head.

"Is that so?" I said. I have about as much interest in football as I do in the Balkan steel industry.

He smiled at me. I tossed the magazine onto the coffee table. "I think I'll change my clothes before we go out."

"Yeah, me too." Jack frowned. "You think I need to shave again?"

I reached up and trailed an index finger along his jaw. "If you're looking forward to any action later this evening, it might be a good idea."

"My God, where's my razor?"

"Where it usually is." I went into the bedroom, yanking my sweatshirt over my head.

"You haven't used this on your legs, have you?" Jack called from the bathroom.

"No, dear. It's all yours." I shimmied out of my jeans, folded them, and dropped them at the foot of the bed. I walked to the dresser and took out a pair of panty hose and a half-slip. Next I opened the closet, frowned at its contents a moment, and then selected a green knit dress that was really nothing more than an oversize turtleneck. With a big leather-and-brass Moroccan belt, it actually looked sophisticated. Anyway, the style and color were right for a tall redhead.

Jack came into the bedroom as I was combing my hair. He had nothing on from the waist up. He went over to the closet and began rummaging through it. "I do have some clean shirts here," he said, digging away. "Don't I?" He and I kept a minimal amount of fresh clothing at each other's houses. I liked the way the muscles under the skin of his shoulders and back flexed and relaxed, and I stopped what I was doing to watch him.

Jack was six-three, with a lean, taut build. Hair and eyes were light brown, the bone structure of his face very well defined. His ancestors were Scots and Prussian, but when I saw him in certain lights and from certain angles, I wondered if there might not be a Plains Indian somewhere in the family tree. It was his cheekbones.

Jack always reacted with surprise when I told him how good-looking he was.

I resumed fixing my hair as he shrugged into a blue cotton shirt. Then I bent forward and peered into the dresser mirror to see if my makeup needed freshening. My face was intact but for lipstick. I reached for it.

"Jack?"

"Yes?"

"Want to walk to the restaurant?"

"Sure." He turned to me and smiled, straightening his tie. "Now I won't lose the parking place right outside."

We left my apartment and walked down the street in the cool twilight.

"So," I said, when we reached the corner, "you were so engrossed in the Patriots all day I never had a chance to ask you what's new in the crime biz."

"Another woman got assaulted on Dana Street late last night."

I paused with one foot off the curb and said, "Oh no. Was it the same guys?"

"Looks like it."

I sighed. "How's the woman?"

"In the hospital with a concussion. Plus assorted cuts and bruises." Jack shook his head, hard. "God. I hate this stuff."

"I know you do." We cut diagonally across the intersection. "How many does this make now?"

"Six."

We were referring to a series of particularly violent attacks on women that had begun that past June. One that month, two the next, two in August, irregularly spaced. Each incident, as the cops called them, followed the same pattern: A woman walking by herself, late at night, would be jumped by two men. After they'd robbed her of whatever cash she was carrying and whatever jewelry she was wearing, the two would beat her until she lost consciousness. One of the women had suffered a broken jaw and three cracked ribs. Another had had her nose and right arm shattered. Another's skull had been fractured; she had stayed in a coma for a week. No one had been raped. No one had died. Yet.

There had been no witnesses (other than the victims) to any of the attacks. The best description of the two guys the women could come up with was that they were in their late teens or early twenties and black. One was about six feet tall and the other about five feet eight or nine. The taller of the pair carried a length of pipe. And used it on the women. Which was probably why none of them had been able to describe their attackers more closely: It's hard to get a really good look at someone when you have blood running into your eyes from a major head laceration.

"Who's investigating?" I asked.

"Teddy and Joe," Jack replied.

I raised my eyebrows. "Not you?"

"Well, I sort of have my hands full as it is." Jack raised one of them, palm up, as if to illustrate his situation. "That nightclub shooting last week," he continued. "The robbery at Cambridge Equity. Then there's always the Hassler murder, in case I get bored."

"How could I have forgotten?" I asked. Edward Hassler had been the president of an up-and-coming biotechnology firm in Kendall Square. Had been, anyway, until someone put a bomb under the hood of his Mercedes one night the previous January. Leaving a late-running board meeting to drive home to Winchester, Hassler only got as far as inserting the key in his car's ignition. A half-second later, he and the Mercedes had disintegrated in a ball of fire.

There were no suspects and no leads, at least as far as Jack had told me. He may well have known something he was keeping to himself, though. That was often the case.

"Well, good luck to you there," I said. "Good luck to Teddy and Joe, too." I shivered a little, remembering the six women and what had been done to them. "You'll all need it."

"I hope," Jack said, "you don't have any reason to go wandering around Dana or Ellery or any of those streets by yourself after dark." He turned his head to give me a close, questioning look. "Do you?"

"No."

"You sure about that?"

I smiled faintly. "The only way I'll go near any of those places at night is if you're with me."

"Well, you'd better not. Alone, I mean. I'm serious, Liz."

We were on a street lined by enormous old maples and beeches. The houses on either side were mostly frame three-deckers. All were expensive, despite their slightly shabby exteriors. The cars in the driveways were of Japanese or German or Swedish extraction.

"We're on the fringes of the attack zone right now, aren't we?" I said.

"I know," Jack said. "Stick right by me."

I laughed. "If you're lucky."

I took his arm. We walked like that the rest of the way to the restaurant. The September night settled cool and still around us.

Monday dawned raw and misty. Not that I was up with the dawn, of course. I was barely up with the noon. Jack and I hadn't gotten to sleep until quite late. He'd left for the police station hours earlier. I don't know how he does it. If I sacked out at two A.M. and had to get up at seven, I'd look like something from the cabinet of Dr. Caligari.

Lucy, my undersized chocolate Lab/Weimaraner cross, was in the living room gnawing on an old tennis ball. She showed no desperate inclination to go outside, so I figured Jack had already walked her. He'd also left a pot of coffee on the stove for reheating. How nice.

I showered, dressed, and had breakfast. Then I went to my work, which entailed a heavy commute back to the kitchen table. At that moment, I had three articles in various stages of composition—a piece for the *Phoenix* on the murder of a Tufts Medical School student; a really depressing (to research as well as write) feature on missing children for *New England Monthly*; and a profile of a woman trial attorney for *Boston Magazine*.

Of the three, the article on the lawyer was the nearest to completion. If I worked steadily, I could probably finish it today. I looked out my kitchen window. The mist hung over the deck like a shroud. It was a definite inducement to stay inside and work.

By five-thirty, I had fifteen pages of reasonably satisfactory material and a terrible kink in my back from sitting so long. I got up and stretched. Lucy was standing by the kitchen door, waving her tail gently and giving me a hopeful look. I opened the door and she raced across the deck and down to the enclosed back yard.

I quickly reread what I had written. I was fairly sure the lawyer would like it. If she didn't, she might sue. But I didn't think I'd libeled her. I slipped the manuscript into a manila envelope and set it aside for mailing tomorrow.

I put out a bowl of food for Lucy and began preparations for Jack's and my dinner. He would probably be here in a half-hour or so. A few minutes before six, I made myself a vodka martini. Lucy returned to the kitchen and dove into her bowl. I took my drink into the living room and turned on the television. The local news was just beginning. I slouched down on the couch to watch it.

The lead story concerned some hearings before the House Ethics Committee. The second story was about a big drug bust in Lynn. They had a lot of drug busts in Lynn. Those and pit-bull attacks on mailmen. The two were probably related.

"And next," the anchorwoman said. "Some serious charges are leveled against members of the Cambridge Police Department. For that story, we go to Louise Traub in Framingham. Louise?"

I sat up straight, nearly spilling my drink.

The next image on the television screen was one of a living room. Wall-to-wall carpet, sofa, coffee table, matching armchairs. The camera panned the room and lingered for a moment on a pink stuffed bunny lying on the floor next to the leg of the coffee table.

Seated on the couch were Louise Traub and a dark-haired man in a plaid sports shirt and jeans.

The reporter said, "I'm here in the Framingham home of Dalton Craig, who has a surprising—and disturbing—story to tell about his years as a detective on the Cambridge police force."

Whatever this was, it sounded interesting.

The camera swiveled to focus on the man sitting next to the reporter. His dark hair was short and receding at the temples, forming a sharp widow's peak. His face was bony, almost skull-like, and

his eyes deep-set. He seemed in good physical shape except for a slight beer bulge.

I set my glass on the end table.

"Mr. Craig," said the reporter. "Could you repeat for our viewers what you told me earlier today?"

Craig appeared to take a deep breath. I leaned forward, as if by doing so I'd be better able to hear what he would say.

"Between the years of 1972 and 1978," he began, in flat, methodical tones, "I was a member of a special, supersecret intelligence-gathering unit within the Cambridge Police Department."

Louise Traub nodded seriously. "And what was the purpose of this unit?"

"It was basically a domestic spy operation. We infiltrated various groups and accumulated information on them."

"And were these groups suspected of committing illegal activities?"

Craig's face was as solemn as Traub's. "No. These were civic groups, political groups, community groups, labor groups. Even some religious groups."

"If they weren't committing illegal activities, why did you spy on them?"

Craig sighed deeply and lowered his eyes. "Because they were all at one time or another, critics of the police department."

"Could you explain?"

"Well, there was one group that was pushing for a civilian review board. We were supposed to infiltrate it and get information on its members."

"And what did the police department plan to do with that information, once it was obtained?"

Craig looked up from his lap and paused a beat before answering. Then he said, "Use it against the people we surveilled. Use it to, uh, discredit the enemies of the department."

"Yes." Louise Traub nodded again. "Mr. Craig, can you tell us the names of the officers involved in this operation?"

Once more, Craig hesitated. "Myself," he said. "Two of the other detectives."

"And they were?"

Craig turned his head so that he was no longer face to face with the reporter but gazing directly at the camera lens. "A sergeant named Samuel Flaherty," he said. "A lieutenant named John Lingemann."

My whole body jerked.

"These are very serious allegations you're making," Louise Traub said. "Have you any proof of them?"

"I've been advised not to answer that question at this point in time, Louise."

"I see. Who else in the police department knew of the existence of this secret intelligence unit?"

"The person who was chief then. It was his idea. He's dead now."

"No one else?"

"No. Like I said, it was a supersecret operation."

"Secret even from all the other members of the police department?"

"That's correct."

My breath was harsh and ragged in my throat.

"Were there any other special targets of this probe?" Louise Traub persisted.

"A man named Albert Parkes."

"And why was Mr. Parkes targeted?"

"He was a suspect in a murder."

"But," Louise Traub countered. "It's not illegal for a law enforcement agency to surveil a suspect in a criminal investigation."

"That's, uh, correct, Louise," Craig said. "But it *is* illegal for law officers to destroy surveillance reports on a subject when those reports would tend to clear the subject of the charges against him."

Louise Traub glanced quickly at her notes. "Mr. Parkes was accused of and tried for conspiracy to commit the murder of newspaper reporter Stephen Larrain, which took place in March of 1977."

"That's correct," Craig repeated. His voice was mechanical. He sounded like someone with no acting talent reading from a badly prepared script.

"And you are claiming that documents that would have helped to

exonerate Mr. Parkes or at least indicated his innocence were destroyed by the Cambridge police?"

"I saw those reports being shredded."

"By whom?"

"You want a name?"

"If you can give me one."

Craig's face was flat and expressionless. "By Lieutenant John Lingemann."

I stopped breathing.

"Was Lieutenant Lingemann acting on his own initiative?"

"I'd prefer not to speculate on that matter, Louise."

The reporter cocked her head slightly and gave Craig an intense look. "Tell me, Mr. Craig. Why, after thirteen years, are you coming forward with these charges against the Cambridge Police Department?"

Craig narrowed his eyes. "Because I've lived with this too long, Louise. Too many innocent people were hurt by what we did to them."

"Are you referring specifically to Albert Parkes?"

"I can't comment on that, Louise."

"Thank you for telling us your story," the reporter said.

The next shot was of Louise Traub standing on the front lawn of a ranch house, Craig's I assumed. A slight breeze fluffed and ruffled her hair. Her face was unremittingly grave. The blond curls dancing around it made an inapposite frame.

She began speaking, but I wasn't listening. I got up, crossed the room, and snapped off the television set, almost hard enough to break the knob. Then I snatched my glass from the end table and threw it into the fireplace as hard as I could.

2

WHEN JACK showed up at a quarter to seven I was practically in tears. He took one look at me and said, "It's not that bad."

"Not that bad? Jack, did you watch the six o'clock news?"

He nodded.

"Then how can you say it's not bad?" I knuckled the incipient moisture from my eyes. "You heard what that Craig—that piece of garbage—said about you?"

"I heard." He shrugged out of his coat and hung it in the closet. Then he came over to me and put his hands on my shoulders. "This is really not the end of the world."

I gestured at the television set. "But—"

He smiled faintly. "I know, I know. Come on. I'll make you a drink."

"No. I'll make you one." I glanced at the twinkling fragments of glass in the fireplace. "And one for myself."

We went into the kitchen. I got out the bourbon and vodka. Jack sat at the table.

"I knew early this afternoon it was going down," he said. "Louise Traub called me."

I took a deep breath. "Well, she would have to get your side of things."

"I told her I had no comment. Very persistent woman, though. Ever met her?"

I shook my head. "No. I don't know too many TV people. I suppose she called Sam Flaherty, too. Did she?"

"Sam gave her the same answer I did." Jack looked at me very closely. "Are you all right?"

I leaned against the counter. "I'm fine," I said. "I'll be even better as soon as you tell me who Dalton Craig is, other than a lying maggot, and what all this is about."

Jack grimaced and shook his head slightly. "Liz, I'll tell you about Dalton Craig later."

I folded my arms across my chest. "All right. But I want to say one thing before you begin. I know you were never a member of any supersecret intelligence-gathering operation that violates people's civil rights. And I also know you never destroyed any evidence in any kind of criminal case."

He inclined his head and smiled. "Thanks for that unsolicited vote of confidence."

"Oh, knock it off." I turned back to the counter and resumed making the drinks. As I reached for the bourbon bottle, I noticed that my hand was trembling slightly.

"I'm not sure how much Louise Traub has dug up already," Jack said, "but this Dalton Craig thing is just part of a long, complicated story. She's going to have her work cut out for her." Jack looked down at the table and then back up at me again. "Does the name Stephen Larrain mean anything to you?"

I glanced at him over my shoulder. "First I ever heard it was on the news tonight. He was murdered in March of 1977 by somebody named Alfred—no, *Albert* Parkes." My fingers tightened around the bourbon bottle. "Mr. Parkes being the individual you were supposed to have helped convict by suppressing evidence that would have proven him innocent."

Jack made a gesture with his left hand as if he were brushing away a gnat. "Yeah, set that aside for a minute. Stephen Larrain was a reporter and a columnist for the *Suffolk Tribune*. Remember that paper?"

"Oh, sure." I couldn't help smiling, very briefly and reflexively, as

if someone had poked the corner of my mouth. "Also known as the *Radical Rag* or the *Suffolk Daily Worker*. Didn't it fold about five or six years ago?"

"Uh-huh. But when it was in its heyday, in the early and mid-seventies, Larrain was one of its stars. He wrote mostly about business and politics from a local angle."

"Before my time as a reporter," I said, "I wasn't even living in this country in the mid-seventies. Much less reading the local papers." I handed Jack a glass of bourbon and ice.

"Thanks." He sipped the drink and set it on the table. "Anyway, Larrain was shotgunned to death in his kitchen one afternoon. Right here in Cambridge."

I finished making my martini and brought it to the table. The tremor in my hands had subsided. I sat down across from Jack. "Go on."

"Three days after Larrain was murdered, we picked up a guy named Joyce for it. Phillie Joyce. A sleaze, a small-time hood."

"How'd you know he'd done it?"

"A witness saw a guy running from Larrain's back door. She came forward the next afternoon and described him, and it sounded a hell of a lot like old Phillie. So we showed her some pictures, and she jumped right on the ones of Joyce. Later she identified him in a lineup. We also found the shotgun, plus there were Phillie's prints all over Larrain's kitchen. So he got charged and arraigned and indicted. Then in December of '77 he made a deal with the prosecutor, which was to plead guilty to a second-degree murder charge and accept a twenty-year sentence in exchange for giving the prosecutor the name of the guy who'd hired him to kill Larrain."

"Albert Parkes?"

"Right. But Joyce also said that Parkes was acting as the middleman for the person who really wanted Larrain taken out."

"Who was that?"

"Otway Gilmore."

"Holy shit!"

Jack smiled. "I sort of thought you'd put it that way."

Otway Gilmore was a local real estate developer. He had money
the way Lake Superior had water. He was sometimes referred to as
Massachusetts's answer to Donald Trump. To me he was more of a
Howard Hughes figure. Gilmore kept a very low profile. Everybody
knew his name, some knew his face, very few knew the man himself.
He was famous without being visible, and he went to great lengths to
keep it that way.

"This is so bizarre," I said. "Did Joyce say why Gilmore wanted
Larrain killed?"

"Yeah," Jack replied. "Larrain had apparently gone after Gilmore
several times in his column. Real scathing stuff about Gilmore being
a crook and a slumlord."

"Was it true?"

"Far as I can tell, yes. What Gilmore would do was buy up
tenements in Somerville and Chelsea and Revere. Then he'd evict all
the original tenants or just drive them out by doubling and tripling the
rents. But he wouldn't do anything to renovate or even maintain the
buildings, which I guess were in pretty crappy shape to begin with."

"So who could he get to replace the original tenants?" I asked.
"Who'd rent a high-priced dump?"

"Illegal aliens," Jack said.

"But how could they afford Gilmore's prices?"

"They could if they had six families living in one five-room apartment."

"Oh," I sighed. "Of course. Naturally. That old dodge."

"Yeah." Jack took a swallow of bourbon. "You know, if you look
at the whole scheme objectively, it's beautiful in a way."

"It is?" I said dubiously.

"Sure. Illegals are the perfect people to gouge. Who're they going
to bitch to about it? They can't go to the Fair Housing Commission
or the Rent Control Board, now can they?"

"No." I could see the point.

"And," Jack said, "if Gilmore let the buildings fall down around
their ears, they couldn't complain to the housing authority about
that, either, could they?"

"No. So Larrain was on to all these shenanigans?"

"Oh, yeah. He interviewed some of Gilmore's tenants—"

"He must have promised them anonymity," I interrupted.

"Sure, and most of them were from places like El Salvador and the Dominican Republic and Ecuador, and with Larrain being a Spanish surname . . ." He shrugged. "You can figure it."

I nodded. "Yeah. In their eyes, Larrain would be more trustworthy than any Anglo, no matter how sympathetic."

"Uh-huh."

I scratched my forehead. "All right. I can see that all this would result in some embarrassment for Gilmore if it became public knowledge. But . . ." I wrinkled my nose doubtfully. "Would Gilmore kill somebody, or rather, have somebody killed, just because that person had embarrassed him?"

"Good point," Jack said. "But it was a little more than that. In the last column he did, Larrain accused Gilmore of murder."

I arched my eyebrows.

"Seems that one of Gilmore's buildings in Chelsea burned."

"Arson?"

"In a way. The fire was caused by overloaded electrical wiring, which was faulty to begin with. This was in January, you know, and everybody in the building had a couple of space heaters going, 'cause of course the furnace didn't work." Jack rubbed his chin slowly. "The place went up like tissue paper."

I was staring at him. "You mentioned murder. Who died?"

"An eighteen-month-old girl."

"Oh, God. And then?"

"Nothing."

"Gilmore wasn't prosecuted?"

"Nope, not even investigated. There was no one to testify against him. The illegals all cleared out. Nobody knew *nada*."

"Shit," I said. "So it all got written off as an accident? Caused by careless tenants?"

"Unfortunately, yes."

"Swell."

Jack nodded. "Well, to get back to Parkes. He was arrested, tried for, and convicted of first-degree murder. Got sentenced to life in November, 1978. *But*—a year later, the conviction got overturned by the Mass. Supreme Court." Jack made a wry mouth. "They ruled that the defense attorneys hadn't been given sufficient opportunity to cross-examine Phillie Joyce. So they ordered a new trial. Then Joyce dropped a bomb of his own."

"Oh, Lord. What?"

Jack looked suddenly tired. "He said he'd only testify against Parkes one more time *if* they'd agree to shorten his sentence."

"Oh, no."

"Oh, yes. So the prosecutor decided, not without some reason, that Joyce could no longer be considered a credible witness. The murder charge against Parkes was dismissed without prejudice."

"Meaning it could be refiled at any future date, right?"

"Exactly. But it never was."

"So where is Phillie Joyce now? Walpole?"

Jack shook his head. "He died maybe eight, nine years ago. Heart attack."

I stretched my legs out under the kitchen table. "What about Gilmore? Clearly no charges were ever brought against him."

"No. When Larrain got shot, Gilmore and his wife and their daughters were cruising around the Adriatic. They'd been out of the country for several months at that point."

"So?" I sat up straight. "That doesn't mean Gilmore couldn't have gotten in touch with Parkes from overseas and arranged the murder. Or maybe they'd worked it out before he went on his cruise."

"Of course," Jack agreed. "But, like you said before, nobody in the prosecutor's office ever really believed that Gilmore had all that much of a motive for wanting Larrain killed. I mean, sure, Larrain had accused Gilmore of murder, but it wasn't a charge with any kind of legal weight."

"No, just moral and ethical."

"Yeah. Well, the point is, Gilmore wasn't in any danger from whatever Larrain wrote about him. All he had to do was ignore it.

Larrain was a hothead anyway. He was always accusing people of being thieves or murderers or swindlers." Jack finished his drink.

"Would you like another?" I asked, indicating his glass.

"Maybe half a one."

As I was making the drink, I had a thought. "Jack? If Gilmore was innocent—at least of conspiring to kill Larrain—that means that Parkes was acting on his own. But if that's true, then why did Phillie Joyce bring up Gilmore's name in the first place? It doesn't make sense."

"Yeah, the one does seem to contradict the other."

"Probably something there we don't know about."

"Probably a *lot* there we don't know about. As per usual."

I glanced at the clock over the refrigerator. It was seven-thirty. "You interested in dinner?"

"Sure. What are we having?"

"Something unbelievably exotic. Fish, rice, and salad."

"Sounds good."

The salad was already made, in a container in the fridge. I put a pot of water on for the rice. "You said that the murder charge against Parkes was dismissed. What had been his defense, originally?"

"Oh, it was beautiful," Jack said. "I've heard some great ones in my time, but this?" He shook his head. "A masterpiece. You understand that Parkes had always maintained Gilmore wasn't involved in the Larrain murder any more than he himself was, that Joyce's story was pure bullshit from beginning to end."

"Right."

"Okay. So—you're going to love this—Parkes's story was that he'd been approached outside his home one morning by, and I quote from the record, a well-dressed stranger. The guy had a briefcase with him that he wanted Parkes to deliver to Phillie Joyce."

"Did this morning happen to turn out to be the one after the day Larrain was murdered?"

"How did you guess?" Jack asked. "Although of course Parkes claims he had no idea of that at the time."

"Of course not," I said.

"According to Parkes," Jack continued, "this stranger handed him a card that identified him—the stranger, I mean—as, and I quote again, a member of a prominent law firm."

"Which one?"

"Well, Parkes couldn't quite remember. Also, he'd managed to lose the card."

"Naturally," I said. "What else?"

"Anyway, the stranger wanted Parkes to deliver the briefcase to Phillie Joyce at a bar in Saugus that night. And Parkes agreed."

"Sure," I said, swallowing some of my martini. "Who wouldn't? I myself hang around the Copley Plaza looking for opportunities to do favors for well-dressed strangers."

"Yeah, me too. Parkes contends that the stranger said he would have taken the briefcase to Joyce, but that he had to go out of town that day and couldn't keep the appointment. And when he, the stranger, told that to Joyce, Joyce suggested he ask his—Joyce's—good buddy Al Parkes to make the delivery. Old Al was the kind of easygoing, stand-up guy always ready to do a favor for a friend, even if it meant going out of his way."

"Parkes and Joyce were *friends?*"

"Parkes owns a construction company. Joyce worked as a foreman for him for a while back in the early seventies. Parkes never denied that he and Joyce knew each other."

"What was in the briefcase?"

"Parkes claims that it was locked and that he never tried to open it. He assumed it was full of important legal papers."

I stopped with my glass midway between table and mouth and peered at Jack. "Come again?"

He snickered.

I shook my head slowly. "And Parkes's attorney actually had the balls to present that case in court?"

"He made it very credible-sounding, Liz, I give him that. Parkes *was* known for being a good old boy. A real down-home type, you know, always ready to pick up the tab for a party or help somebody out of a jam. And the lawyer played up that angle very well."

The water was boiling. I measured out a cupful of rice and dumped it into the pot. Then I got the pan of halibut steaks from the refrigerator and shoved it under the broiler.

"Joyce must have had his own version of what you just told me," I said. "What was it?"

"Up to a point, it didn't differ a whole lot from what Parkes said. They *did* meet that night at the Blue Star on Route One in Saugus, and Parkes *did* give Joyce the briefcase. Only, according to Joyce, Parkes knew damn well what was in it, which didn't happen to be legal papers."

"More like, legal tender," I said.

"Uh-huh." Jack nodded. "A fifteen-grand payoff."

"Wow." I finished my drink. "Pretty high-ticket assassination."

Jack rattled the ice in his glass. "And Joyce claimed that when Parkes handed him the fifteen thousand, Parkes thanked him on behalf of Otway Gilmore. The exact quote, as Joyce told it, was 'Thanks for a job well done, from Otway Gilmore.' "

I leaned sideways to open the broiler door and check on the fish. "Interesting," I said. I let the broiler slam shut. "But Jack, it still doesn't explain why thirteen years later a sleazebag ex-cop decides to crawl out of the woodwork and accuse you of destroying evidence and committing civil rights violations."

Jack let out a deep breath. "Can it wait till after dinner?"

I was silent for a moment. Then I said, "Whatever you like." I rose. "I'll toss the salad."

He smiled at me. "And I'll wash the dishes."

I had just opened the refrigerator door when the phone rang. I was about to say something smart like, you bet your ass you will, but I stopped and looked at Jack.

"Oh, shit," he said. "I hope that's not for me."

"I'll see." I shut the refrigerator.

As I walked to the living room, it occurred to me that the caller might be one of my reporter acquaintances who knew about my connection with Jack and was hoping to get in touch with him here. Hoping perhaps for a quote or comment from Jack for the Dalton

Craig story, which would probably be appearing in both of tomorrow's papers.

The caller wasn't a reporter; it was the lieutenant on the desk at the police station. He *did* want to speak to Jack.

I went back to the kitchen. "For you," I said. "Lieutenant Holdsworth."

"Damn."

I was tossing the salad when he returned. He was putting on his trenchcoat.

"Oh, no," I said. "You're kidding." I waved the wooden spoon I was holding at the broiler. "We're just about to eat."

"You can have my share," Jack said. "Somebody just got stabbed to death on Columbia Terrace."

3

HE DIDN'T come back that night. I knew he wouldn't. I gave the leftover rice and fish to Lucy, and stored the salad for tomorrow's lunch. Then I went to bed. I slept surprisingly well.

The next morning, with some trepidation, I went out for the papers. My nervousness turned out to be unfounded, because neither the *Globe* nor the *Herald* ran articles on the Dalton Craig mess. I thought that odd; both papers adored stories on police corruption. Then I realized that they must have been holding off in anticipation of new and even juicier revelations. I know how newspaper editors work.

At nine-thirty I called Jack at the station. The secretary told me he was out on the street and not expected back till very late in the afternoon. I didn't leave a message. I'd see him in the evening.

I let Lucy out to gallop around the back yard and sat down at the kitchen table with my writing materials. I was astonished to find I was actually able to do some work. Perhaps I'd been infected by Jack's play-it-as-it-lays stoicism. I cranked out five decent pages for the *Phoenix* on the death of the Tufts medical student. Another three and it would be done. But by early afternoon, I'd run out of steam. In any case, it was a depressing piece to write, although not nearly so much so as the one for *New England Monthly* on the missing children.

A little before two o'clock, I walked to Central Square. I took the

article on the lawyer to the post office for mailing to *Boston Magazine*. Then I went to the police station.

Sergeant Samuel Flaherty was a tall, thin guy in his early fifties, with graying red hair and a long pallid melancholy face like that of an Irish basset hound. He was at his desk in the C.I.D., eating a take-out burger and fries and browsing through the *Cambridge Chronicle*. For someone who'd just been slandered on the six o'clock news he didn't look particularly traumatized.

As I approached his desk, he glanced up and smiled.

"Hey, doll," he said.

"Hi." I smiled back at him. "I heard there was some excitement over on Columbia Terrace last night."

"Oh, that." Flaherty shook his head disgustedly. "Assholes. Nothing you'd want to write about."

"What happened?"

He popped a French fry into his mouth, chewed, and swallowed. "Asshole Number One parked his moped in the hallway of his apartment building. Asshole Number Two came along and told him to move it. Asshole Number One told Asshole Number Two to go fuck himself. Asshole Number Two stuck a knife into Asshole Number One."

I made a face. This was the kind of crime the cops always referred to as "two guys doing it to each other." I said, "Was Asshole Number Two arrested?"

"Oh, yeah. No problem."

"That's good."

Flaherty took a bite of his hamburger. I felt very comfortable sitting around schmoozing with him. I did with most Cambridge cops, but Flaherty was special. He was Jack's partner and closest friend. They had gone through a lot of cases together. And now they were in trouble together.

"Dalton Craig," I said.

"For Chrissake," Flaherty said. "Not while I'm eating."

I laughed. "Be right back," I said. I went to the far corner of the room, where an alcove had been fixed up as a makeshift kitchenette

and where coffee was always kept brewing. I found a Styrofoam cup
and poured myself some. It was pretty good stuff, in contrast to the
television-movie-detective fiction cliché that all cop coffee is invari-
ably lousy.

I snagged a chair from behind one of the empty desks and hitched
it up beside Flaherty's. The detectives' desks weren't actually desks,
but library carrels. I always wondered if they'd bought them at the
Widener Library Discount Daze.

Flaherty crumpled the paper his burger had been wrapped in and
tossed it into the wastebasket.

"How you doin'?" he said.

"Fine," I replied. "Then again, I wasn't slandered on the six
o'clock news last night, so why shouldn't I be fine?"

Flaherty made a face. "Buncha bullshit." He held out the little
bag of French fries.

"No, thank you."

"Don't tell me *you're* on a diet."

"No." I smiled. "But I just had lunch."

Flaherty poked the last three limp potato sticks into his mouth and
tossed the little grease-spotted bag after the burger paper. He swigged
from a can of sugar-free Dr Pepper and said, "What else can I do for
you?"

"I agree with you—this business with Craig is a big bunch of
bullshit. But that doesn't make it any the less troublesome, does it?"

Flaherty shrugged. "Don't make it any the less a pain in the ass,
that's for damn sure."

"How seriously is the department taking it?" I asked.

Flaherty shrugged again. "As seriously as it has to. We have the
lawyer for the Superior Officers Association. And there's the City
Attorney. If it comes to that."

I hesitated a moment. Then I asked the question I hadn't wanted
to ask Jack. "You and Jack," I said. "You're not going . . . ah, you're
not going to get into any trouble over this? I mean, within the
department?"

"What do you mean?"

"Well," I said awkwardly. "You're not—" I brought the rest out in a rush: "You two won't get suspended or fired or anything, will you?"

Flaherty stared at me, and then, amazingly, laughed. "No, doll," he said. "We won't." Reading my face, he added, "Liz, people are always accusing cops of crap. It's a fact of life. Sometimes it's justified and sometimes not. Mostly not. But what you gotta see is if the department automatically suspended somebody every time some jerk went on TV with a story about this or that, you wouldn't have a very large working police force. Well, that's an exaggeration. But close, doll."

"Oh," I said. "All right. That's good to know."

Flaherty shook a cigarette from the pack lying on his desk and lit it. There was a big NO SMOKING sign on the doors of the C.I.D. The city had banned it in public buildings, and there was a fine for violators of the ordinance. Flaherty didn't seem worried about being busted, though. He leaned back and blew a large puff of smoke at the ceiling.

"Can I ask you some more questions?" I said.

Flaherty smiled, showing yellow teeth. "Sure you can. Shoot."

"Well, now that you're finished eating, who's Dalton Craig?"

"A bag of shit. Pardon my French."

"I'll buy that. But . . . what's the rest of the story. Who *is* this guy?"

Flaherty leaned over and tamped out his cigarette on the inside of the wastebasket. A small shower of sparks wafted down onto the discarded food wrappings. Then he pushed back his chair to give himself room to put his feet up onto the writing surface of the library carrel. He took another gulp of Dr Pepper.

"Dalton Craig," he said, "worked for the Cambridge Police Department from 1968 to 1983."

"Oh, he started the same year Jack did."

"Yeah. He put in fifteen years and then left to join a private security company." Flaherty finished his soda and set the can on the windowsill. "Can't say the department was sorry to see him go, either."

"Why was that?"

"Guy turned into a fuckin' lunatic his last few years. We were getting citizen complaints about him every two minutes. And, I mean, you know, ninety percent of those complaints are crap. Like somebody always claims they been pushed around or verbally abused or they had their civil rights violated. Or, Jesus, somebody calls up on Saturday night to bitch about a noisy party, and we go out there and tell them to keep it down, and then the fuckin' guy who called up gets pissed because we didn't arrest and execute everybody at the party on the spot, and he starts yelling at one of the cops, and—" Flaherty stopped abruptly. He looked at me and then said, "You've heard this stuff before."

"Once or twice," I said, smiling. I'd heard it more than that, and very seldom from Jack. I'd taught report writing in the police academy for two years. One of the things I'd taught the recruits was how to write up complaint forms.

"Okay," Flaherty said. "Craig was something different. Like I said, he was a maniac."

"What was he doing?"

"Oh, stuff like arresting people for trespassing, and banging them around, and threatening to shoot them—or so they said. Or like this other time—this was really good—he busted a pregnant woman standing on a street corner for loitering. She was a teacher from Rindge and Latin who was waiting for her husband to pick her up after work. That was nice. We almost *did* get sued over that one."

I sipped my coffee. "And now he's accusing Jack of destroying evidence in a major criminal case," I said.

"Yeah," Flaherty replied. "Bag of shit, like I said."

"But what made Craig such a crazy?"

"Ah, who the hell knows? He was an okay guy at the beginning. Sometimes cops just get that way."

It was certainly possible. I'd met up, in my time, with crazy doctors, and mad CPAs, and psychotic academics, none of whose dementia had been detected by any kind of professional distant early-warning system. The brother- and sisterhood of writers to which I currently belonged had more than its share of bedbugs. So why shouldn't there be cuckoo cops?

I knew the answer to that. Deranged teachers and medics and accountants and authors didn't automatically carry guns. And under no circumstances had they the power of arrest and detention. That made a big difference in the public's eye. As it rightly should.

I leaned forward and put my elbows on my knees, giving Flaherty a very intense look. "Do you think it's Craig's being cuckoo that accounts for why he's doing what he's doing to Jack now?"

Flaherty took out another cigarette and lit it. He dropped the match into the slot in the top of the empty Dr Pepper can. I heard a faint *ting* and an even fainter hiss as the match hit bottom and expired.

"I don't know," Flaherty said. "Maybe. There was trouble between them even before Craig went off his rocker, I know that."

"Like what?"

"They went through the academy together," Flaherty said. "They both did fine there, maybe Jack did a bit better, but there was no great big gap between them."

"Uh-huh."

"The thing was," Flaherty continued, in an almost musing tone, "at the time, Craig—it was like he looked up to Jack, you know? I mean, here was Jack, this big tall strong handsome guy who could shoot straight and top-score in all the unarmed combat classes, and had the street-smarts, but he also, you know, he had a like . . ." Flaherty paused for a moment, his basset-hound face scrunched in thought. "Oh, hell," he said, finally. "Jack is . . . I mean, hell, he's an educated guy. Craig wasn't."

I had the feeling that Flaherty was trying to say something more, only he didn't quite have the words to do it.

"Was Craig *jealous* of Jack?" I asked.

"In the beginning?" Flaherty looked thoughtful. "I don't know. Maybe. If he was, it didn't show. Toward the end, yeah, there was a lot of resentment."

"What was it like in the beginning?"

"They were friends. Buddies. What can I say?"

I nodded. "When did things start to go sour?"

Flaherty's reflective frown became a scowl. "Seems like it was about two years after they were out of the academy."

"Did something happen then?"

"Jack got assigned to the detectives."

"Oohh," I said. "And I suppose Craig was still on the patrol force? And not happy about being there?"

"You got it."

"*Was* Craig eventually moved to the detectives?"

"Yeah, a couple years after that. By that time, Jack was a sergeant, though."

"Which didn't help the situation, I suppose."

"Nope."

I shook my head, slowly. "So things were pretty tense, huh?"

Flaherty pursed his mouth as if he had a bad taste in it. Metaphorically speaking, he probably did. Either that or the memory of the greaseburger had come back to haunt him. "Okay, to give you one example. One night Craig went out with some of the guys, you know, to sit around and have a few beers and gas about the department. Anyway, Craig got pissy-eyed drunk, and in the middle of things, stood up and proposed a toast, to Jack, the best ass-kisser in the Cambridge Police Department. 'Cause why else would he have gotten such quick promotions?"

I was speechless with disbelief for a moment. Then I felt a smoky curl of anger inside me. "What crap." I could hear my voice becoming high and furious. "Jack wouldn't know how to toady if you gave him a card with printed instructions."

"Well, sure," Flaherty replied. He looked a little taken aback by my vehemence. "Everybody knows Jack knows that. I'm just telling you where Dalton's head was at the time."

"Yes, I understand," I said, making an effort to calm down.

"I could tell you other stories about Craig," Flaherty said. "But you get my drift."

I drank the rest of my coffee and dropped the cup into the wastebasket. "When did Craig start to go really crazy?"

Flaherty smiled sardonically. "I think it was around the time Jack made lieutenant."

"In—what? 1981?" I did some mental arithmetic. "So Craig must have left the department two years later."

Flaherty considered that for a moment. "Yeah, sounds right. Also, Liz, you know Craig finally did get promoted to sergeant. But then he got transferred back to uniform."

"Oh, God," I said. "That must have been a blow. And there was Jack, staying on in the C.I.D., only as a lieutenant, of course. Oh, that must have made the whole situation really jolly."

The phone on Flaherty's desk rang. As he reached to answer it, I got up and moved over to the window. I looked out at the intersection of Western Avenue and River Street. Some workmen were busy tearing up the island there.

Flaherty concluded his call. I walked back to his carrel and stood beside it, leaning my right elbow on the top shelf of the desk.

"You know, Sam," I said. "What you've told me is sort of reassuring."

Flaherty gave me a look that was initially one of puzzlement. Then, slowly, his features regrouped into an expression of understanding.

"You see," I said, "when it comes out that Craig had a thirteen-year-long totally unjustified grudge against Jack, that's going to blow him and his story out of the water."

"We can hope," Flaherty said.

"It will," I replied firmly.

He smiled as if he wanted to believe me.

I gathered up my shoulder bag. "I have stuff to do this afternoon. And I imagine you do, too."

"A few things." He rose and took my free hand, with a kind of clunky gallantry that I found absolutely endearing. "Thank you for coming to see me, doll. It's always a pleasure."

"Likewise," I said, grinning.

"I don't have to tell you not to be a stranger."

"Of course you don't."

I was halfway through the swinging doors, one foot in the hall and the other still in the C.I.D., when the little red you-forgot-something-dummy light flashed on in my brain. I backed into the room.

"Sam?"

"Yuh?" He looked up from the reports he was reading, surprised to see me still there.

I crossed the room to his desk slowly, feeling troubled.

"What's on your mind?" Flaherty said.

"Well, I'm not exactly sure," I said. "Probably nothing. But . . ." I hesitated. "Well, it's this. Last night, when Jack was telling me about Stephen Larrain and Albert Parkes, he gave me a pretty detailed picture of things. But he seemed—oh, I don't know—reluctant, I guess, to talk about Craig." I shrugged. "I was surprised that he was so unforthcoming, that's all."

Flaherty nodded.

"Craig was a creep," I said. "You guys were glad to get rid of him. Why should Jack be reluctant to tell me that?" I made a small circle in the air with my hand. "All right, I know, normally you have to torture Jack to get him to say something bad about a fellow cop. But this situation—well, it's different, isn't it?"

Flaherty looked at me for a moment, and then sighed, long and heavy. "I forgot, you didn't know. I guess I thought for some reason you did."

I returned his stare. "You're right. Obviously I don't know. Know what?"

"Craig was best man at Jack and Diana's wedding. He was her stepbrother."

4

OUTSIDE ON GREEN STREET it was bright and blowy. I turned right and walked against the wind to Western Avenue. There was a luncheonette on the opposite side of the street. I went in there to get some coffee and to try to compose my thoughts.

In my mind, I kept repeating the sentence "Dalton Craig is Jack's stepbrother-in-law" over and over, like a mantra, in the hope that by so doing I could blunt its edges and assimilate its impact.

A waitress in a polyester uniform that had fit her snugly two sizes earlier offered me a menu. I ordered a tuna sandwich on toasted wheat and coffee. I'd lied to Flaherty earlier; I hadn't had lunch.

I folded my arms on the Formica counter. A few seats down from me, a wizened old man in a well-pressed brown suit studied the race results in the *Herald*.

The waitress brought me the coffee first, along with two miniature plastic buckets of light cream and a pink paper packet of artificial sweetener. I stirred them both into the coffee in time to the rhythm of my silent chant.

Although Jack and I talk about a lot of things, including our pasts, I wasn't particularly surprised that he'd never mentioned Craig's existence to me. Above and beyond his ingrained reluctance to criticize even a bad cop, he might have thought the whole subject too petty and sordid to bear discussion. If I were Jack, I'd have wanted to

forget the fact that I'd ever known, much less been friends with, somebody like Craig.

Craig had been a family member of sorts. And the question this gave rise to was how the situation had affected not just Jack himself but Diana and Jack as a couple. It must have been a source of tension between them, or at least a strain, especially if Diana had cared at all for Craig. God, what a charming position for her to be in, loving a husband and a stepbrother and having the two of them at sword's point. Of course your first loyalty went to your husband. Still . . .

Jack didn't talk about his marriage very much. Enough, though, for me to have gathered that it had been a good one. As far as I knew, it had ended only because of Diana's death. Crossing Garden Street on foot one evening, on her way to a photography class, she had been hit and killed by a car driven by a drunk with seven DUI convictions behind him. There had been an arrest and trial. The drunk got sentenced to an alcohol abuse awareness program and Diana got put in the ground.

The waitress slid a platter with my tuna sandwich and a few pickle slices in front of me. My appetite wasn't at its keenest, but I ate the sandwich anyway. The bread hadn't been adequately toasted and the pickles tasted tinny. I paid the bill and went home.

Jack showed up at seven to take me out to dinner. His mood was cheerful, even expansive.

As we walked to his car, I said, "Did you win Megabucks today or something?"

He laughed. "That'll be the day. No, I didn't win the lottery." He unlocked the car's passenger door and held it open for me. "Remember that nightclub murder I was telling you about on Sunday?"

"Sure."

"I think I got a witness who'll talk."

"Congratulations." I smiled at him. "I knew you would."

"Yeah, well," Jack said. "I hope he sticks." He started the car.

As we were riding down Hampshire Street, I said, "Any fallout today from last night's television spectacular?"

Jack shook his head. "Not really. A few reporters called and left messages for me."

"Did you return the calls?"

"Nope." He glanced at me. "On the advice of the attorney for the Superior Officers Association."

"I see."

Jack tapped the horn and raised his right hand to the car that passed us going in the opposite direction.

"Who was that?" I asked.

"Teddy and Joe. The detectives."

I nodded. "Are they still looking for the guys who've been assaulting and robbing all those women around Eliot and Dana?"

"They're trying."

I sighed. "How's the most recent victim doing?"

"Recovering," Jack said. "Coming along. She doesn't remember much about the attack. She probably never will, with a head injury."

I shook my head. "How's your other stuff going?"

"Like the Edward Hassler murder? That guy who was killed in the car bombing? Nowhere."

"You must be getting discouraged."

"Well . . . yes, I am."

I reached over and patted his arm. "Hey, look. At least the business last night on Columbia Terrace got cleaned up quickly."

"That's true."

We were a block from the restaurant.

"By God," Jack said. "Is that a parking place I see?"

I squinted out the window. "I think it is."

"Son of a gun," Jack said. "That's the second stroke of luck I've had today."

We went back to my place after dinner.

"You want some coffee?" I asked. "There's decaf."

Jack let Lucy outside to run around in the back while I got out cups and put the kettle on to boil.

"You seemed a little quiet while we were in the restaurant," Jack said.

Lucy barked at the kitchen door. Jack opened it and she burst into the room, tail thrashing. She flung herself at him and he reached down and patted her, then closed and locked the door.

"Jack?"

"Mm-hmm?"

"Why didn't you tell me that Dalton Craig is your brother-in-law?"

He stood motionless before the kitchen door, his back to me. "How'd you find that out?"

"When I was at the police station this afternoon. Sam told me."

He turned. His face was expressionless. Rather carefully so.

"Do you want to hear what Sam said?"

He shrugged. "If you feel like telling me."

He sat down at the table. I leaned against the counter and repeated the gist of the conversation I'd had with Flaherty that afternoon. Jack listened without interruption, his face still impassive.

"So?" I said. "Did Sam tell me true?"

"There was a bit of trouble around the department when Dalton was there, yeah."

"According to Sam, it sounded like a lot of trouble, Jack. Craig was obviously rabidly jealous of you. He still must be. Of course that's why he's done what he's done." I shook my head and took a deep breath. "The guy is sick, sick, sick."

"There's a little more to it than that."

My eyebrows arched. "Oh?"

"Well," Jack replied, in very measured tones, "Dalton always thought I was responsible for Diana's death."

I stared at him. Then I said, very softly but with emphasis, "What?"

Jack's face was still neutral, as his voice had been, but I thought I could see something dark flickering behind his eyes.

I leaned toward him. "Why did he think that?"

Jack ran his hand back through his hair. Then he gave me a quirky half-smile. "You really want to hear all this?"

"Yes, Jack, I do."

He nodded. "All right. There's some family history that comes first."

"Whatever."

"Growing up, Diana and Dalton were very close. Diana's father died when she was a baby, and a few years later her mother married again, a guy named William Craig. He was a widower with just the one son. Anyway, Di was about three and Dalton was about five when their parents got married. Mr. Craig was in the army, and so they were always moving around—you know, a year in one place, then two years in another, and then off again someplace else for six months."

"Uh-huh."

Jack's face had gone from neutral to pensive. "I remember Di telling me once, this was when I was just starting to get to know her, that she always felt that she and Dalton had never stayed long enough in one place to form any real friendships. So they more or less grew up each other's best friends. Or at least . . . you know, close."

"I know what you mean."

"Also, Dalton was just enough older than Di to feel very protective of her. When they were in high school, he even beat up some kid because he thought the kid had made a dirty crack about Di. The kid was one of Dalton's best buddies."

"*Had* he offended Diana?"

"According to her, not at all. It was nothing. Just some dumb wiseass teenage joke. She thought it was funny, in fact. But I guess it bugged Dalton, because he knocked about six of the kid's teeth out. Also told him never even to look at Diana again, much less talk to her."

"That's not protective, that's pathological." I had an odd, pungent thought. "Jack?"

"Hmmm?"

"You don't suppose that Dalton was jealous of you because . . ."

I paused, feeling awkward. "Well, not because you were such a terrific cop, but because you took Diana away from him?"

"Jesus." Jack gave me a strange look. "What a weird idea. No, honey. That never occurred to me."

"It's possible," I said. "If he and Diana were extremely close."

"What are you getting at?"

"Nothing kinky," I said. "It's only that men very often have a kind of, um, funny feeling about the men who marry their daughters or sisters. Even if they like the guy. It's natural. But in Craig's case, the feeling may have been exaggerated, that's all."

"I wouldn't know about that," Jack said flatly. "I never had any sisters or daughters."

"Okay." It would clearly be unwise, at this point, to speculate further on the nature of whatever attachment Dalton Craig had felt toward his stepsister. "Tell me the rest."

"Di and I got married," Jack said. "And it was fine between us, and then there was the accident."

"And Craig blamed you for that," I said. "Why? What did he think you could have done to prevent it?"

"That I could have taken Diana to her photography class that night rather than let her go by herself."

"Are you *serious?*"

"Well, in a way Dalton was right," Jack said. "If I'd driven Diana over to the Adult Ed center, instead of letting her walk down Garden Street, what happened would never have happened."

His tone was very matter-of-fact. "Oh, God," I said. Jack's face was closed and quiet. Whatever had flickered behind his eyes before was gone now.

"There was a kind of bad scene at the funeral," he said. "Dalton was . . . he was distraught, I guess."

I had known Jack long enough to be fully aware of his ability to understate the facts of a situation. "What did he do?" I asked. "Accuse you of—" I stopped, unable to say the rest.

Jack hesitated a moment and then nodded. "Yeah."

I went over to him and put my hand on his shoulder. "What else?"

"We were coming out of the church," Jack said. He raised his right hand and rubbed his forehead with the index and middle fingers.

"Did Dalton start a fight?" I asked.

"Something like that." Jack gave his head a slight shake. "The person I really felt the worst for was Helen. Diana's mother. She wasn't in the best of health at the time to begin with."

"And seeing her stepson go berserk at her daughter's funeral didn't make her feel much better, I suppose."

"I guess not," Jack agreed. "She had a heart attack that night."

"Oh, Christ. Did—"

"No. She recovered."

I looked down at Jack for a moment. Then I moved my hand to the back of his neck and massaged it gently.

"Honey," I said, "I wish you had told me all this before."

"Why? There was no reason to."

"There is now. For one thing, it makes it even more clear why Craig is out to get you. My God. This has been festering in him for—what? Sixteen years?"

Jack was silent. Resisting the idea? I couldn't tell.

I leaned forward to hug him, briefly but hard. Then I stood up straight, resting my hands on his shoulders. "You okay?"

"Of course I am." He tilted his head back so that it pressed against my breast. "Didn't I tell you that before? I'm fine."

"All right," I said, and gave his left shoulder a squeeze.

I knew what it cost him to dredge up those memories and their attendant private, interior pain. I knew because I was that way myself.

What I didn't know was whether he, along with Craig, blamed himself for Diana's death.

5

THE STORY DALTON CRAIG had told on television broke in the next day's papers. I read both versions over breakfast. They were doozies. They also had a dimension to them that, if I'd been thinking straight, I'd have anticipated. On the second page of the Metro section of the *Globe* was an article headlined CAMBRIDGE POLICE OFFICERS MAY BE NAMED IN LAWSUIT.

The print seemed to waver in front of my eyes. I shut them for a moment. Then I took a gulp of coffee and began to read:

> The *Globe* learned yesterday that one of the two men convicted in the 1977 murder of a newspaper columnist may seek damages from the city of Cambridge and two of its police officers. Allegations that then Detective-Sergeant John Lingemann fraudulently concealed and destroyed evidence that might have cleared Albert Parkes. . . .

I hurled the Metro section to the floor, grabbed the *Herald*, and flipped through it until, on page seven, I found an article entitled CAMBRIDGE HERO COP POSSIBLE LAWSUIT TARGET.

The *Herald* article said substantially the same thing as the *Globe*'s. When I'd finished reading, I folded the papers neatly, set them carefully to one side of the table, and stared at the kitchen wall.

Lucy ambled over to my chair and put her muzzle on my thigh.

I reached down and smoothed back her ears. She raised her tail and swung it back and forth, like a fur metronome.

I retrieved the papers and opened them to the relevant pages. I checked the bylines on both articles. The *Globe* reporter was a fairly good acquaintance; the writer for the *Herald* a slightly better one.

I got up, went to the living room, plucked the phone off the end table, and dialed the *Globe* number. When the switchboard answered, I asked to speak to John Ouellette. He wasn't in. I left my name and number, but no message. I figured I didn't have to do that. Ouellette didn't know me inside out, but he knew me well enough to figure why I wanted to speak to him.

I had better luck calling the *Herald*. Harvey Searle was at his desk in the city room.

"It's Liz Connors," I said, when he picked up the extension.

There was the briefest of pauses on the other end of the line. Then Searle said, "Oh, hey, hi, kid, how you doing?"

"Not great," I replied. "Can I talk to you? Like soon? Like today? Like in an hour?"

Another tiny silence. "Make it two. I'm in the middle of something."

"Okay." I glanced at the clock on the mantel. "Twelve-thirty, then? At the *Herald*?"

"Yeah, okay. That sounds all right."

"See you."

I went back to the kitchen and reread the *Globe* and *Herald* articles. Both recapped the Stephen Larrain murder case, beginning with the arrest of Phillie Joyce. Both gave a full account of Albert Parkes's role in the matter—his arrest, trial, conviction, and the ultimate dismissal of the murder charge against him. Dalton Craig was quoted as being opposed to police corruption.

Neither paper said much at all about Otway Gilmore, except for brief references to the fact that Joyce had named him as the prime mover behind Larrain's murder.

I set the papers aside and dredged through my memory for what I knew about Gilmore. Since I don't write about big business, and am

not really interested by it, I'd never followed his doings closely. Still, he was famous enough so that you'd have to have been an anchorite not to have been familiar with the outline of his career.

The archetypal self-made tycoon, Gilmore had started a gravel-hauling business sometime back in the late nineteen-forties. This he had parlayed, in ten or so years, into an immensely successful general contracting operation. Sometime in the early sixties, perhaps foreseeing the high-tech revolution, or maybe just bored with building roads, Gilmore had sold the contracting outfit and bought a moribund business that manufactured office equipment. His prescience, or ennui, had paid off. Within a year, the office-machine business was not only still alive but flourishing, and within ten years had become one of the leading producers of computer parts in the northeast.

But it hadn't ended there. Not content to be merely a computer mogul, Gilmore had gotten into land development in the mid-seventies. He was now the biggest holder of commercial and residential properties in the Boston area. Sometimes it seemed as if he were the only one. What buildings weren't owned or operated by Otway Development Corporation were those owned and operated by Gilmore Realty Trust. At least that was my impression.

There were questions I had about Gilmore. Maybe Harvey Searle could answer some of them.

At eleven-thirty I walked to Kendall Square and took the subway from there to Broadway in South Boston, the Irish enclave of the city. I crossed a bridge over a canal of nearly motionless opaque olive-green water and God knew whatever other nauseating effluvia and some railroad tracks and ties. Then I darted through an intersection beneath the expressway. The *Herald* plant was to my left on the corner of Herald Street and Harrison Avenue. Atop the building was a billboard declaiming SAY NO TO DRUGS.

It was twenty past twelve when I walked into the *Herald* lobby. I checked in with the security person at the desk, who then called up to the city room to ensure that Searle was truly expecting me. Perhaps, looking at my red hair, the guard feared I might be the advance

woman for a terrorist attack by the Fenians on the other side of the canal.

The lobby had on display some antique printing apparatus. I went to inspect it. At twelve-thirty-two Harvey Searle came bounding down the stairs from the city room. He was wearing a gray warm-up suit.

"I usually run during this hour," he said. "But we can't run and talk. You wanna compromise and walk and talk?"

In his mid-thirties, Harvey Searle was a little over six feet tall, with thick curly black hair and a square, ruddy face. At some point, his nose had been broken. It gave him a tough look, which I and a lot of other women found attractive.

The last time I'd seen him had been about three months ago. I could swear that then he'd been at least twenty pounds heavier.

"Harvey!" I exclaimed admiringly. "You've been saying no to food."

He sucked in his stomach and threw out his chest. "Nice, huh?"

"Better stay out of the dating bars or you'll be sexually assaulted."

He slapped me lightly on the shoulder with his left hand. "Come on, let's walk."

We trotted out of the building and onto Harrison Avenue.

"Which way?" I asked.

He pointed. "Down there." He bounced lightly back and forth on the balls of his feet.

"Harvey," I said. "If you want, we can do a slow jog. I won't collapse in the gutter."

He looked at me doubtfully. "You sure?"

I'm not a runner. But I do happen to be a practiced long-distance walker—anyone who doesn't have a car becomes one by necessity— and that gives me staying power. Anyhow, I was wearing jeans and a sweatshirt and sneakers.

We thumped in lower gear across Harrison Avenue and down Herald Street, toward the South End. The South End is not to be confused with South Boston. Ever.

"Read your article this morning," I panted. "Also John Ouellette's in the *Globe*."

"Yeah, I figured you had." He threw me a quick sideways look. "You upset?"

"At you and John, for writing the stories? No, of course not. At the situation? Well, Harv—what do you think?"

He nodded.

We pounded down another four blocks. At the end of them, I could feel a stiffness beginning over my ribcage. Some athlete.

"Left," Searle said.

I grabbed his forearm and stopped running. Harvey didn't, and his forward momentum yanked me staggering along with him a few paces. He spun around in front of me, jogging in place. His face was about a foot and a half from mine. It was a crisp day, but perspiration had beaded his forehead and chin.

"Harvey," I said, "you've been a police reporter for the past ten years. You've known Jack longer than I have. Do you think, do you really, honestly think, that Jack would do what he's accused of doing? Do you?" My grip on his arm tightened.

Harvey didn't stop his side-to-side bobbing immediately, but rather slowly, like a mechanical toy winding down. "Ah, shit," he said. "I knew it'd be a mistake to run and talk."

"Harvey!"

"Rest for a minute," he said. He looked around for a place to do that, then tilted his head at the crumbling cement stoop of a boarded-up brick tenement.

We walked over to the steps. Harvey eased himself down on the lowest and began massaging his thighs with long, slow strokes of his palms. I leaned against the rusted iron railing and watched him.

"I don't make the news," he said, methodically rubbing his hams. "I just report it."

"I know that, Harv. I'm in the same business you are, remember?"

"Yeah. Sorry."

I nodded. "Okay. Do you think Jack would"—and I quoted from Searle's own article—" 'destroy evidence in a criminal case'?"

He looked at me for a moment. Then he looked away, squinting down the street. "No."

I dropped down onto the steps beside him. "That makes two of us. So, Harvey . . ."

"Yeah?"

"What the hell is all this about?"

Searle raised his hands from his thighs and slumped backward, resting against the step behind him. He closed his eyes and began inhaling and exhaling in deep, measured breaths. "You have a specific question in mind?"

"Lots of them. But I'll begin with the second most important one, since I already asked you the first most important one. How much do you know about this business?"

Searle let his head hang back, opened his eyes, and stared up at the sky. His breathing became a bit more shallow.

"Liz, the Larrain murder was a big deal for us," he said. "He was a news person. One of the family. Every reporter in town was working on that story, officially or unofficially." Searle lowered his head and glanced at me. "Like when a cop gets shot and dies, all the other cops, even the ones who might not have known him, want to be the ones to get the guy who did it."

"Sure."

"It was like that with us." Searle shook his head, very hard. "No way were we going to let up on those sons-of-bitches who killed Larrain. No *way*. We were gonna be walking up their heels twenty-four hours a day."

I noticed his use of the plural. "So you don't think Phillie Joyce acted on his own initiative when he shot Larrain?"

"Ah, Liz. Are you shitting me? Albert Parkes is as guilty as hell. No question there." Searle reached up with his left hand, grasped the decaying railing, and pulled himself to his feet. "Come on," he said. "Let's walk."

I followed him.

"All right, Harvey," I said to his back. "So Parkes wanted Larrain killed. Why?"

Searle turned and looked at me as if I were speaking in tongues. "He had his orders and he was acting on them."

Searle walked fast, his feet slapping hard and flat against the concrete. I cantered up beside him. "Orders from Otway Gilmore?"

"Well, who the hell else?"

We moved briskly past a row of elegantly renovated town houses.

"The DA for Middlesex County at the time Larrain was murdered didn't seem to think that Gilmore was involved."

Searle made an ugly face. "That corrupt wimp? He was probably on Gilmore's payroll."

I drew a sharp breath. "Harvey—seriously?"

"Yeah, of course seriously. There's a lot of people on Gilmore's payroll."

We chugged past an expensive-looking wine-and-cheese shop and a seedy little variety store. The latter was shuttered with a heavy iron grate that seemed to protect nothing more than windows grimed by five years' worth of soot. The wine shop had a sign on its door advertising a special on Pouilly-Fumé.

"I know Larrain wrote some nasty articles about Gilmore," I said. "But I guess I have the same problem as the corrupt wimp did with seeing that as a sufficient motive for murder. Wasn't there anything else?"

We had reached an intersection. Traffic through it was heavy, and we stopped on the corner waiting for the stream of cars and trucks to break. Searle turned to me.

"What do you know about Gilmore?"

I shrugged. "Only what everyone does. He's a sleaze and a crook. I know he's morally responsible for the death of a baby girl in one of his tenement fires, if not for the death of Larrain."

"Right."

The traffic eased, and we sprinted across the street.

"So?" I said.

We were standing in front of the shell of a red-brick building that looked as if it had once been an elementary school.

"Liz," Searle said. "Gilmore not only has the ethics of a cockroach, he has an ego the size of Rhode Island."

"What are you saying?"

Searle wiped some perspiration from his forehead with the back of his hand. "Shit, I know it sounds melodramatic. But, yeah—I know Gilmore and I know about Gilmore, and, yes, I believe that a guy who thinks the way Gilmore does would arrange the murder of somebody who publicly criticized him. Yes, goddamnit, yes, I think he had Larrain killed just because Larrain wrote bad stuff about him. For Gilmore it would be like swatting a fly."

I stared. "Can you prove it?"

Searle made a quick, irritated gesture. "No, for Christ's sake, of course not. If I could, Gilmore would be in prison."

We started walking again, past another row of rehabilitated town houses.

"Why do you suppose you never read any bad press anymore about Gilmore?" Searle asked.

The bitterness in his voice brought me up short.

"Everybody's afraid?" I said, after a moment. "Of getting blown away like Larrain? Come on. You people spend your lives writing about bad guys."

Searle didn't answer.

"All right," I said. "Gilmore's an evil person. You know that. I know that. We all know that. So how does he stay out of trouble with the law?"

Harvey sighed. "Liz, Gilmore has huge money and even more power. If he went down, he'd bring at least six mayors in this state with him. Plus an assortment of legislators, judges, and possibly a few police chiefs and, for all I know, newspaper publishers."

"Christ," I said. "He can't have bought off every public figure in Massachusetts."

"Damn near," Harvey replied. "The point is, if Gilmore gets in hot water, they all do. And they're not gonna let that happen."

"Course not."

"Also, Gilmore does good works."

"What?"

Harvey smiled. "He's a big contributor to various charities. And to the right cultural stuff, like the Symphony and the Museum of Fine

Arts. All of which obligates other rich powerful people to him, or at least puts him in their corner."

"Well, he sure doesn't publicize his good works. The guy is a recluse. You know, I don't think I've ever seen a picture of him. What's he look like, anyway?"

"The last glimpse I caught of him was about five years ago." Searle picked up speed a bit, so that we were almost jogging again.

"He's tall," he said. "Maybe six-four. And very fit, especially for a guy his age."

"How *old* is he? Mid-sixties?"

Searle frowned. "I'd guess around there. But he could pass for ten years younger."

"I see. Well, go on."

Searle glanced at me. "His appearance is very distinguished. If I were a woman, I'd probably think he was attractive. The Yul Brynner type."

"Gilmore's bald?"

"Uh-huh. Probably when he had hair, it was black or very dark brown, because that's what his eyebrows are. I don't know what color eyes he has; I never got close enough to tell. But I was pretty damn sure that last time I saw him he'd had a face lift somewhere along the line. I asked one of the society reporters on the paper, and she thought so too. His skin had that sort of tight look."

We increased our pace. I tried not to pant too obviously.

"Still," Harvey said. "He's a good-looking guy. Hope I look that good when I'm his age."

"Can you tell me something about his background?" I asked. "Not his business career. I know most of that. What do you know about *him?*"

"I don't think he has a lot of formal education. In fact, I don't think he ever finished high school. But his manner is very—he speaks very well, for example. His tastes are refined. Well, not his architectural tastes. Some of those buildings he's put up are pretty grotesque. But he's supposed to have an outstanding personal art collection. Not enormous, but whatever's in it is the best of its kind."

"Self-cultivated," I said. "And self-educated."

"Yeah, I heard he's a book collector, too. First editions. Stuff like that."

I made a face. "I hate hearing that loathsome people are book-lovers," I said.

"You'd prefer it if Gilmore only read *Hustler* and the comics?"

"Absolutely. And if he's an admirer of Yeats, I don't want to hear about it."

Harvey laughed. "Okay, I won't tell you."

"When did you last see Gilmore?"

Searle frowned slightly. "It was at the ground-breaking for that complex behind the Prudential Center."

"The Bay State Plaza?"

"Yeah."

"Gilmore built that?"

"He owns it."

"Good God." The Bay State Plaza was a multilevel mélange of expensive retail stores, offices, chi-chi restaurants, and residential condominiums, plus two hotels that charged three hundred dollars per night for their cheapest rooms. It combined, to my eyes at least, the tackiest features of Caesar's Palace and a suburban shopping mall. There were fountains and waterfalls everywhere, and the one time I walked through the Plaza the constant splashing and trickling had aroused in me nothing more than an urgent desire to find a ladies' room.

"Gilmore showed up for the ground-breaking," Searle said. "Unusual for him, because, as you say, he avoids public appearances. But I guess for political reasons he had to make this one. Anyway, he had with him the wife and kiddies—you see them in public even less than Gilmore—an aide, and a bodyguard."

Searle slowed his pace somewhat, for which I was grateful. The stitch in my side was giving indications of an imminent resurgence. We hustled in lower gear past a brand-new and very Art Deco-looking restaurant called Iris.

"Can we drop Gilmore for a minute and talk about Albert Parkes?"

"Sure."

"Okay. According to your story, Dalton Craig says that the Cambridge Police Department had Parkes under surveillance the morning after Larrain was murdered. But, Harvey . . . the cops didn't pick up Phillie Joyce until two days *after* that. *He* was the one who told them about Parkes, and he didn't even do that till months later. So why would they have gone after Parkes so early?"

"Can we hang a left here?" Harvey said. "I have to get back."

We loped across the street and started back up it on the opposite side.

"All right," he said. "Parkes will probably claim that he was an associate of Joyce's, and Joyce was a suspect in the murder from the beginning, and so they put Parkes under surveillance just like they did all of Joyce's other known associates."

"There's one thing wrong with that story."

"Oh?" Searle threw me a sideways look. "What's that?"

"I'm positive the cops didn't have Joyce as a suspect in the murder as early as the morning after Larrain died. I remember distinctly Jack's telling me that it wasn't until the afternoon of the next day that the woman who saw Joyce leaving Larrain's apartment went to the cops and described him and picked him out of a mug book."

"Shit," Searle said. "You sure about that?"

"Absolutely."

Searle's face cracked in a slow grin. "Nice," he said. "Very nice. You know this woman's name, Liz?"

"Jack didn't say."

"Doesn't matter. I can probably get it from our morgue. If not, the trial transcript."

"What are you going to do?"

"If she still lives around here, I'll go talk to her. See what her recollection of events is. If what you just told me is true . . ."

"It'll put a big hole in Albert Parkes's story. It also won't do much for the credibility of Dalton Craig."

We were back on Harrison Avenue now, moving toward the *Herald* plant.

"Well, it may not be that simple," Searle said.

"Huh?"

"Just don't count your chickens, Liz."

We slowed to a stop in front of the *Herald*. I felt a prickle of unease. "Harvey," I said. "Do you know something you haven't told me?"

He looked at me a moment. Then he said, "Parkes claims to have a witness who can support his alibi."

"What part of it?"

"Well, you know how Parkes said some guy gave him a briefcase to hand over to Phillie Joyce?"

I waved an impatient hand. "Oh, yeah, that bullshit. What about it?"

"Parkes says a former neighbor of his is willing to testify that he saw the briefcase exchange take place."

"Oh, yes? And who might this creature be?"

"Now he's Parkes's son-in-law. He married Parkes's eldest daughter a year after Parkes was convicted."

"Oh, Harvey. You're fooling me."

"I swear to God." Harvey blotted some perspiration from his forehead with his sweatshirt sleeve. "Six months ago, the son-in-law and daughter moved into a seven-hundred-and-fifty-thousand dollar house in North Andover. Which was custom-built for them free of charge by Parkes's construction company."

"Oh, my God," I said. "No wonder the son-in-law's so willing to speak up on Parkes's behalf."

"Well, it could be fishy. Then on the other hand, the whole thing could be perfectly aboveboard. Why *shouldn't* a guy in the construction business build a house for his kids?"

"Yeah, sure. When did you find out about the son-in-law?"

"This morning."

I nodded, then said, "Well, that's good news."

"It is?"

"Of course. There's no decent judge in the world, at least I hope there isn't, who's going to entertain for a minute a lawsuit where the

plaintiff's best witness happens to be an after-the-fact relative by marriage. Come on. Even if a judge bought it, a jury wouldn't."

Harvey shrugged.

"All right, why didn't the son-in-law come forward during Parkes's original trial? Who's going to believe he just happened to remember now, twelve years after it was supposed to have happened, that Parkes accepted a briefcase one morning from a mystery man?"

"You better hope nobody," Harvey said.

It occurred to me as I was riding home on the subway that Harvey apparently didn't know that Dalton Craig had a family connection with Jack.

He would almost certainly find out sooner or later.

God, Jack would hate that.

Still, it would probably be to his benefit if the disclosure were made as quickly as possible.

6

I MADE THAT POINT to Jack at seven o'clock that evening, as we were having a drink in my living room.

"You're probably right," he said. He paused for a moment, and then shook his head. "No one's going to hear it from me, though."

"But . . ."

"Liz, it's not something I want to discuss with a bunch of reporters."

I sighed. "I'm a reporter."

He gave me a slight smile and patted my thigh.

"The only thing is," I said, "the fact that Craig has an insane grudge against you really calls his credibility into question."

"Then let that come up when the lawsuit—if there is one—gets to court. If it does." He drank some of his bourbon.

"You seem remarkably blasé about that," I said. "It doesn't bother you, the prospect of being sued by Albert Parkes for God knows how much money?"

"Do you realize how long it takes to get a suit like that rolling? Christ, I could be retired by then. And it's all horseshit anyway." He grinned at me. "You think so yourself."

I returned his smile, a little reluctantly. "I just hate seeing your integrity publicly impugned, that's all."

He made a dismissive gesture. "I'll survive." He took another sip of bourbon. "Seriously, the papers and the TV will lose interest in

this after a little while. Something else will come along to grab their attention."

I wasn't so sure about that, but I didn't say so. What I *did* say was, "Do you mind if I continue to try to find out—sub rosa—what I can about Parkes and Craig and the rest of that crew?"

"Be my guest," Jack said, finishing his drink. "Even if I disapproved, I wouldn't try to stop you. Go ahead. You have good contacts. You may find out some interesting stuff. Just be careful not to stomp too hard on the wrong toes."

I gathered up our empty glasses to take them to the kitchen.

"One thing," Jack said.

"What's that?" I stopped in the doorway.

"Don't tell anybody about me and Dalton, okay?"

"I won't."

As I walked to the kitchen I thought, *I will if it becomes necessary to get you out of this mess.*

When I returned to the living room I said, "What would you like to do this evening? Everything on television is crap."

"So what else is new," Jack said. He looked thoughtful. "Tell you what. You want to go to a movie? We haven't been in a long time."

It was a lousy movie. I hate it when the female lead is such a sap. On the way back to my house, we turned onto Trowbridge Street, residential and, at this time of night, mostly somnolent. I cranked down my window a few inches to let in a rush of night air. It was cool and laced with the perfume of wood smoke. I loved that sweet, ashy autumnal smell. I leaned back and closed my eyes and took a deep breath. Over the river and through the woods—

"Jesus *Christ*," Jack said. He swerved the car to the right and braked it to a tire-screeching halt in front of the entrance to someone's driveway. I lurched forward, reflexively flinging up both hands to brace against the dashboard so I wouldn't hit the windshield. My right palm smacked the glove compartment at an awkward angle, and I felt a needle thrill of pain dart up into my wrist.

Jack threw open the car door and ran over to the sidewalk.

"What . . ." I said.

I blinked, straightened up, and shook my head slightly. Then I got out of the car, peering after Jack.

I walked to the curb. "What's the matter?" I said, bending my wrist back and to ease the stinging kink in it.

Fifteen feet away, Jack was crouched beneath a thick-trunked maple. Sprawled before him was the body of a woman. I felt my chest contract as all the air in my lungs escaped in one long horrified exhalation.

Jack looked up at me, then jerked his head in the direction of the nearest house. "Tell them to call an ambulance," he snapped. "Quick. My radio isn't working."

I ran up the footpath to a white-frame three-decker. The front porch was dimly illuminated by an overhead light. I went up the stairs two at a time. There were three bell buttons beside the door. I pressed all of them simultaneously.

A few frantic moments later, I heard the thud of hurried footsteps from within. Then silence, as if whoever had responded to the clamor of the doorbell was having second thoughts about answering the summons.

I made a fist, pounded on the door, and screamed, "Help me!"

The door opened about six inches and an alarmed, angry male face appeared in the crack.

"Call an ambulance," I shrieked. "There's someone badly hurt just outside."

The face gaped at me.

"Please call nine-eleven."

"Was it a car accident?"

"I don't know. Would you call an ambulance? Please?"

The man looked at me as if trying to decide whether I was a clever practical joker or a robber with a mad scheme to gain admittance to his house.

"Oh, hurry, will you?"

My frenzy must have struck him as legitimate, for he nodded, finally, and said, "Right away."

"Thank you."

The man was still sufficiently careful, or suspicious, to shut the door in my face and bolt it before going to the phone.

I ran back down the steps and out to the sidewalk. Lights had gone on in two of the houses across the street. I had a sure sense that pale, curious faces were peering out at me through slitted draperies and from between the slats in Venetian blinds.

I hurried toward Jack and the injured woman. He had taken off his coat and draped it over her. From this angle, the body was in deep shadow. I stopped about five feet away and said, "How is it?"

Jack looked up at me briefly. "Bad."

"Can I do anything else?"

He shook his head.

I walked to his side and dropped to my knees. Then I bent forward to look at what lay beneath the maple tree.

"Oh, God," I said. I jerked upright and clamped a hand over my eyes.

"Where the fuck is the goddamn ambulance?" Jack said.

As if in answer to his question, a siren wailed. A white van with flashing red lights came racing up Trowbridge Street. Behind it was a cruiser.

I pushed myself to my feet, darted to the curb, and waved my arms.

The ambulance drew up in front of me. A man and a woman in blue EMT uniforms emerged from it. The woman trotted around to the rear of the ambulance and yanked open its doors.

The man who'd telephoned nine-eleven was standing on his front steps, looking out at us. I felt a tug on my sleeve and turned. A woman in an ankle-length flannel nightgown and paisley wool shawl was gazing anxiously up at me.

"What happened?" she asked.

I shook her hand from my sleeve and walked over to Jack's car. I crossed my arms on the top of it and rested my head on them.

What I'd seen under the maple tree would stay with me for a long time.

A face darkened and swollen like a rotting melon, nothing recog-

nizable as a nose, the lower lip torn or bitten through and hanging loose, the jaw pushed crazily to one side.

I raised my head and looked over at the group beneath the maple tree. The two cops from the cruiser had joined them. The EMTs had gotten the woman onto a wheeled stretcher and suspended some sort of intravenous device over her. I heard the woman EMT say to Jack, "You did the right thing." She and her partner wheeled the stretcher to the ambulance and hoisted it, with the aid of the two police officers, into the back of the vehicle.

The number of spectators had increased. I put my head back down on my arms I heard the metallic thunk of the ambulance doors being slammed shut, and, a few seconds later, the rising keen of the siren. Cambridge Hospital was only a few blocks away. I pressed my forehead against the wool sleeve of my blazer.

"Come on, let's get you home."

I looked to my right. Jack was standing beside me, his coat slung over his arm. Even in the inadequate light the dark splotches of blood on it stood out.

Another police cruiser had arrived.

"If you're needed here," I said. "I can walk down to Mass. Avenue and call a cab."

"Don't be idiotic. I'll drop you and come back here."

I opened the car door and slumped down onto the passenger seat. Jack went around to the driver's side. He bunched up the coat and tossed it through the open window onto the rear seat. Then he got in behind the wheel. A third police cruiser passed us, moving very slowly. Jack put the car in gear and we followed it up Trowbridge Street.

As we turned onto Broadway, I said, "If it's not a stupid question, what happened?"

"She got beaten up."

"Pulped would be a better word, wouldn't it?"

"Yeah, I think it would."

"Mugger?"

"I don't know."

"This is mid-Cambridge. Same part of town where all those other six women were attacked."

"Uh-huh."

"So it was probably the same guys who did this, right?"

"I can't say yet, Liz."

I nodded. "Do you think this woman will—do you think she'll be okay?"

Jack took his left hand from the steering wheel and rubbed it over the lower half of his face. "I think her neck was broken. That was why I didn't want to try moving her."

I shuddered. "God. What did they *use* on her?"

Neither of us spoke again the rest of the way to my house. Jack wouldn't let me go into the apartment by myself. Even though it wasn't in mid-Cambridge.

In my living room, I said, "Jack?"

"Yes?"

"Come back here tonight, if you can."

"I will."

7

AT THREE-FIFTY-SEVEN that morning, Paula Young died at Cambridge Hospital of massive trauma.

At eleven that morning, John Ouellette from the *Globe* returned the call I had made to him the previous day.

I was thickheaded from having gotten only three hours' sleep. "John, can I see you?"

"I have to be over in Cambridge this afternoon."

"Well, that's fine. Can I meet you some place?"

"I have some business in City Hall at two. Shouldn't take more than an hour."

"I'll be hanging around outside there at three."

"Sounds good. I'll let you know if there's a problem."

I dropped the phone receiver back into its cradle and lay back on the couch, listening to the blood pound through my temples. I didn't close my eyes, though. If I did, I'd see Paula Young's shattered face.

At three o'clock exactly I was sitting on a bench outside City Hall. At three-twenty, Ouellette came out of the building.

"Sorry," he said. "I got hung up."

"Doesn't matter." I rose from the bench. "Hi. How are you?"

"Good. You look like shit, though."

"Thanks, pal. I had a rough night."

"Uh, listen, Liz, I'm running late and I have an appointment over

in Kendall Square at a quarter to four." Ouellette was already moving toward the street.

"So that's twenty-five minutes from now. What's your hurry, John?" I smiled. My facial muscles felt stiff. "You have your car here? Let's ride around and talk for a bit."

He shrugged. "If you want."

John Ouellette had covered Cambridge—politics, crime, education, and human interest—for the *Globe* for over a decade. But his reporting roots in the city went back further than that—as a Harvard undergraduate, he'd worked on the *Crimson*. Like Harvey Searle, the police reporter for the *Herald*, he'd known Jack longer than I had.

Ouellette was my age, a husky guy of medium height with very broad shoulders, a moon face, and very pale, thin, almost pinkish-blond hair. He was divorced and had a son who lived with the ex-wife somewhere in western Mass.

As we walked down Inman Street to the car, he said, "What's the matter with you anyway? You really do look sick."

"You know about that murder on Trowbridge Street last night?"

"Sure. I'm doing a piece on it for tomorrow's paper."

"I was with Jack when he found the body. Only she was still alive."

Ouellette grimaced. "Jesus. I hope to hell they catch those two guys soon." He glanced at me. "Just stay the hell out of that part of town at night."

"We're in that part of town now," I said.

Inman Street ran right through mid-Cambridge. Trowbridge was on the other side of Harvard Street. To our left was the City Hall Annex, where you went to get dog licenses and parking permits. There was an elementary school on the corner of Harvard and Antrim. The rest of the neighborhood was upscale residential, with a scattering of high-priced antique stores and law offices in renovated Victorian houses. Some kids were horsing around on the jungle gym in the elementary school playground.

"Doesn't look like the right setting for violence, does it?" Ouellette said.

Ouellette's car was a badly decayed seven-year-old white Toyota station wagon. The dents and rust patches gave it the look of an unevenly toasted marshmallow. A Chapman lock decal was plastered to the driver's window.

"Don't tell me you're afraid this heap will be stolen," I said.

Ouellette held up two fingers. "Twice already. Once right out of the *Globe* lot."

I shook my head. "The chop shops must be desperate."

He started the car. "You want to fasten your seat belt?"

I did. Then I said, "So what did you think of the Dalton Craig show the other night?"

Ouellette reached into the pocket of his tan windbreaker and took out a package of cigarettes. Then he punched in the lighter on the dashboard. "Let me put it this way: I knew Craig slightly when he was a cop, and the guy was a fuck-up from the word go."

"I've heard that." We drove past the playground on the corner of Antrim.

The lighter popped from its holder. Ouellette touched the glowing end to the tip of his cigarette. "On the other hand, just because Craig's a fuck-up doesn't mean he can't tell the truth on occasion."

I sat very still. "What do you mean?"

"Well, hell, it's possible that a police department in a city like Cambridge was—still could be—running some kind of domestic spy operation. I mean, Liz, Cambridge has been the radical-subversive-Communist-liberal Mecca of the East Coast for the past twenty-five years."

"So you actually believe Craig?"

"No, actually, I think he's a lying sack of shit." Ouellette took the cigarette from his mouth and pointed it at me. "But that's only because I know your boyfriend, and I know Sam Flaherty, and neither one of those guys is the type you'd put in an illegal secret spy unit."

We were rolling down Memorial Drive now, the Charles River to the right and the Harvard Houses to the left. It was a postcard day, the sky a lucent blue, but I still wasn't in the mood to be distracted by scenic splendor.

"I have a theory about why Craig has come out with this story about Jack and Sam," Ouellette said.

I tensed, I hoped not noticeably, wondering if Ouellette knew about the family relationship between Craig and Jack. "Let's hear your theory."

Ouellette tossed the butt of his half-smoked cigarette out the window. "Simple. Craig's being paid big bucks to dump on Jack and Sam by Albert Parkes."

I felt myself relax.

"And speaking of lying sacks of shit," Ouellette continued, "there's another one for you. Albert Parkes."

"You don't believe his story, either?"

Ouellette just laughed.

"How could you prove a payoff had taken place?" I asked. "By finding out if Craig had made any recent heavy deposits in his bank account that didn't have an easily explained source?"

Ouellette blew out a whoosh of breath. "That would be one way. Or if he traded in his Chevette for an El Dorado."

"*Does* Craig drive a Chevette?"

"Now how the hell do I know what he drives, Liz? I was just giving you an example."

"I was teasing, John."

"However," Ouellette continued, "Craig is probably too shrewd to flash any cash that way. He'd know how it would look. My guess is, if he *has* come into some payoff money, it's well hidden somewhere—for the time being, anyway."

We turned off Memorial Drive. Around us the older M.I.T. buildings rose in neoclassical serenity. Monuments to science and reason.

"John, tell me—what do you know about Otway Gilmore? Harvey Searle is convinced Gilmore was behind Stephen Larrain's murder."

Ouellette pushed out his lower lip. "It's possible."

"*Only* possible?"

"Liz, what do you want from me, an affadavit? Okay, I think it's *probable* that Gilmore had Larrain killed. Happy now?"

I tapped the end of my nose with my index finger. "What exactly *is* the connection between Gilmore and Parkes? I've never gotten that entirely clear."

"The two of them started doing business together around—oh, say fifteen years ago. Parkes's construction company put up a bunch of buildings for Gilmore. Did some restoration on some of Gilmore's other properties."

I nodded. "And they kept on doing business together?"

Ouellette grinned nastily. "Of one sort or another."

"Yes indeedy."

"Another thing you'll find interesting," Ouellette said, "is that after Parkes was released from prison, he started getting very rich very quickly."

I raised my eyebrows. "Oh, really?"

"Yeah, Parkes said he'd gotten some excellent investment tips from his old buddy Otway Gilmore."

"Holy God. Where'd you find that out, John?"

"Guy who writes for our business pages told me."

"Now isn't that an interesting coincidence. Parkes takes a fall for Gilmore, goes to jail, gets out of jail, and gets rich through the offices of Gilmore. I love it."

We were in Kendall Square now, home not only of M.I.T. but Polaroid, Bell, Draper Labs, and Biogen. The tech was ultrahigh here. It made Route 128 look like a cowpath.

Ouellette pulled up in front of the Marriott Hotel.

"Shacking up with someone?" I asked.

"Naw, I'm meeting my interview in the cocktail lounge."

"Better than a deserted pier at midnight in the rain." I undid the seat belt and opened the car door. "John, thank you for the ride. I'll return the favor."

He smiled. "I'm sure you will."

I walked down Mass. Avenue to Central Square. Tired as I was, my spirits were a little higher than they had been an hour ago. Not surprising considering what Ouellette had told me about Parkes and Gilmore.

It was just four o'clock. I decided to stop in the branch library on Pearl Street and browse for a while. Then I'd wander over to the police station and collect Jack.

About six Indian restaurants were gathered in a row along a two-block stretch.

As I passed the second of them, a young woman with long floaty red hair, distended pupils, and a beatific smile wafted in front of me and said, "Hello, I am your perception of me."

"Yes, I suppose you are," I said, moving sideways.

She thrust a yellow leaflet at me. "Wouldn't you like to debut into an expanded life?"

"Oh, I don't think so. I came out at the Junior Assemblies when I was eighteen. That was enough."

"Well, then, love and intimacy to you."

Hell, it was better than "Have a nice day."

I looked at the leaflet in my hand. It was an invitation to come stretch my mind, body, and heart, and experience total renewal at a polarity therapy workshop. For only fifty bucks a throw.

Two Ecuadorian teenagers came bopping down the sidewalk toward me. "*Aqui,*" I said, and shoved the leaflet at one of them. Maybe they could figure it out.

I spent forty-five minutes at the library, checking out the new books, then strolled down Franklin Street to the police department. I had to wait for several moments at the corner of Western Avenue for an opportunity to cross. The street seemed even busier than usual at this hour.

The traffic island in front of the police station was still partially excavated. On the unripped-up part was a gathering of maybe twenty-five to thirty people. They were apparently being addressed by a woman standing on a crate. I was too far away to hear clearly what she was saying. I crossed the street.

Maybe it was an antiapartheid rally. Or prochoice. Or antimilitary research. Or protenants' rights. Or against U.S. involvement in Central America or the Middle East. Maybe it was an outdoor polarity therapy workshop. In Cambridge, it could be anything. Funny place

to hold a rally, though. Holyoke Center would have been much better.

My curiosity aroused, I moved closer to the edge of the throng. An Eyewitness News van cruised down the street.

The demonstrators were giving their full attention to the speaker. She was an attractive early-fortyish woman, with curly light-brown hair and fair skin with a spattering of freckles. She was quite impassioned.

A man standing about ten feet away from me had a large square of poster board dangling like an oversized pendant against his chest. The string around his neck was secured to the upper corners of the sign. I sauntered around in front of him to read it:

CITIZENS' COMMITTEE TO END POLICE REPRESSION

I gave my full attention to the speaker.

"And we will no longer tolerate such trampling of the rights guaranteed us by the law of this country," she was saying. "For too long the police department of this city has been allowed to systematically harass and pry into the affairs of its citizens . . ."

Oh, no, I thought, *this can't be for real.*

The reporter for Channel Four was making his way around the fringes of the crowd, looking for a good sound bite. I sidled off quickly in the opposite direction.

"We demand," the speaker shouted, "the immediate resignation of the two police officers guilty of the most flagrant abuses of our civil rights . . ."

I left. I couldn't bear to listen anymore.

"Gee," Jack said. "This looks like a nice place. You think they're willing to seat civil rights violators?"

"Oh, stop it," I said.

He laughed and put an arm around me. With his free hand he pulled open the door and ushered me into the restaurant foyer. The hostess came toward us, smiling.

"Two?" she said.

"Son of a gun," Jack whispered to me. "They *do* seat civil rights violators."

"Oh, will you shut up," I hissed back irritably.

The hostess led us to a banquette. When we were seated, she handed us menus and recited, "The waiter will be along right away to take your orders for drinks, if you care for a cocktail."

Jack looked around the room. "Nice table," he remarked. "It must be at least twenty-five feet from the kitchen door."

I had been reading the menu. I threw it down on the seat beside me. "How can you laugh about this?"

He leaned back against the vinyl padding of the banquette, crossing his arms. "Can you think of anything better to do?"

"Oh, Jack."

A waiter who looked like a recent graduate of Hollywood High struck an elegant pose beside the table. Jack ordered drinks for us. Then he opened his menu. "Oh, great," he said. "They have duck." He closed the menu and smiled at me.

I folded my hands on the tabletop and turned my head away from him, so that I was gazing at the bar on the opposite side of the room. A moment of dense silence passed. The candle in the middle of the table flickered inside its glass dome.

"Ah, come on, honey," Jack said. "Lighten up." He put his hand on my wrist and shook my arm gently. "If *I'm* not getting upset about this, *you* certainly shouldn't be getting upset about it."

"That's just it," I said. "I can't understand why you're not bouncing off the walls. If I were you, I would be. Jack, I hate to keep harping on this like some dreary nag, but"—I faced him—"I'm worried about what will happen to you. I can't help it. And it bothers me that you just keep brushing this whole thing off, as if it were some kind of stupid joke."

"Nothing bad will happen to me."

I closed my eyes. "Jack, there was a woman standing outside the police department this afternoon shrieking at the tops of her lungs for your resignation and Sam Flaherty's. And she was on the six o'clock

news afterward, still yelling the same thing. How can that not bother you?"

The stylish young waiter glided up to the table bearing our drinks. I opened my eyes and smiled at him reflexively. He beamed back at me and took our dinner orders. Sweet of him to lavish a smile so enchanting on two people who clearly weren't talent scouts just in from the coast.

Jack leaned across the table. Even in the semidarkness I could see that his eyes were very bright.

"Liz," he said. "They can set up all the Citizens' Committees they want. They can scream all they want about civil rights abuses. There's no way anyone will ever prove that there was any kind of illegal secret spy unit within the Cambridge Police Department. Because there never was one. And even if there had been, I wasn't part of it, and neither was Sam."

"Well, I know that," I said.

"So what are you worried about?"

"Jack, how do you prove to the public that something that never existed, never existed?" I shook my head. "Excuse me. That locution's sort of confusing, isn't it?"

He straightened up slowly. "No, I can follow you."

I slid along the banquette, edging up closer to him. "Of course there are no department records that are going to show you were in a spy unit. But what good will that do? The Citizens' Committee will simply say the lack of recorded evidence was meaningless because a secret operation would by definition leave no written record of its existence."

"So?" Jack took a sip of his bourbon. "That pretty much means the Citizens' Committee has no substantiated case against me or the department, doesn't it?"

"Jack, they don't need to have a substantiated case against you. It's not a question of them proving you guilty. It's a question of you proving yourself innocent."

"I can do that, Liz. I can pull files and schedules showing what I was doing during the years I was supposed to have been in the spy unit. So can Sam."

"The Committee will say that the department faked them to cover you."

Jack laughed. "It's not easy to fake some of that stuff. Look, if, say, I happen to have arrested a rapist on a night when the Citizens' Committee claims I was infiltrating a bingo game at Saint Anthony's, the DA's office will have a record of the fact that I was arresting a rapist that night, not hanging around a church recreation hall trying to bust some eighty-year-old Portuguese lady."

"They could say the DA's office was in on the cover-up."

"Yes, they could. They could also say the Attorney General's office was in on it, and the governor was in on it, and the president of the U.S. was in on it. So what?"

I shook my head, biting my lower lip. "You're making everything I say seem trivial."

"No I'm not. I'm just trying to show you that the situation isn't all that desperate."

I looked at him hard. His face was relaxed, expressing nothing more than mild good humor. I searched his eyes. They were steady, calm.

"Okay," I said. "You win. Subject closed. For the time being."

The waiter delivered our food. Actually, he didn't deliver it so much as present it, laying the plates before us with choreographed precision. As he angled his body deftly around the table, I realized I was watching a performance. I was almost tempted to applaud.

"All right," I said to Jack. "What else is new, then, in your life?"

He laughed. "Not much." He picked up his fork and held it poised in midair. "Actually, that's not true. I got a call this afternoon from the DA's office."

"Oh? What did they want?"

"I'm supposed to go on special assignment."

I raised my eyebrows. "Sounds like the title of a TV show. *On Special Assignment.* I like it. What does it involve?"

"Starting tomorrow, I'm going to be spending all my time investigating the Edward Hassler murder. The car bombing."

"But what about the other stuff you were working on?"

"It'll get divided up among Sam and the others."

"Well, that's very interesting," I said. "I mean that the DA's all of a sudden so hot to have you dig into Hassler's murder. What's it been—nine months since the poor man was killed?"

"Yeah, just about."

I frowned. "Why is the DA's office so revved up about getting the case solved *now*? Or at least worked on at high intensity?"

Jack laughed. "I think it's their way of getting me out of the public eye for a while."

"By sending you on a wild-goose chase?"

"Sure. Makes perfect sense. They can't fire me or suspend me. But they can take me off the front line."

I nodded, toying with my glass. "And you're not upset about being shunted around that way?"

"Oh, hell, no. I'm pleased. How often do I get to devote all my time and energy to just one case?"

I raised my glass to him. "Well, if anyone cracks Hassler, it'll be you."

"Thanks, Liz. You're a very supportive girl."

I leaned my head back against the banquette and smiled lazily. "And incredible in the sack, too, Jack. Don't forget that."

He raised his glass to me. "To forget that," he said, "would be impossible."

8

I WAS AT MY KITCHEN TABLE the next afternoon, finishing up the article on missing children, when Jack phoned to tell me that two arrests had been made in the mid-Cambridge assaults case.

"Oh, that's wonderful," I said. "That's terrific. I'm so glad. Who made the pinch?"

"Teddy and Joe, the two guys who were working on it, with an assist from a couple other guys."

"Well, that's great. I meant to ask you earlier, can I come down to the station this afternoon? What I mean is, Jack, things must be pretty hectic down there."

"No more so than usual. Bunch of reporters underfoot, though, if that's what you mean."

"Who's around that I know?"

"Well, I saw Ouellete from the *Globe*. And Searle from the *Herald*."

"Maybe I'll join them in a bit."

"Okay. Catch you later."

I went back to the kitchen table and typed the last paragraph of my article. I was glad it was done. And I fervently hoped no one would ask me to do another piece on the same subject for a long while. I numbered the last page and pulled it from the typewriter.

It was a little after three when I left the apartment. The day was cold and industrial gray, with a damp edge just beneath the chill.

Had this been November, I'd have said we'd be expecting snow. But we were only at the end of September.

I stopped at the post office to mail the article and continued on to the police department. On impulse, I went in the front entrance rather than the rear as I normally did. John Ouellette was hovering by the desk, chatting with one of the cops behind it. I waved at him. He said something to the cop and they laughed. Then he walked over to where I was standing, a few feet from the entrance to the office of the Day Operations captain.

"Well, John," I said. "You'll have a nice piece for the front page of the Metro section tomorrow."

"Yeah," he agreed. "Good, isn't it, that they caught those two maggots."

"Mm-hmm. There are going to be an awful lot of relieved women in that part of Cambridge tonight."

He nodded. Then he glanced idly around at the main desk with the television monitors above it, and at the traffic desk. "This police department's been getting a lot of press lately, with this arrest today, and the Albert Parkes and Dalton Craig stuff, and the Citizens' Committee."

I curled my upper lip. "Oh, yes, the Citizens' Committee."

"I haven't been able to get any of the guys here to comment on that," he said. "At least comment on it in a way that I could reproduce word-for-word in a family publication. I wonder," he concluded with heavy irony, "why not?"

"Yeah, that's a real puzzle."

He smiled briefly. "Well, in any case, I'm interviewing the spokesperson for the Committee tomorrow. Linda Crosbie."

"The one who was standing on the box in the traffic island yesterday ranting about Jack's resignation."

"Yeah." Ouellette looked at me with a kind of rueful sympathy. "For what it's worth, I still don't think Jack was ever a member of any kind of illegal spy unit. I doubt one even existed, pretty much." He shrugged. "Maybe I'm not as paranoid as I should be about things like that."

"That's all right—Linda Crosbie's paranoid enough for two."

Ouellette shook his head. "I don't know about that. I spoke to Crosbie last night, and Liz, she didn't sound like a crackpot to me."

"What sort of evidence against Jack and Sam does she think she has?"

"That's what I'm hoping to find out when I talk to her."

"Well, if her only source of dirt is Dalton Craig, then you know exactly how much credence to put in it, don't you, John?"

"I'm sorry," he said.

I believed him. I even managed a smile. "I have to go now. Good to have run into you again so soon."

"Yeah, you too."

I'd gone a few paces when he said, "Liz."

I stopped and looked at him over my shoulder.

"I forgot something. Remember yesterday how you were asking about Otway Gilmore?"

"Sure."

"Well, I found out something else about him. It's probably no big deal. But—he's apparently been buying up parcels of land in East Cambridge and Kendall Square recently. What's left there to buy."

"For what reason?"

"Development, what else? Condos, offices. God, that fucker's going to own Massachusetts one of these days."

I nodded. "Yes, that property down by the river and Lechmere is very hot, isn't it?"

"I'll say."

"Probably explains why Gilmore wants to grab himself as big a hunk of it as possible. Thanks for telling me."

"You're welcome."

My mood had been upbeat when I'd arrived at the police station. While talking with Ouellette, though, I'd felt depression settle over me like a fine layer of grit. I made an effort to shake it off as I walked past the desk. I shoved open the heavy wooden door that led to the first-floor landing and went up the stairs to the C.I.D.

The cast-iron steps weren't nearly as littered with crushed cigarette

butts as they had been before the no-smoking-in-public-buildings ordinance had been passed. Perhaps someone should point that fact out to the Citizens' Committee.

Jack was at his desk, mulling over some report forms. He looked up as I walked into the office.

"A vision of loveliness," he remarked.

"Funny, all the guys say that to me."

"No, they don't. You wouldn't let them." He tossed the sheaf of papers in his right hand onto the desk blotter and leaned back in his chair. "You run into any of your little buddies from the fourth estate downstairs?"

"Just John Ouellette." I perched on the corner of his desk. "Sooo. Tell me about the big arrest."

"It's not complicated. Teddy and Joe were out last night, riding around about midnight, and they saw this beat-up old Buick go trolling the wrong way up Maple Avenue. Also, it was going very slowly, which looked funny to them. So they went to pull it over."

"And?"

"It accelerated, and skidded, and hit another parked car. Not hard, but enough to stop it."

"Go on."

"All right, there were two guys in the car. Black, young. The one in the driver's seat jumped out and tried to run. Teddy grabbed him and they mixed it up a little. At that point, Fox and Creighton showed up. They searched the Buick, and Creighton found a little cocaine in the glove compartment and a couple of half-empty cans of beer on the floor. And then he fished around under the front seat and hauled out a piece of lead pipe."

"Oh, boy."

"So Teddy said to the driver of the car, 'What's this for?' And the guy said, 'You know.' And Teddy said, 'No, I don't. Tell me.' And the guy said, 'Well, you got us, man.' And Teddy said, 'Got you for what?' And this clown answers, 'You know, man. All them ladies we done.' "

"My God," I said. "They admitted to the assaults?"

"Yeah," Jack said, his voice sounding as if he were having trouble believing what he was telling me. "It was like they weren't even bothered about being arrested. As if it were all part of the game. As if they were expecting to be picked up sooner or later." He grimaced. "Why am I surprised? I've seen this before."

"What? Guys being arrested for terrible crimes and not minding being arrested?"

"Sure. It's like they don't give a shit. Oh, given a choice, yeah, they'd probably prefer not to be arrested. But, basically, what do they care if they get sent to prison? They've been there before." He shrugged. "What does ten or twenty years in Walpole mean to someone like that?"

"A bed, three square meals a day, and all the sex and drugs you can consume."

"Right."

"So why did one of them try to run, then? And punch Teddy?"

"Pavlov reaction, probably. Liz, you should see these two cruds. I've met acorn squashes with bigger intellects."

"Are they locals?"

"No, turns out they're both from Boston. Mattapan."

"What brought them to Cambridge?"

Jack shrugged again. "Fresh turf. Probably ran out of assault victims in the home territory."

"I assume they both have records in Boston."

"Oh, sure. Armed robbery, assault with a deadly weapon, auto theft, possession of a controlled substance with intent to sell . . . you name it."

"Setting up a graven image and worshiping it?"

Jack smiled. "Not unlikely."

"Well, now they can add murder to their list of accomplishments."

"You mean Paula Young?"

"Well, yes. Who else?"

Jack got up, went over to his filing cabinet, and pulled open the top drawer. He removed from it a worn and thickly stuffed manila

folder and glanced at the contents. Then he slapped the folder shut and tucked it back into the top drawer. He turned to me.

"I'm not too sure those two clowns committed a murder," he said.

I stared at him. "But, Jack—you just told me. . . ."

"I said they admitted to assaulting a series of women. *Six* women."

"But they didn't admit to killing or even to attacking Paula Young?"

"No."

"Did anyone ask them if they'd killed her?"

"What do you think, Liz?" Jack gave the filing cabinet drawer a shove and it rolled back into place with a muffled clunk. "Of course, somebody asked. And they said no, no way." He went back to his desk and sat down again behind it. "No way did they kill Paula Young."

"They could just be saying that because they don't want to face murder charges."

"They could."

I cocked my head. "But you don't think they're lying, do you? You believe them."

"I think I do." He sounded surprised at himself.

I frowned. "But why?"

He rested his elbows on the arms of his chair. "Go back. What happened to those first six women? I mean, other than that they all got beaten to hamburger."

"Well . . . let's see. They were all robbed, weren't they?"

"Right."

"And Paula Young wasn't. Is that what you're telling me?"

"Yes. When you and I found her the other night, something I noticed right away was that she was wearing a gold chain around her neck with a pendant that had a diamond on it about the size of an aspirin. Now a necklace like that has to be pretty valuable, doesn't it?"

"I would say."

"Plus she also had on a gold watch. And when I went through her purse, she had a hundred and two dollars in her wallet. You really think a robber would pass up any of those items?"

"No."

"And the two guys who got arrested last night were most definitely robbers. Now that proves zilch, I know. But what does it seem to suggest?"

I slid off the desk. "Do I have to bother to tell you?"

The cops found out a great deal about Paula Young over the next few days. All of it was innocuous.

She had been a month past her thirty-fourth birthday when she'd died. She had been born and brought up in Rumson, New Jersey. She was the second of three daughters. She had never been married. She had no police record, nor had she ever served in the military.

By profession, she was a C.P.A. A business administration major from New York University, she also held a master's degree in taxation from Pace. For the past six years, she'd been employed by one of the largest and most prestigious accounting firms in Boston. Two years ago, she'd bought a condo on Trowbridge Street, the third floor of a renovated three-decker.

People who knew her said there was no special man in her life, although she dated occasionally. She worked out twice a week at a health club near Porter Square. She had a subscription to the Symphony. In the summer, she sailed. In the winter, she cross-country skied. She liked Thai food and Caribbean vacations. She drank only sparingly and didn't touch drugs. She liked to give small dinner parties. She shopped at Saks and Barsamian's, and belonged to the Book-of-the-Month Club.

All in all, she was your typical affluent, unattached, hard-working young Boston-Cambridge career woman. Of course, none of her friends could think of a single reason why anyone would want to beat Paula Young to death.

Neither could the cops.

Not only had Paula Young not been robbed, she hadn't been raped. Almost always it was one or the other or both with a female street crime victim. But Paula's murder, as far as I could see, seemed to have been committed for the hell of it.

A nice thought. What it meant was that even though the two subhumans from Mattapan were under lock and key, the women of mid-Cambridge still weren't safe from random attack on the street.

John Ouellette had a piece in the *Globe* on the Citizens' Committee. It was short and, given the inflammatory nature of the subject, remarkably understated. Then again, Ouellette as a reporter was supposed to take an objective point of view, wasn't he? I read the article with equal amounts of trepidation and fascination.

Ouellette was right: Linda Crosbie didn't come across as a crackpot or a hysteric. Intense, yes. Incorrect in her assumptions? That, too. But far from silly or paranoid-sounding.

The gist of the article was that, while the Citizens' Committee had not yet gathered concrete examples of the alleged misdoings of an alleged spy unit within the C.P.D.—and in fact had only the assertion of Dalton Craig that such a unit had existed—the Committee would be actively seeking further information on this score. Crosbie also invited any resident of Cambridge who had been subject to any form of harassment by the C.P.D. to get in touch with her or any other Committee member.

Good luck to them, I thought, and set the paper aside to show to Jack.

While the police were going after the killer, or killers, of Paula Young, and Linda Crosbie was going after the police, and Jack was going after the murderer of Edward Hassler, I was going after Otway Gilmore and Albert Parkes. The first part of the search entailed spending an entire day in the public library looking at microfilmed back issues of the *Globe* and the *Herald* in its previous incarnations as the *Herald-American*, the *Herald-Traveler*, and the *Record-American*.

The articles on the Stephen Larrain murder and the arrest of Phillie Joyce and Albert Parkes were big stuff, but they didn't tell me anything I didn't already know. The business pages of both papers yielded up the occasional piece about a recent divestiture or acqui-

sition or merger or leveraged buy-out or whatever on the part of Otway Gilmore. It wasn't exactly riveting reading.

A wedding announcement in the *Globe* gave me the name of the man who'd married Parkes's daughter, the man who'd just recently offered to testify in court that Parkes had been framed by Jack. The man for whom Parkes had built a seven-hundred-and-fifty-thousand dollar house. Stanley Watters. I wrote that down in the little notebook I carry everywhere with me.

The library also had, on microfilm, back issues of the *Suffolk Tribune*, Larrain's paper. I combed through them for his columns on Gilmore. There had been six on that subject between November 1976 and February 1977. I enjoyed reading them. They were very vitriolic and very well written.

The last column about Gilmore concerned the fire in Gilmore's Chelsea tenement, the one in which the eighteen-month-old girl had died. It was a masterpiece. In it, Larrain had traded his characteristic irony for a kind of driving, controlled savagery. His commentary was brilliantly interspersed with quotes in broken English from the dead child's mother, quotes whose inarticulacy merely rendered them the more eloquent.

I read the column twice. When I'd finished, I let my body sag down into the uncomfortable library chair, with its low wooden back and creaky orange plastic cushion. I ached for the dead kid and her mother, and also for the loss of a writer as good as Larrain.

9

IT WAS MONDAY afternoon and I was standing on the corner of Newbury and Arlington Streets in Boston, waiting to meet another reporter friend, Anna-Grace Carpenter. Anna-Grace had spent most of her long career writing for a variety of publications about the connections between politics and big business. She might be an excellent source of information about Otway Gilmore. She had a well-justified reputation for not only knowing where all the bodies were buried but for disinterring them as well. She was also tough, abrasive, and salty, traits that didn't endear her to people who thought that women reporters ought to be confined to the society pages. I knew of at least three bank presidents and five state legislators who turned pale at the mention of her name. My kind of girl.

From the corner I watched well-dressed people, individually and in groups, enter and leave the Ritz. This section of Newbury Street was a sort of toned-down, miniaturized version of Rodeo Drive. Or, more accurately, Fifth Avenue between 48th Street and the Plaza. Across from me was a shop that sold seven-hundred-dollar shoes and a confectioner's where you could buy a single chocolate truffle for five bucks. Both were doing a brisk business.

I felt something brush my elbow and turned. Anna-Grace stood behind me. I grinned at her. "I thought you were a pickpocket."

She surveyed my six-year-old windbreaker and faded jeans. "If I

were, I'd give you a miss. Why don't you buy yourself some decent clothes, for Christ's sake, Liz?"

"In real life I'm a rich matron from Chestnut Hills," I said. "I just like to masquerade as an impoverished writer."

We began walking down Newbury. The wind was at our backs and chilly. I buttoned my jacket.

"You want to know about Otway Gilmore," Anna-Grace said. I nodded.

"He's an awful person." She shook her head slowly as she spoke.

I was struck by the seriousness, almost the solemnity of her tone. Usually Anna-Grace tended toward a sardonic contemptuousness when speaking of bad guys.

We walked past a jewelry store open by appointment only. Across the street a woman was alighting from a limousine double-parked in front of a furrier's.

"Practically all of what I can tell you about Gilmore is hearsay," Anna-Grace said. "I've never actually met the man."

"Who has?" I shrugged. "That's okay."

"He's married. He has two daughters. One's a sophomore at Wellesley. The other's married and living out west somewhere. California, I think." Anna-Grace glanced at me. "If you're looking for dirt there, I've never heard any."

We passed a hair and skin salon said to be favored by visiting actresses. It offered makeup instruction. I wondered what it would be like to have my face painted by a professional. Would hordes of dazzled and lustful men follow me down the street afterward? Maybe I'd buy some new jeans first.

"I've heard Gilmore collects art and books," I said. "And supports fashionable charities. Does he have that other rich man's pastime?"

"What's that?"

"Women. Does Gilmore have any expensive playmates?"

Anna-Grace laughed. "None that I've ever heard of. Liz, the guy has only two real lusts—more land and more money."

"And his reputation."

She gave me a puzzled look. "What?"

"Well, he killed Stephen Larrain to protect it, or at least to avenge it, didn't he?"

"Oh, is that your theory?"

There was an edge to her voice that made me frown. "It's several people's. You don't agree with it?"

Her lips curved briefly in the shape if not the spirit of a smile. "No, I don't. Gilmore never gave a shit whether people thought he was good, bad, or ugly. Oh, I know he's a colossal egomaniac. But the only time he'd ever care if somebody said anything nasty about him would be if it would lose him business. Or put him some place where he couldn't do any business at all."

I looked at her. The small acid smile had vanished from her face, leaving it flat and rather tight around the eyes.

"What does that mean?" I asked.

"This is nothing I could ever prove," Anna-Grace said. "But I'm willing to bet my pension that Larrain had some hard, verifiable information that Gilmore had committed some crimes other than the ones Larrain had already accused him of. I'd also bet that this information was the sort that could either send Gilmore to prison for a long time or cost him a hell of a lot of money." Anna-Grace took a deep breath. "And Gilmore found that out, and had Larrain killed before he could write a story about it or go to the Attorney General's office or . . . or whatever Larrain would have done under those circumstances. Probably he'd have written his story first."

We walked past the Harvard Bookstore Café. There was a poster outside the entrance advertising an upcoming wine-and-cheese party in honor of John Updike, Sue Miller, and James Carroll.

"If Larrain had that kind of information," I said, "what happened to it? He apparently hadn't filed anything with his editor at the *Suffolk Trib.*"

"Maybe the guy who got hired to kill Larrain—that sleazebag Joyce—also got hired to steal Larrain's notes."

I shook my head. "I don't think so. If he had, it's something he would have mentioned to the district attorney when he was negotiating his plea. And he didn't." I paused, recalling what Jack had told

me. "Anyway, Joyce seemed to think that Gilmore wanted Larrain taken out because of the columns Larrain had *already* written about him."

"Well, that's probably the story Parkes fed Joyce. Maybe Parkes believed it, too. Maybe the information Larrain had was such bad dirt that Gilmore didn't want even Parkes and Joyce to know what it was. Or even that Larrain had it."

"I don't know," I said. "You still haven't explained how Gilmore found out that Larrain had the goods on him. Or how Larrain got the goods to begin with, if there was no documentation."

Anna-Grace twitched her shoulders, irritably. "Oh, for Christ's sake, Liz, what does it matter?" There was a harsh note in her voice now. "Maybe Larrain got a tip that Gilmore was involved in some kind of major real estate scam, and he started poking around trying to verify the rumor. And Gilmore got wind of what Larrain was doing, and got nervous about it, and decided to take Larrain out of action." Anna-Grace let out a long breath. "I'm not saying that's exactly what happened, but it could have."

I looked at her thoughtfully. "The whole subject really disturbs you, doesn't it?"

"Of course it does. Do *you* like the idea that somebody like Gilmore can not only get away with murder but thumb his nose at the rest of us?"

We were at the corner of Newbury and Exeter. What had been the Exeter Street Theater when I was in preparatory school was now a Conran's, selling hi-tech housewares. I had a brief, vivid memory of climbing the building's fire escape on a dare from a boy who was a student at the Berklee School of Music. I even recollected that I'd been wearing a blue Villager sweater and skirt at the time. I'd been nineteen then, and nothing had seemed impossible.

Anna-Grace and I walked over to Commonwealth Avenue. The pedestrian mall in the middle—it was too long and too wide and too much like a garden to be called a traffic island—was furnished with wooden benches. We found one that wasn't completely encrusted with pigeon droppings and took it.

"Anything else on Gilmore?" I asked.

Anna-Grace put her hands in the pockets of her trenchcoat and crossed her legs at the ankles. "There was a story going around two or three years ago . . ."

"Yes?"

"I'm sure it's true. But it's another one of those goddamned things that's completely unprovable, which is why you never saw anything in print about it. Actually, I don't think that many of the reporters know it. I only heard it because . . ."

"You have incredible contacts and everybody tells you everything."

Anna-Grace pulled herself up straight against the back of the bench. "There was a man in Quincy; Merton Holmes his name was. He was a developer like Gilmore, only on a much smaller scale. Anyway, he owned a bunch of land, not only in Quincy but in Milton, and in a couple of other places on the South Shore. Hingham and Cohasset, towns like that. All this property was very valuable, of course. Holmes was going to build residential condos on the parcels in Quincy and Milton and, from what I heard, was intending to turn the other land on the South Shore into vacation communities."

"Sure," I said. "There're a lot of places like that in those towns. I see them advertised all the time."

"Well," Anna-Grace said, "Gilmore was apparently very eager to cash in on the real estate boom down there. So he made an offer to buy up some of Holmes's property. And Holmes turned him down."

I grimaced. "Gilmore's not the kind of guy to take no for an answer."

"Gilmore made a second offer, and Holmes refused that, too. Then he upped the ante a third time, but Holmes still wasn't willing to sell. So . . . Gilmore backed off."

"Huh," I said, surprised by Anna-Grace's last words. "Was he nasty about it?"

"No, he was the soul of graciousness. Said he regretted Holmes's decision, but that he understood perfectly the reasons for it."

"What a gentleman."

Anna-Grace ignored the interruption. "About a month later, somebody broke into one of Holmes's construction sites in Milton and trashed it."

I wrinkled my forehead. "How do you trash a construction site? They all usually look as if they've been hit by bombs to begin with."

"By sabotaging the heavy equipment, for one thing. Also, by torching the site office—you know, the mobile home sort of things they always have parked on those lots?"

"Right."

"This one got burned to the ground. It was definitely arson. Somebody'd broken into it and poured gasoline all over everything."

"How nice."

"Yeah." Anna-Grace shifted around on the bench. "Anyway, Holmes figured it was random vandalism; he didn't, as far as he knew, have any enemies who might be out to get him. The cops and the state fire marshal's office investigated, but never came up with anything." Anna-Grace took her hands from her coat pockets and held them out, palms up. "Holmes put in an insurance claim for the destroyed equipment, chalked the whole episode up to bad experience, and went out and bought some guard dogs to patrol his property." Anna-Grace glanced at me. "Now I'm going to get to the ugly part of the story."

"Okay."

"A couple of weeks after the business in Milton, somebody broke into Holmes's construction site in Quincy. And"—she gave me another quick look—"this is going to bother you, Liz."

I shook my head impatiently. "Go on."

"Whoever it was, slit the throat of one of the watchdogs and then hung the body on the fence like a—like a side of beef or something."

I cringed.

"An autopsy was done on the dog, and they found that it had been shot with a tranquilizer dart or gun or whatever before it was . . . you know."

I felt queasy. "Yes. You couldn't get near a trained guard dog unless you'd drugged it first," I muttered.

"Whoever killed the dog," Anna-Grace said, "also did the exact same kind of destruction job on the Quincy site as had been done on the one in Milton. Again, the cops and the state fire marshal's office investigated. And again they didn't come up with any suspects. But . . ."

"But what?"

"They started looking a little askance at Holmes."

"My God." I drew a sharp breath. "They thought he might have done it himself? Burned down his own property and killed his own dog?"

"Insurance fraud." Anna-Grace shrugged. "It happens, especially in the building trades. I suppose if I'd been the cops, I'd have wondered, too. Maybe."

"Yes, but to slit the throat of *your own dog* . . ."

"I told you that part would bother you."

"Go on. I'm fine." Nonetheless, I felt my lips clamp together and I could taste bile in the back of my throat.

"Things started getting worse and worse for Holmes," Anna-Grace said. "There was no more vandalism or dog butchering, but when he applied for loans to begin construction on the vacation places on the South Shore, he kept running into all these stone walls."

"The banks wouldn't lend him the money?"

"Nope. It was very strange. Holmes had always been considered a good risk in the past. But at this point, he was having a hell of a time trying to find someone to finance him. He sure couldn't finance himself, because however rich you are, you can't pay one hundred million dollars out of your own pocket to subsidize a major development."

"No, you can't."

"Holmes wasn't quite in that league, anyway. I mean, he was well-off, but most of it was in land he'd inherited from his father."

"This story isn't going to have a happy ending," I said. "I can just feel it."

"I told you it wouldn't. Holmes started having problems again with his developments in Milton and Quincy."

"Not more vandalism," I pleaded. "I don't think I can take another dead dog story."

"No, this was different. He started having labor difficulty. Sometimes half the crew wouldn't show up. And then there was some screw-up with the utility permits in Quincy. All of which resulted in a lot of delay. It ended up costing Holmes a lot of money."

I nodded.

"Well," Anna-Grace said, "the worst for him was yet to come. He and his wife and son went out to dinner one night—probably to forget their troubles for a few hours—and when they got home, they didn't have one any longer."

"What?"

"It had burned in their absence."

"You're kidding." I knew she wasn't.

"I wish I were. Luckily, it was the maid's night out, or else the fire department would have found a charred corpse in the ruins." The corners of Anna-Grace's mouth turned down. "But the fact that there was no one home when the house went up only made things look that much worse for Holmes. Because the place had definitely been torched."

"And Holmes was the number-one suspect for the torching?"

"Oh, sure. He was known to be in financial straits, and at that point, he'd had a history of arson jobs done on his properties."

"What happened after that?"

"Holmes spent the next few days following the fire putting his business and legal affairs in the best shape he could. And then he got into his car and went for a long drive and parked in a rest area off Route 495. And then he blew his brains out." Anna-Grace stood up abruptly, brushing off the skirt of her trenchcoat. "Come on. I have to get back to work."

We walked in silence, heads down, across the mall and Commonwealth Avenue.

On the corner of Exeter and Newbury, in the Gothic shadow of the old theater, I said, "It was Gilmore, wasn't it?"

Anna-Grace's smile looked as if someone had drawn a straight-

edged razor across the lower half of her face. "So they say. And I believe it."

I bent over and hit both knees with my fists. "What kind of power does that man have? Okay, so he could hire people to burn down houses and slaughter dogs. I'm sure he has that kind of muscle on hand. But"—I straightened up—"is he that strong, that potent, that influential, that he could order the banks not to give loans to someone? And just walk into the city offices anywhere and tell them to hold up or delay a building permit, and they'd do it? And cause a work crew to strike? Just because he told them to?"

"Men like Gilmore have tremendous clout," Anna-Grace observed, in rather prim tones.

"They sure as fucking well do," I said bitterly.

A stronger wind had blown up and a huge bank of purple and charcoal clouds had boiled up in the eastern sky. The light had changed to a queer greenish-yellow, the sure precursor of a major storm. I hurried for the subway. Leaves and bits of paper swirled and skittered along the sidewalk, driven by the wind.

I tried as hard as I could, during the ride, to keep my mind a total blank. But the magic lantern in my brain kept flashing alternate shots of a man with a shattered head sprawled across the front seat of a car and the limp corpse of a dog dangling from a chain-link fence like a discarded sweater. I squeezed my eyes shut and tried to concentrate on the little pinpoints of light and amoeboid spangles that danced and swam on the inner surface of the lids.

I got off the train at Porter Square. I was supposed to meet Jack— he was going to stop at my place on his way home from work and pick up Lucy. I looked at my watch. Four-thirty. I should do some grocery shopping; there were a few staples we needed. Offhand, I couldn't think of anything I felt less like doing.

The sky was solid steel as I dashed across Somerville Avenue to the shopping center. I hoped the rain would hold off till I got to Jack's. The prospect of trudging five blocks in a downpour clutching a sodden and disintegrating grocery bag didn't thrill me.

Oddly, my mood began to lighten a bit as I moved through the aisles of the supermarket. Maybe it was the sheer banality of the exercise. Or maybe it was the sight of housewives—and, since this was Cambridge, an equal number of men, mostly bearded and backpacked—knocking on cantaloupes and scrutinizing lettuce heads. Whatever it was, I could feel myself becoming tranquil as I browsed over the cheese selection. All the same, I avoided the meat counter.

The sky had gone from steel to lead. I checked out of the supermarket and, on impulse, stopped at the liquor store and bought a bottle of wine to go with dinner. Thus provisioned, I scurried across the intersection of Somerville and Massachusetts avenues.

It was just beginning to rain in large, glutinous drops when I got to Jack's. I set the grocery bag down on the front porch, fished the key from my purse, and unlocked the front door. Lucy was standing on the other side of it, tail performing boy scout flag maneuvers.

"Well, hello," I said, startled by the sight of her. It was just five o'clock. Early for Jack to be home. I picked up the grocery bag and stepped into the foyer. The interior of the house was dim.

"Jack?" I called.

His voice came from the living room.

"You're back early," I said, and carried the food into the kitchen, snapping on the overhead light switch with my elbow. I put away the milk and coffee and set the cheese on the counter to soften. The wine I put in the middle of the table, as if it were a centerpiece.

I walked down the hall to the living room. Jack hadn't turned on any of the lamps. I stood for a moment in the doorway, letting my eyes adjust to the lack of light. As they focused, I saw Jack in one of the chairs before the fireplace. He was sitting as he always did, legs stretched out and shoulders slightly slumped.

"Put on a light, if you like," he said.

"Maybe just a little one," I said. "I like this cavern effect." I walked into the room, and leaned over to flick on the end-table lamp by the couch. A few of the shadows in the room receded.

I went to the chair across from Jack and sat down.

"You're early tonight," I repeated.

"I know."

I crossed my legs and leaned sideways against one of the chair wings. The rain that had been tentative a few moments ago was now rattling like birdshot against the windowpanes. This would be a good evening to give the fireplace a workout.

"Like a drink?" Jack said.

"Sure."

He made a move to get up and I held out a hand to him. "No hurry. It's nice here. Warm." I turned my head to look at him, feeling suddenly soft and weary. It was a good sensation.

"Jack, I had a talk with Anna-Grace Carpenter this afternoon. It was very interesting, but, oh, so depressing. I'll tell you about it later."

Jack was settled motionless in his chair.

"What did you do today?" I asked. "Whatever it was, it had to have been more uplifting than what I did."

"I got suspended," he said.

10

I DIDN'T REACT to his words, mostly because I couldn't. A moment of silence yawned between us. Then Jack pushed himself up from the armchair and walked out of the room. His footsteps receded down the hall to the kitchen. I continued to sit, listening to the sound of my breathing. Faint as it was, it seemed louder to me than either Jack's footsteps or the insistent clatter of the rain against the window.

The room seemed too dark now. I switched on the pole lamp next to my chair.

"Here."

Jack's voice made me jump. I looked up and to my right. He was standing over me, a glass in either hand. He gave the one with vodka in it to me.

"You startled me," I said, in the vague manner of someone emerging from a deep sleep or general anesthesia. I took the glass.

He sat down on the arm of his chair and stared at me. "I shouldn't have dropped it on you like that. I'm sorry."

I wriggled upright as the waking sensation became stronger. "Don't apologize." I took a sip of my drink. The icy astringency of the vodka catapulted me further into sensibility. I shook my head. "You didn't do anything to apologize for."

He gave a short laugh in which there was no lightness and very little humor. "Some people would disagree with you very strongly there."

"Jack, what is this? Will you tell me, please, without being funny or elliptical?"

He nodded, and there was no more death's-head amusement in his face.

"I don't understand," I said. "Is it because of Dalton Craig and Albert Parkes? The Citizens' Committee . . . is *that* it? Jack, you *told* me you wouldn't get into any trouble with the department over that."

"This has nothing to do with Dalton or Parkes."

I leaped on the omission. "The Citizens' Committee?"

"Well, yeah, they've gotten into it." He leaned forward, his elbows on his knees, the glass held in both hands. I was clutching mine, too, as if it were a talisman. An eighty-proof rabbit's foot.

"What?" I said. "What is it?"

The full dark weight of his gaze was heavy on me. "A woman says, that, three years ago, I raped her."

The glass in my hand tilted and a small cataract of liquor slopped down my leg. I opened my mouth. Nothing came out of it except a little air.

Jack reached out, took the glass from me, and set it on the small table between the two chairs. Then he glanced at his watch. "We can catch the whole story on the news in a few minutes, if you'd like."

I found my voice, except that it didn't sound like mine. "No. You tell me." My lips and throat felt stiff as they formed the words.

"Yeah." He was still watching me very closely, as I was him. Reading each other's faces. There was nothing in his. I don't know what he saw in mine, other than maybe the rigid blankness of shock.

"All right," he said. "Well, this woman—she lives here in Cambridge, name of Yolanda Sims—filed an official complaint that, on three separate occasions in April of 1986, I forced her to have, uh, sexual intercourse with me."

I drew a long, shuddering breath.

Jack raised his glass and took a swallow of bourbon. "The first of these incidents," he continued, sounding as if he were reading from

a police report, "she claims took place on the evening of April tenth, in her house. The second, two nights later, in the same place. The third, a week after that. Also in the same place."

He put his glass on the table, got up, and paced slowly over to stand before the empty fireplace. His back was to me. He had his arms folded and was looking down at the hearth tiles.

"She doesn't say I held a knife to her throat or a gun to her head, or that I threatened to beat her up, or anything like that." He uncrossed his arms, let them drop to his sides, and then shoved his hands into his pockets. "What she says is that I extorted the sex from her." He turned, slowly, to face me, rocking back a little on his heels. "In exchange for offering not to testify against her son in a robbery case."

"What?"

He shrugged. "Yeah, well, she's got this kid, Joey, he must be about twenty-two by now, who'd been in and out of the courts since he was, oh, I guess, fourteen. Started out his criminal career with stuff like malicious destruction of property, then on to possession of drugs, then car theft . . . finally, he graduated to armed robbery." Jack made a sour, disgusted face. "He and these two shit-for-brains buddies of his decided it would be fun to hold up a convenience store wearing Halloween masks, just like the bad guys on TV. So they did—it was the store at the intersection of Prospect and Broadway, if you care—and everything would have been cool, except that the elastic on Joey's mask snapped, and it fell off his face."

My mouth twitched reflexively. I made a fist and pressed it to my lips.

Jack noticed. He walked to the table and picked up his drink. "You can laugh," he said. "It *is* pretty funny, the picture of that little schmuck pointing a gun at the clerk, trying to look like a bad-ass, and then his disguise ends up on the floor."

I was silent.

"Anyway, Joey got scared, and he told the clerk he'd blow her head off if she didn't give him all the money in the register. So she did, and then he and the other two desperadoes took off." Jack sat down again on the arm of the chair. "The point is, the clerk recognized Joey as one of the local kids." Jack shook his head. "Apparently it didn't occur to the little prick to try to rob a place where the people behind the counter didn't already know him. Then again, I suppose he figured wearing a mask would make him invisible. Which, who knows, maybe it would have if the damn thing had stayed on." Jack lowered his head and brought the glass of bourbon to his mouth. I reached for my own drink.

"Anyhow," Jack said, "I *did* arrest Joey the morning after the robbery." He glanced up at me. "That was the morning of April tenth."

"I see."

"Uh-huh. Okay. Well, Yolanda Sims claims that I came to her that night, around seven o'clock, with a proposition." Jack looked away from me, at the fireplace. "She says that I told her that if she let me fuck her, I'd arrange to have the charges against Joey buried."

The word "fuck" came very harshly from Jack's mouth.

I closed my eyes. When I opened them, Jack was peering at his watch. "Time for the show," he said. He got up, crossed the room to the television set, switched it on, and pressed the channel selector button. Then he moved back a pace and stood watching as the maze of colored dots on the screen coalesced into an image. I levered myself out of my chair and joined him. Side by side, we gazed at the television like a pair of nineteenth-century aborigines presented with a microwave oven.

The picture was a little fuzzy. Jack leaned forward, fiddled with the aerial, and the picture sprang into immediate crisp focus.

Most of the screen was taken up by a close-range shot of the head and shoulders of a brightly blond woman in her late forties. She had a narrow, pointed face. Her features were small and sharp.

Jack looked at his watch again. "Didn't I time this perfectly?" he said. "Five minutes into the newscast. That's her." He nodded at the television. "Yolanda Sims."

"Turn up the volume," I said, in a tight voice.

He did so. "Must be a slow news night," he commented dryly, "for them to put this on so early."

Yolanda Sims and another woman sat side by side on wooden stools against the backdrop of a white wall. The other woman was Linda Crosbie, Director of the Citizens' Committee Against Police Repression. She looked grave.

Yolanda Sims looked . . . hard. She might in actuality have looked like Joan of Arc just before they torched the kindling, but not to my eyes. She wore rust-colored slacks and a rust-and-white long-sleeved sweater with padded shoulders and a low V neck. Her makeup was a bit too brilliant and her hairstyle—deep bangs and a bouffant mass of short, sculpted curls—was a bit too elaborate for the occasion. Next to her, Linda Crosbie—who wasn't much younger than Sims—seemed like a dewy faced and slightly windblown child.

Staring at Yolanda Sims, I thought, God, Jack has better taste in women than *her*. She looked to me like an aging floozy. Who would believe that he'd be interested in . . .

I cut off the thought, appalled that my reaction could be so facile and snobbish.

Jack was gazing at the screen.

Linda Crosbie was speaking. "Ms. Sims," she said. "We're all certainly horrified and disgusted by the suffering you've experienced. But can you tell us why you waited three years to seek justice in this case?"

Good question. I was wondering that myself. I moved a little closer to Jack and took his hand.

Yolanda Sims arranged her face to look diffident, yet earnest. "Well, I . . ." Her voice was low and hesitant. "I heard about the Citizens' Committee, and how they would help people like me." She stared down at her lap. "I guess I was afraid to say anything, before now."

"I see." Linda Crosbie's voice was sharp, yet sympathetic. "Why were you afraid?"

Yolanda Sims was quiet, her face puckered.

"Had you been in some way threatened?" Linda Crosbie prodded.

Sims chewed at her lower lip and then nodded, just once.

"In what manner?" Crosbie asked, sounding grim.

Yolanda Sims looked up from her lap. "The police officer said that if I didn't do what he wanted, he'd fix it so that my boy went to jail for a long, long time. And then he told me what it was like in the prisons, and what would happen to my Joey if he went to someplace like Walpole." She closed her eyes and shook her head violently. Linda Crosbie reached across and patted her hand.

"Did this police officer, John Lingemann, then arrange to have the charges against your son dropped?"

"No. He even testified against Joey before the grand jury."

Linda Crosbie's mouth set in a tight line. "I see. Did you have any contact with the police officer after that?"

Sims's throat moved, as if she were swallowing hard. "I . . . I tried to call him at the police station. He wouldn't answer none of my calls. Then, one night, it was, oh, I guess a month after the grand jury, he came to my house."

"What happened then?" Linda Crosbie's face looked as if it had been carved from granite.

Yolanda twitched her shoulders. "He told me that I should stop bothering him, or . . ."

"Or what?"

Yolanda put a hand to her face. "Or something bad would happen to Joey. And maybe to . . . to me."

"Did he specify what?"

Yolanda looked puzzled.

"Did he say exactly what bad things might happen?"

Yolanda shook her head. She took a deep breath. "He just laughed at me. Then he told me what a good reputation he had in the city, and about all these important friends he had, and how no one would believe me if I tried to tell them about what he'd done to me. Be-because I wasn't nobody and he was—" Sims's voice cracked and burst on a sob.

I released Jack's hand. My head felt thick and dizzy.

The criminal statutes of Massachusetts defined rape as "having sexual intercourse or unnatural sexual intercourse with a person and compelling such person to submit by force and against his will."

According to Yolanda Sims, Jack had forced her, on repeated occasions, to have sex with him.

She hadn't claimed he'd threatened her with a deadly weapon. She didn't have to.

Jesus God. This woman could get Jack arrested. She could also get him indicted, tried, convicted, and sent to prison. Cops who got sent to prison for any charge were always fair game for the other prisoners. Cops who got put away for a sex crime had about as much chance of surviving their interment as a snowball did of flourishing in hell.

Even if Jack were acquitted of the rape charge, his life would be ruined. Sure, he'd be reinstated—grudgingly—by the police department. Maybe he'd even advance in it, though that was doubtful. But whatever happened, there would always be people to say, *Oh yeah, there goes that piece of shit, the cop who raped somebody and got away with it.*

11

JACK WENT into the kitchen and dumped our unfinished drinks into the sink. I followed him like a somnambulist and sat down at the kitchen table.

His back was to me. "You all right?" he asked.

"Yes." I was quivering inside. "How about you?"

"I'm okay." He washed the glasses, wiped them with a towel, then folded the towel and put it on the counter. His movements were precise, economical.

How can you be okay? This is the worst thing that's ever happened to you since Diana died. It's the worst thing that's ever happened to us.

He was leaning against the counter, hands braced on its edge, staring at the window as if its rain-smeared panes were the source of some irresistible fascination. I got up and went over to him, put my hand on his arm. He turned his head toward me.

His expression was, well, it was one I'd never seen before, a kind of wary tentativeness, perhaps uncertainty. Only the barest shadow, but it was there, and it grew more intense as we looked at each other.

A moment went by before I realized that Jack was waiting for me to give him what his pride and reserve wouldn't allow him to ask for, or acknowledge that he needed—my assurance that I believed he was innocent.

Jack, don't you know that without my telling you?

I put my arms around him and pressed my face into his shoulder. For a second he resisted, stood still and unyielding, then I felt his arms slide around me. I rubbed my face slowly against his shirt. His hold tightened, and we leaned into each other. The warm silence of the kitchen closed around us, made denser by the clatter of the rain against the windows.

When we drew apart, it was in slow motion. I examined Jack's face. The shadow had retreated.

But something had passed between us as we'd held each other, something strong and intangible, like a spark of electricity. My inner commotion eased just a bit.

Jack smiled faintly. "You didn't finish your drink," he said. "Want another?"

I shook my head. "Let's go sit down," I said.

We went back to the living room and dropped down side by side on the couch. Jack put his arm around me and I settled against him.

"Now what do we do?" I said.

"I don't know what *we* do," Jack replied. "But I can tell you what's going to happen to me."

"Yes?"

"I can be suspended up to five days without a hearing. After that, I can request one, and they'll have to give it to me."

I raised my head slightly. "A hearing? What kind of hearing? In court?"

"No. This would be before the City Manager or," he said, assuming the tone of someone reading from a rule book, "his designated representative."

"Who else would be there?"

"My lawyer, somebody from the Superior Officers Association. Possibly the chief."

"What about Yolanda Sims?" I felt the corners of my mouth turn down as I pronounced the name.

"She wouldn't have to be there."

"She *wouldn't?*"

"No. It's not a hearing to establish whether I raped her—although I guess they think they have some cause to suspect that—but to establish whether I should continue to be suspended."

"What do you think will happen?"

He shrugged slightly, lifting his arm momentarily from my shoulders. "I don't know. It's something I can't predict."

I took a deep breath. "Suppose they decide to continue the suspension?"

"Then that's what they'll do."

"Oh, God. And after that?"

"Either way, there'll be an investigation."

"By Internal Affairs?"

"To begin with, yes."

I raised my head and stared at him. "Who else would get in on it?"

"Well, the DA's office. They'd do their own independent investigation."

"Oh, God," I repeated. I lowered my head and burrowed it against his shoulder. His arm around me tightened.

"But how can they investigate a crime that never took place?" I asked.

"It's a very serious charge, Liz. They *have* to treat it that way."

"I know, but . . . I mean, what are they going to *do*?" I bit my lower lip, hard. Maybe it was only the pain of that that made my eyes sting. "Do they think they'll line up a parade of witnesses who'll all say they saw you throw Yolanda Sims across a bed?"

"They do have one witness. Of a sort."

"Who?"

"Joey," he said. "Yolanda's kid. She says she told him, after he got indicted by the grand jury, that I forced her to go to bed with me because if she didn't, I'd make sure he'd end up doing bad time."

"Where is he, anyway? I assume he *did* get sent to prison?"

Jack gave a little snort of a laugh. "Walpole."

"That certainly makes Joey a credible witness, now doesn't it? Do either he or Yolanda seriously think anyone will take him at his word? A convicted felon getting up and testifying that the cop

who busted him is a bigger criminal than he is? Who'd believe that?"

"It's happened before," Jack said, his voice tired and quiet. "You know that, Liz."

I did, and being reminded made me grow cold inside.

We were silent for a moment. The rain seemed to have let up a little. At least it no longer sounded as if someone was hurling fistfuls of gravel at the windows. But the wind had risen. I was shivering.

"Want me to make a fire?" Jack said.

"Only if you feel like it."

He made no motion to get up and go to the fireplace. I pressed a little harder against his side.

"Jack?"

"Yes?"

"I'll go to the hearing with you."

I felt something brush lightly over my hair, and then he gave me a kiss on the forehead. "I know."

"I mean, I'll be there, whenever it is."

He didn't respond. I moved my head to look up at him. "Jack?"

"Hmmm?"

"Did you hear what I said?"

"Sure."

"Well, don't you want me to go with you? To the hearing?"

He inhaled, and then let the breath out very softly. "I think it would be better if you stayed away, sweetheart."

I didn't move for a while. Then I said, "Why?"

"It would just be . . . better if you weren't there, that's all." He smiled down at me.

I struggled upright, squirming against the encirclement of his arm. "*Why* would it be better, Jack?"

He shook his head.

"Jack—"

"No," he interrupted. "I'll go by myself."

"But I want to be there with you."

"I know you do. That's enough for me."

"Jack—"

"Ssh," he said and gave me another squeeze.

I was about to argue with him. I'm not sure what stopped me. But instead, I closed my eyes and nodded a slow and extremely reluctant assent.

12

THE FOLLOWING MORNING we slept late. There was no reason not to. I never had to go to work, and now Jack didn't, either.

He woke first, brought me a cup of coffee in bed. I sat up, put a pillow behind me, took the mug, and inhaled; Jack made the world's best coffee.

"I should be doing this for you," I said.

"What the hell for?" he asked.

I put the cup on the bedside table, leaned forward, and gave him a hug. "You're all dressed up."

"I have an appointment with the lawyer and the union representative at eleven. I'll probably be tied up with them for a few hours."

I nodded.

"I wondered why you were wearing a suit."

"Well, I have to look like a responsible person, you know."

"Oh, yes. Absolutely correct."

He leaned down and kissed me. "You have plans for today?"

I shrugged. "Just the usual. Research, write."

"Uh-huh. Well, have fun." He inevitably said that when we parted in the morning, just as I always told him to behave himself.

"Behave yourself."

"Got no option," he said.

*   *   *

I hopped out of bed and into the bathroom. I was showered, toothbrushed, dressed, combed and made up in twenty minutes. I downed my coffee and a small glass of orange juice. Then I grabbed my jacket, left Lucy in the living room with a great piece of rawhide, and ran five blocks to the subway station in Porter Square.

The police station, when I got there, looked as staunchly solid as it always had. I felt vaguely surprised—without Jack, I'd expected it to collapse overnight. I went in the Green Street entrance and up the short flight of stairs to the desk. Sam was standing by the elevator, talking to another detective named Joanne DeMarco. They both fell silent at my approach.

The three of us stared at one another, and an odd look flitted across Joanne DeMarco's face. She and I had a kind of breezy acquaintance; we'd had a drink together once, and she'd regaled me with a string of anecdotes about what a swell time she'd had when the male cops finally accepted her as one of the guys.

Jack had always thought highly of her. I thought she'd make a great article subject. She was the first and, as yet, the only female night narcotics investigator in the C.P.D.

Joanne was perhaps two inches shorter than I was, with a slim, athletic figure and dense, black, shoulder-length hair.

"Hi, Jo," I said, smiling deliberately. " 'Morning, Sam."

The smile she returned didn't, to my eyes, have much zip in it. Then she murmured something to Sam, wheeled, and hurried off to the muster room.

That just left me and Sam to contemplate each other.

Flaherty's basset-hound face was creased, as if he'd slept with it pressed against something hard. He cleared his throat. "Whatcha doing?"

"I wanted to talk to you," I said.

"Thought you might."

"I haven't had breakfast. Would you join me for coffee? You pick the place," I added. "Anywhere, just as long as it's not upstairs in the C.I.D."

The place we chose was one of the nine or ten coffee-and-doughnut shops that flourished within a two-block radius of the police station. It was run by a large and ebullient Lebanese family. A daughter took my order for eggs over easy and rye toast, and Mother brought Sam a large black coffee. We were seated at a booth in the back, in a little alcove. Perfect for a private chat.

"Joanne looked embarrassed to see me," I said. "What have I become, a pariah by association?"

Flaherty regarded me silently over his Styrofoam cup. He blew gently across the surface of its contents.

"Sorry," I said. "That was a cheap shot."

He shrugged, and sipped his coffee. "You're worried and you're pissed off. Can't blame you for that."

I bit the corner off a triangle of toast, chewed it, and swallowed. I was actually ravenous.

"Okay," I said. "I'm not going to fool around with this." I put the toast back on the plate and wiped my hands on a paper napkin. "Sam, do you think Jack raped Yolanda Sims?"

"Christ, Liz." He set his cup down. "What the hell kind of question is that?"

"How about your colleagues?"

"What?" He grimaced.

I ate some egg. "How about your brother and sister officers? What are their feelings on the subject?"

Flaherty let out an impatient breath. "As far as I know, the same as mine. I haven't heard anything different."

"Oh? Then why the suspension? And the Internal Affairs Investigation?"

"Because there has to be."

"Right." I finished an egg and a slice of toast, eating both without tasting either. Maybe I was fueling the rage inside me. It was there, just as Flaherty had noticed, and I could feel it expanding like a rogue tumor.

I slammed my fork down on the Formica tabletop.

"Liz," Flaherty said.

"What?"

"Calm down." He drank some coffee. "I'm on your side. And Jack's."

A spurt of guilt went through me. "I know you are." I looked down at my platter. Why was I venting my fury at this man? He was Jack's closest friend, not only inside the police department but out of it. They had been partners for ten years. If it had been Sam accused of rape and corruption, Jack would have been there for him, just as Sam would stand up for Jack now. Automatically and without question.

"Sorry," I said. "You're in some hot water yourself. I keep forgetting."

"That's all right. Anyway"—Flaherty shook his head—"the water I'm in ain't half as hot as Jack's is. Finish your breakfast. Then we'll talk some more."

"Yeah. Okay."

I ate what was left of the food and pushed my empty plate to one side. Flaherty lit a cigarette. He gave me a squinting smile through the smoke.

"You all settled down now?"

"I think so."

"Good." He stirred half a packet of artificial sweetener into his coffee.

"Sam, if Jack didn't do anything to Yolanda Sims, then why is she saying he did?"

He took another long drag on his cigarette. "Doll, people are always suing cops, or trying to sue them."

I scowled. "Yolanda Sims isn't suing Jack. She's trying to get him put in *jail*."

"That ain't gonna happen, and she knows it."

"Then what the hell is her point?"

Flaherty raised his left hand and rubbed the thumb against the index finger in a brisk circular motion. "Money," he said. "I bet you, Liz, whatever you want, that after the internal investigation's over, and they find no evidence against Jack, that Sims is gonna launch a

suit against him, the department, and the city. For about seven zillion bucks."

"But why bother, if you have no basis for the suit? If you know you can't win?"

"Oh, it'll never get to court." Flaherty gave me a nasty, horse-toothed grin. "The city will settle with Sims before that point. They'll give her a couple hundred grand or whatever just to get her off their backs and go away and shut up."

"Really."

"They almost always do, when something like this happens." Flaherty stubbed out his cigarette in the plastic ashtray beside the paper napkin dispenser. "Look, Liz, Yolanda Sims has had a grudge against Jack for the past three years for busting that fuck-up kid of hers. So she wants to get back at him, right? Only she don't know how. Then all this bullshit with Dalton Craig and Albert Parkes comes down. Right after that, we get a Citizens' Committee formed to protect all the folks in Cambridge from getting their rights violated by the police department. And their leader goes public, asking anybody who's ever been hassled or beaten up or—"

"Raped."

"Yeah, right—or raped by one of us animals, to come forward and see that the cop who did it gets brought to justice. Just to make sure he don't get the chance to commit any more crimes, you understand." Flaherty lit another cigarette. "They all got real pure motives. None of them are interested in the bread. Oh, my, no."

I picked up my coffee cup and pressed it against my chin. "So what you're saying is that Yolanda saw an opportunity to wreck Jack's career, plus cash in on the deal, and grabbed it."

"Yup."

"You think she has something going with the Citizens' Committee?"

Flaherty's eyes, slitted against the smoke from his cigarette, flared open at my last words. "Like a conspiracy?" he said. "Oh, Christ, no. She made up her sad story, took it to them, and they bought it."

"Without questioning any of the details?"

Flaherty smiled, again not pleasantly. "Why should they? She told them exactly what they wanted to hear."

"I suppose." I drank the rest of my coffee. "Sam, what about Joey Sims?"

"Don't worry about him," Flaherty said. "There's no prosecutor gonna trust that little bag of shit enough to even give him the right time of day, much less an Internal Affairs investigator."

I remembered having made the same observation to Jack the previous evening. Nice to have it confirmed by an objective party.

The waitress brought the check. Flaherty wanted to pay it. I told him there would be hell to pay if he even tried.

We walked out onto Western Avenue. I had my head down and my hands shoved into my jacket pockets. Slouching along, I must have looked as if I was sunken into the deepest well of depression. In any case, he paused on the sidewalk, just before the bus stop, and gave me a pat on the back. I glanced up at him, a little startled.

His long, seamed face wore what I supposed was an encouraging smile. "It'll turn out okay," he said. "It will. You wait and see."

I nodded. "I believe you." And added to myself, *I don't have a choice about that, do I?*

The hearing was held three days later. I hugged Jack hard before he left, and told him to break a leg. He said, "Yeah, with the way life has been going recently, that's probably exactly what I *will* do."

The whole thing would be over by five, give or take a quarter of an hour. I was supposed to meet Jack at the Harvest for a drink afterward. If things went well, we'd get loaded to celebrate. If things did not, we'd get loaded, period.

The afternoon passed for me with aching slowness. I went to the library to do preliminary research for a new article—on the short-comings of the Massachusetts correctional system—but had no concentration. I ended up wandering for an hour or so around the library grounds and the adjoining Rindge and Latin High School

campus, kicking through piles of brown and crumbling leaves and mumbling to myself. I must have looked demented.

At four, I went home to feed Lucy and change. I traded my jeans and tweed blazer for the green turtleneck dress, some gold jewelry, and my favorite perfume, for the time being, Pavlova. The last time I'd worn the green dress was the Sunday evening before Dalton Craig had gone on TV to accuse Jack of framing Albert Parkes for murder. I was beginning to think of that day as the Last Good One.

The Harvest, if not the most expensive, is certainly the chic-est restaurant-*cum*-bar in the city. It's Cambridge's subdued variation on the Le Cirque-Lutèce-Four Seasons theme. It is *the* watering hole for local and visiting celebrities and those who have the wherewithal and the desire to rub elbows with them. It is also the singles spot of choice for the affluent and *au courant*. Jack and I visited it only very infrequently, but when we did, we got a lot of laughs.

When I arrived at five after five, the bar was half full. I didn't see Jack, but I did see a tight end for the Patriots, the second lead of a television crime show filmed in Boston, and a reporter I recognized from the Channel Five newscast. The remaining clientele were well-dressed folk of either sex and whatever preference discreetly checking out the potential and the competition. I got a table for two as far away from the mating game as possible and ordered a vodka martini.

Jack appeared at five-fifteen. Three women and one man inspected him as he walked past the bar. I waved quickly at him. I was a little nervous about the Channel Five reporter. I had the feeling she might recognize Jack, and, even though she was obviously off-duty, she might try to get an interview.

Jack sat down opposite me and put his elbows on the table. We looked at each other, and for a moment we were alone in the middle of a vast and silent chamber.

"They lifted the suspension," he said.

I felt my insides melting and dissolving. I closed my eyes. Then I leaned across the table and grabbed Jack's wrists. He sat still for a moment, then pulled his arms gently from my grasp and took hold of my hands. We each squeezed, hard.

"Thank God," I said. "Oh, that's wonderful. I'm so happy. Oh, Jack."

The waiter brought me my martini. Jack asked for a bourbon on the rocks.

When the waiter left, I said, "Was it awful?"

Jack leaned back in his chair. "Not too bad."

"Was Yolanda there?"

He shook his head. "No. But I didn't think she would be. I told you she had no reason to show up."

"Oh, I'd have thought she might like to be present just to rub it in."

He smiled slightly. "Well, she wasn't."

We let go of each other's hands. "Tell me about it," I said.

"There's really not much to tell. The City Manager had reviewed the complaint. I answered some questions. My lawyer talked. The guy from the Superior Officers Association talked. The chief put in a few words. They consulted and deliberated and all that shit. Then, at the end . . ." He shrugged.

"They all obviously realized what was the truth."

"Who knows? There's still going to be an Internal Affairs Investigation."

"Yet they're letting you go back to work."

"Yeah, well, innocent until proven guilty."

"More like guilty until proven innocent, I'd say."

The waiter came to the table with Jack's bourbon.

"I have a feeling about this," Jack said. "I could be wrong. *But.*"

I widened my eyes at him.

"What I think it is," he said, "is not so much that those people today thought I'm being screwed, but more that, at the moment, they need me to keep on being useful to them. So that's why the reinstatement."

"You always have been useful to them, Jack. That's no news."

"That's not what I mean. You remember I'm on special assignment with the Hassler murder?" He looked thoughtful. "They want

me to keep working on that. I think there's big pressure on them to get it cleared up."

I sipped my martini. "Who's pushing the city to get Hassler solved?"

"I don't know, exactly. Probably other members of the Kendall Square and East Cambridge business community. They have the economic clout. And they don't like having one of their number get blown up. It makes them nervous about their own prospects."

"I suppose poor Mr. Hassler's wife and children would like to see an arrest made, too."

"Oh, sure." There was a sardonic note in Jack's voice. "But they aren't paying huge taxes to the city, are they?"

"No. But they have a larger interest than anyone else does in finding out who killed their husband and father, don't they?"

"Yeah," Jack replied. "And we all know what that's worth."

13

As it happened, we didn't get loaded. We had a second drink, dinner in the café (the exotic burger of the month), and went home to bed. The real celebration took place there. The next morning, Jack returned to the C.I.D. I had this vision of his colleagues greeting him with tears of joy and relief in their eyes. If they did, I'd never hear about it from him.

I spent the next morning riding around Cambridge with John Ouellette. He'd called me as I was finishing breakfast to tell me he had some new information on Otway Gilmore. He delicately refrained from mentioning anything about Jack's situation. But I knew him well enough to know that he, like all reporters and writers, always had some kind of not-so-well-hidden agenda, and that Lieutenant Lingemann's problem would be a red-letter item on it. In agreeing to meet him, I'd be, in effect, agreeing to some eventual trade-off of information.

He picked me up on the street outside my house at ten. As I got into his ancient Toyota, he gestured at a brown paper bag on the seat beside him. "Coffee in there. There's cream and sugar or artificial sweetener."

"Thanks." I reached into the bag. It also held a discus-sized Danish pastry, wrapped in wax paper and wedged between the two coffee cups. I held it up and said, "Oh, I see you're on a health-food kick."

"Breakfast of champions."

We drove out from my little comma-shaped street onto the main road.

"What've you got for me on Gilmore?"

"We got a press release the other day. Seems his next big project is going to be some development on the waterfront. Sort of a miniature version of the Bay State Plaza. Hotel, shops, condos, the works."

"That's nice." I ripped the lid from my coffee cup. "How many people did he slaughter or pay off to get the go-ahead for this one?"

Ouellette laughed. "I couldn't say. He's got a partner in this gig. A guy named Arthur Barrow."

"Who's he?"

"Senior partner of Barrow, Showalter, and Stevens. Big venture capital outfit."

"I see. Is this Barrow a murderer and a crook, too?"

"Far as I can tell, he's Mr. Clean."

I sipped my coffee. "Then why's he partnering with Gilmore?"

"Fucked if I know. Maybe Gilmore's decided to get involved in an honest enterprise for a change."

We turned left off Cambridge Street and onto Felton, then right onto Broadway, and left again up Quincy, past the Fogg Art Museum, the Harvard Faculty Club, and the Yard.

"Look on the backseat," Ouellette said. "There's a manila folder with a copy of the press release in it. Also a photo of Gilmore I dug up from our file."

It took me a while to find what I was looking for: The station wagon's backseat contained a gym bag, a cardboard carton full of empty Molson bottles, a tape recorder, a green sweater, three spiral-bound notebooks, and at least a week's worth of newspapers. The manila folder was under a pair of running shoes. I flipped it open. An eight-by-ten black-and-white photo of a bald man with thick, black caret-shaped eyebrows gazed up at me.

"You can keep the picture if you want," Ouellette said. "It's a copy. The release too."

"Thanks."

I stared down at the photograph. It was a full-length shot, taken from about ten feet away. Maybe the camera had created an illusion, but Gilmore's image seemed to project tremendous physical force. He was as tall, fit, and distinguished-looking as Harvey Searle had described him. He was dressed in what must have been a hand-tailored business suit. He was also scowling, apparently at the photographer who had caught him emerging from the revolving doors of a building. I shut the folder and tucked it on the dash. We turned right onto Mass. Avenue.

"I understand Jack's hearing went well yesterday," Ouellette said.

Here comes the trade-off, I thought. "I knew you weren't riding me around just for the pleasure of my company."

He smiled slightly. "They lifted the suspension."

"Yes."

He glanced at me. "Must have been a reason why."

"Because they know the charge against him is bullshit," I said curtly. "Anyway, they need Jack in the department."

We bore right on Mass. Avenue, past the Cambridge Common. On the outer edge of the park a peddler of handmade jewelry was setting up shop.

"Liz, before I picked you up today, I had another interview with Linda Crosbie. She's foaming at the mouth that Jack's been allowed back on the cops again. I mean, she's wild about it."

"I expect she would be." I turned my head so that I was looking, without seeing anything, out the window on my side of the car. "What's she saying about him? That he's the worst menace to society since the Boston Strangler?"

"Liz." Ouellette's voice was quiet and deadly serious. "This is bad stuff we're talking about here. It would be good if Jack gave his version of the events. Or if you . . ."

"No. If he isn't saying anything, *I'm* not saying anything."

Ouellette sighed. "Okay."

We rode by the law school, a block of small businesses, and the Lesley College Graduate School offices. I picked at a loose thread on the outer seam of my jeans.

"You understand why I don't want to talk about it."

"Sure."

We turned right onto Wendell Street.

"There is one thing," I began.

"What's that?"

"I wanted to go with Jack to the hearing. And he wouldn't let me."

Ouellette was silent for a moment. Then he said, "I can also understand that."

"You can?"

"Oh, sure." He looked over at me. "Probably the primary reason was, he didn't want to subject you to something that could have been hard for you."

"I could have dealt with it."

"Sure, but I think that's beside the point as far as he's concerned."

We turned right onto Oxford Street.

"What's the secondary reason?" I asked.

"What's the best way to put this?" Ouellette said to the windshield. "Okay, I know. He didn't want you to see him in diminished circumstances."

"Diminished circumstances," I repeated.

"Sure. He had to go defend himself before a group of people who might very well believe that he committed a disgusting crime. You think he wanted you to see him in that position?"

"I don't know?" I said. "How would *you* know?"

Ouellette smiled faintly. "I'm a man."

We were back on Cambridge Street again. I supposed Ouellette was going to drop me back at my place. I finished my coffee and put the empty cup back in the paper bag. I took the manila folder containing Otway Gilmore's photo from the dashboard and set it in my lap.

As we passed Trowbridge Street I glanced down it automatically. Two police cruisers were parked at an angle midway up it. The blue lights on their roofs were revolving.

"Jesus," I said. "Look there. Don't tell me someone else got murdered."

"Let's see," Ouellette said. He pulled the station wagon over to the corner of Trowbridge and Cambridge, parking it before someone's driveway entrance. A gray-haired patrolman stood in front of a red-frame three-decker. Ouellette got out of the car and moved toward him very purposefully. I stood on the sidewalk, glancing around much less purposefully. I wondered if I would ever be able to walk or ride down this street again and feel easy about it.

Ouellette came back to me.

"What happened?" I said.

"Bunch of housebreaks."

I nodded. Ouellette went to speak to another cop.

I spotted a young woman in a gray suit leaning against the waist-high picket fence that bordered the tiny front garden of a white duplex. I walked over to her. As I approached, I could see that her face had a red, congested look, as if she'd been crying. She probably had been, if she were the occupant of one of the burglarized condos or apartments. No one who's never had his or her home broken into and all their belongings rummaged through can even begin to imagine what it's like to be hit with the knowledge that some creep has violated your own private corner of the world. The loss of privacy is worse than the loss of property.

The woman looked up at the sound of my footsteps. Her cheeks were wet.

"You . . . ?" I ventured.

She bobbed her head once.

"I'm sorry," I said.

Her eyes were wide and their expression wild. "Goddamnit," she said. "I saved six years to make a down payment on this house." She flung her hand toward the duplex. "Six years. I thought I was buying a beautiful place in a nice neighborhood. Then I move in and somebody three houses down gets murdered. Terrific. That means I'm not safe on the street. Now I find out that I can't go to work without . . . without this shit happening." She put her hands to her face.

"I'm sorry," I repeated.

If she heard me, she didn't acknowledge it. I went back to the car to wait for Ouellette.

He returned in about twenty minutes. As he slid behind the steering wheel, he was shaking his head, slowly and portentously.

"Somebody went on a real rampage there," he said. "I've seen places that have been broken into before, including my own, but this . . . ?" He whistled.

"Really trashed, huh?"

"And how." He nodded in the direction of the woman in the gray suit. "See her? She was the one who found out first. Came home from work to get some papers she'd forgotten, walked in, and saw everything torn to pieces. I mean literally torn. All the furniture and the bed were slashed to ribbons, and all her kitchen stuff was smashed on the floor. All her jewelry was taken, of course." Ouellette sighed. "Same thing happened in the place downstairs from her."

"Was that the only building broken into?"

"Nope." He pointed down the street. "That red one with the veranda got hit—the cops discovered that—and the yellow house next to it."

"The *yellow* one?"

"Yeah." He frowned at me. "What's wrong?"

"John, what's the number for that place?"

"Lemme check." He took out his little reporter's notebook. "Let's see. Oh, here it is. Ninety-eight."

"Jesus Christ."

"What's the matter?"

"That was where the murdered woman, Paula Young, lived."

14

THE GREEN LIGHT on my answering machine was winking. There were three plaintive requests from Harvey Searle to call him ASAP and Jack's voice informed me that he was going to be tied up for a while at work and that he probably wouldn't see me until around eight-thirty. I smiled. Was he enjoying being back in the detective business enough to start keeping twelve-hour days?

It was closer to nine when he let himself in my front door.

"You wouldn't believe the shitload of paperwork I had to catch up on," he said, as he hung his trenchcoat in the closet.

"I thought you were supposed to be going hammer and tongs on the Hassler murder," I said, walking over and kissing him.

"I am." He rolled his eyes at the ceiling. "But nothing takes precedence over arranging vacation schedules."

I laughed. "Come on in the kitchen."

Jack sat down at the table. Lucy ambled over to him, tail waving, and put her muzzle on his knee. He scratched her behind the ears.

"I don't have anything special for dinner," I said. "And it's kind of late to start making anything elaborate. So what do you say to soup and sandwiches?"

"Fine."

"On the assumption you'd say just that, I already made some bacon for BLTs."

"Better still." He got up and took a bottle of beer from the refrigerator.

I'd set a pot of homemade vegetable soup on the stove. I turned the flame on beneath it to low. Then I took two tomatoes out of the oven, washed them, and put them on the cutting board.

"You know," Jack said, "in all the time I've known you, I've had this burning question I've wanted to ask you, but I keep forgetting."

"What's that, dear?"

"Why the hell do you keep tomatoes in the oven?"

I smiled at him. "To ripen."

"They get ripe in the oven?"

I held one up for him to inspect. "See?"

"Son-of-a-gun," he said. "I guess they do. Learn something new every day. Who taught you that trick?"

"My mother's younger brother's wife's mother told my father, and he told me."

"Don't even bother running that one by me again," Jack said. "I'm not smart enough to follow it."

"Of course," I said didactically. "If you preheat the oven, you gotta remember to take the little buggers out of it before you do."

"I'm not that dumb, cookie."

I sawed the tomatoes into nice quarter-inch slices and arranged them on a plate. I fetched a head of lettuce from the refrigerator and began pulling leaves from it. "My God," I said.

"What's the matter?"

I shook my head. "Talk about forgetting to ask questions. Jack, what about those housebreaks on Trowbridge Street this morning?"

He gave me a quick sharp look. "How do you know about them?"

"Well, I was there."

"You were?"

I told him about my drive with Ouellette, omitting all references to the discussion John and I had had of why Jack hadn't wanted me to attend the hearing.

"And Paula Young's was one of the condos that got broken into," I finished. "I mean, bizarre, right?"

"Yes, it was a very odd coincidence."

I got out a colander and dropped the lettuce leaves into it. "Was it only that? Just a coincidence?"

"As far as I know, it's being treated as one. It's not my case, though."

I put the colander in the sink and sprayed water over the lettuce. "Still . . ." I said. "Was much stolen from her place?"

"Hard to say. She isn't around to tell us if anything's missing, is she? But from what I understand, it was trashed just as badly as the other three condos were."

I wrapped the lettuce in some paper toweling. "I'm surprised someone from Paula's family hadn't already packed up her stuff before today. At least the clothes and the books, and, you know, portable things."

"I think one of her cousins was supposed to come this weekend to do just that."

I grimaced. "Christ, what a nice surprise for whoever. Just what her family needs on top of everything else. I've heard of grave-robbing, but this is . . . really sick."

"Yeah."

The soup was simmering. I got two mugs from the cupboard. Then I took a loaf of oatmeal bread from the counter and handed it to Jack. "Think you can swing making toast?"

Jack grinned. "Liz?"

"Yezzz?"

He gestured at the toaster oven. "You don't have any kumquats or whatever ripening in there, do you?"

"No, angel." I smiled. "Just passion fruit."

"Oh," he said. "I thought you kept that under your mattress."

The next morning was Saturday. Jack left at nine. He wanted to clear a few bits and pieces of paperwork off his desk. I was pouring myself a second cup of coffee when the phone rang. It was Harvey Searle.

"Don't you listen to your messages?" he said, sounding aggrieved. "I called you *three times* yesterday."

I sighed. "I know, Harv. I'm sorry. I've been a little busy, that's all."

"Well, this is important."

"Harvey?"

"Yeah?"

"I have nothing to say about why Jack was suspended or why he was reinstated. Though the reason for the latter should be obvious. Talk to the City Manager, okay?"

"I already did."

"Oh."

"Liz, I'm not calling you to pump you. I *have* something for you."

"Yes, your colleague from the *Globe* used much the same ploy yesterday."

"Oh, shit, do you want to hear what I've found out about Yolanda Sims or not?"

"Harvey." I gripped the receiver and pressed it against my ear. "Where are you?"

"About five minutes away from your house."

"I have a fresh pot of coffee."

Harvey was rapping on my front door just as I was opening the kitchen door for Lucy, who was returning from her mid-morning patrol of the back yard. She dashed ahead of me, barking, as I went to admit Harvey. He was wearing the same warm-up suit he had on the last time I'd seen him.

"You live in those duds?" I asked.

"Hey, they're comfortable. What can I say?"

I nodded at the couch. "Sit down. I'll get the coffee. How do you take it?"

"Black."

"Okay. Be back in a second."

I loaded up a tray and brought it to the living room. Searle had his notebook out and was riffling through it. I set the tray on the coffee table.

"So," I said. "You've been checking into Yolanda Sims, have you?"

He nodded and, without looking up from the page he was reading, accepted the cup I offered him.

"So what've you found?" I prodded.

He shut the notebook and tossed it onto the table. "I went to try to interview her last Wednesday. She wouldn't talk to me. Said I should direct all inquiries about her case to the Citizens' Committee." He grinned. " 'Course, she didn't put it quite that elegantly."

"I would guess not."

"So, you know me, Mr. Intrepid Investigative Journalist, I kept at it. Kept calling her. Even went over to her house again." He took a sip of coffee. "She told me to fuck off and slammed the door in my face."

"You must have had that happen to you before."

"Yeah, frequently. Anyway, I got a little irked by that so I figured, what the hell, here's somebody acting like she has something to hide, so maybe I should try to find out what it is."

"You sound like a cop."

"I'm a crime reporter."

"Mmmm. Well, tell me about Yolanda Sims." I settled back against the couch cushions and gazed at him expectantly.

He ran a hand over his dark curly hair. "Okay. I guess you already know she's got this dirtball kid down in Walpole."

I nodded.

"He's her only child. Been divorced for ten years now. Ex-husband moved out of state right after the divorce, for financial reasons."

"Cute euphemism." I snorted. "You mean he skipped to avoid alimony and child support."

"Yup. Anyway, Yolanda's lawyer filed a Complaint of Contempt against the husband, Joseph Sims, Senior, and a subpoena was issued, but it was returned unserved. Nobody could find him."

"Harvey, how on earth did you dig up this stuff?"

"Well, I knew Sims was divorced, so I went down to probate court, ran her name in the card file, got the docket number of her case, gave the number to the clerk. The clerk pulled the docket, and I read it."

"Oh."

Searle drank the rest of his coffee. I offered him more, but he shook his head. "I also talked to some of Sims's neighbors."

"What kind of a reception did they give you?"

"Unenthusiastic, mostly. I *did* luck out, though, with one old witch who's clearly the local gossip."

"Yes?"

"God." Harvey grimaced. "What a charmer that one was. A real dirt data bank."

"Forthcoming?"

"I couldn't shut her up," he said wryly. "She couldn't wait to drag me into her kitchen, sit me down, and tell me about what a tramp Yolanda was."

I raised my eyebrows.

Harvey made his voice into a cracked falsetto. " 'That woman has a different man in her house every night. To *stay*,' " he quoted.

I snickered.

"Yeah, I know it sounds funny when I tell it," Searle said. "But this was one vicious old bitch. I mean, I could see she was really getting off on trashing Yolanda. Not that I have any great sympathy for her, but . . ." He shook his curly head. "This was really sick to listen to, even if true."

"Hmm."

"Anyway, one thing useful I got from the hag was that Yolanda had been laid off her last job as a doctor's receptionist and was collecting unemployment." Searle grimaced again. "Only, of course, according to the hag, Yolanda didn't really get laid off. She got fired because she was banging the doctor and the doctor's wife found out."

"I see. Well, why is that useful information?"

Searle gave me a strange look. "Yolanda needs bread."

"You mean—oh, of course. She's unemployed and her ex-husband's not subsidizing her, so there's an additional motive beyond simple greed to try to sue Jack and the police department and the city."

"Sure."

"But Harvey, she wouldn't see any of that money—granted she were awarded it—for quite some time."

Searle shrugged. "So she's thinking long-term."

I sighed. "Maybe."

Searle said, "I guess I might have just a little more coffee."

I watched as he poured himself a third of a cup. Then he broke a saccharin pill in two, dropped the smaller piece in his coffee, and returned the other to the bottle. I did the same myself.

"Harvey?" I said.

"Uh-huh?"

"Am I to gather that you don't think Jack raped Yolanda, either?"

He stared at me, and then scowled. "Aww, Liz—"

"That means you don't?"

"No. I don't. Jesus!"

I nodded. We drank our coffee in silence. Lucy padded into the room and lay down before us in the space between the coffee table and the couch. I reached down and patted her haunch absently.

"Goddamnit," Searle said.

I jumped, spilling coffee onto Lucy, who wiggled under the table. "What is it?"

"I'm gonna go see her again," he said, standing up. "Now. I don't like having doors slammed in my face."

"Harvey."

"What?"

"Take me with you."

I could swear he blanched.

He studied me dubiously. "Oh, Liz, I don't know if that's such a hot idea."

"Oh, Harvey, *please?*"

He looked unhappy and uncomfortable. "Liz, remember what this woman has said about Jack."

"How could I forget it? Why do you think I want to see her?"

"That's *exactly* my point. You can't be objective about this, and . . ."

"And what?" I stood up to face him.

"I know you, kid. When you lose your temper . . ."

"For Christ's sake, I have *some* self-control."

"Yolanda will strain it, believe me."

"Harvey, I swear that even if she calls Jack a child molester, you won't hear a peep out of me. I just want to look at her and listen to her and form my own impressions. Okay? Besides, she probably won't talk to us anyway, so what's the harm in my going with you?"

We stared at each other. Searle was the first to look away.

"Shit," he said. "All right, all right. You can come." He shook his head slowly. "Why do I have the feeling I'm making a huge mistake?"

"You aren't." I smiled. "Thanks, Harv. Just let me get my jacket."

Out on the sidewalk, he said, "Just how do you want to be introduced to Yolanda, on the off chance she lets us darken her door?"

"Well, it would probably be wise not to tell her I'm her alleged rapist's girlfriend."

"Jesus, no." He eyed me speculatively. "I could tell her you're one of my colleagues."

"Sure. I'm a rookie reporter, and I'm following you on your rounds to observe your technique. How's that sound?"

"Implausible," Harvey said. "But she might buy it."

I giggled.

"What's funny?"

"Suppose," I said, "just suppose Yolanda decides to unburden herself to a sympathetic female reporter. I can look very sympathetic, you know."

He crossed his eyes. "Yeah, I know."

"Well, she might end up wanting to talk to me and me alone. Then *you'll* be out in the cold."

"I've been there before," Searle replied. "I can handle it."

Yolanda Sims lived in East Cambridge, on Hurley Street between Sciarappa and Third. Her house was a smallish two-story aluminum-sided white box set at right angles to the sidewalk. On the way over, Searle told me that Yolanda had inherited the place from her father.

That kind of primogeniture was common in East Cambridge. I knew
of families in this area who'd been living in the same house for three
or four generations.

We went up the steps to the front door. Searle rang the bell. Then
he turned to me. "Remember," he said. "You've made a solemn
promise to behave yourself."

I grinned at him. "Go take a flying fuck at a rolling doughnut."

He shook his head and pressed the bell button once more, this
time for a little longer.

A few moments passed. Searle put his ear to the door. "Can't hear
anything," he announced.

I was disappointed, but, oddly, also a little relieved. "I guess she's
not home," I said, and prepared to leave.

"Wait a sec; not so fast," Searle said.

I looked at him curiously.

"Maybe she's in the bathroom," Searle said. "Or in the cellar. Or
maybe she saw us—me—coming—and she's just not answering the
door."

"So do we wait her out?"

"Maybe," Searle said. "Let's try something else first." He beck-
oned to me and started down the steps. I followed him around to the
back of the house. There was another door there, one that led out
onto a tiny flagstone patio and, fairly obviously, into the kitchen.
Searle banged on it. The curtain over its window was closed and
completely motionless.

No response.

"Damn," Searle muttered. "I know she's in there."

"How?"

"A feeling."

I nodded.

A yard or so away from the door was a casement about six feet off
the ground, and, beneath that, a weathered gray bulkhead. Searle
walked up the bulkhead and bent forward to peer in the window,
cupping his hands around his face to shut out the sunlight shining on
the pane.

"If you aren't careful," I joked, "that witchy neighbor of Yolanda's will think you're one of Sims's more ardent boyfriends."

Searle grunted and canted his head to change his view.

"Holy shit," he said. His head jerked.

"What—"

He jumped down off the bulkhead, landing with a thump on the flagstone patio. He bounded past me to the kitchen door, grabbed the knob, and wrenched it back and forth a few times.

"Harvey, what—"

He backed up a pace, raised his right leg, and kicked violently at the door. It vibrated slightly in its frame, but the lock held firm.

"Fuck," he said.

The downspout on the corner of the house had a small pile of rocks at its base for drainage. Searle grabbed one about the size of a tennis ball and hurled it at the window in the door. The diamond-shaped pane nearest the knob shattered. Searle yanked the cuff of his sweatshirt down over his right wrist and then, very carefully, put the protected hand through the jagged hole in the glass. He flipped the lock on the doorknob. Then, just as slowly and cautiously, he pulled his hand back through the saw-toothed hole in the window.

He took a deep breath, opened the door, and stepped into Yolanda Sims's kitchen. I crowded after him. Our shoes crunched on shards of glass.

"Oh, my God," I said, and put my hands to my face.

Yolanda Sims lay, partly on her side and partly on her back, in front of the stove. One leg was bent at the knee and slightly raised. Her arms were flung up over her head, looking pallid and boneless against the bright orange and yellow linoleum. Her eyes were open, their gaze fixed glassily and forever on the ceiling fixture. She was wearing black slacks and a white blouse, and, on the blouse, a great irregularly shaped bib of dried and darkened blood.

15

"FROM WHERE I was standing, all I could see was a pair of legs," Searle said. "I thought maybe she'd fallen down and hurt herself, or had a heart attack, or a stroke. Or something." He took a gulp of straight Scotch. "Jesus Christ."

I was huddled in one of the wing chairs before Jack's fireplace, working on a drink of my own. Harvey Searle was slumped in the chair opposite me. Jack was leaning against the mantel, watching the both of us.

Searle looked up at him. "Two shots right in the heart."

Jack nodded.

"They know what kind of gun?" Searle asked.

"On the basis of the size of the wounds, maybe a thirty-eight." Jack shrugged. "The autopsy and forensic tests are the only way to tell for sure."

"When will they have the results of those?"

"Could be a while," Jack sat down on the arm of my chair and put a hand on my shoulder. "How you doing?" he said to me.

"I'm okay."

Searle finished his drink. The Scotch bottle was on the table next to him. He poured himself a refill.

"Do they have any idea when she was shot, Jack?" I asked faintly.

"Judging by the condition of the body," he replied, "sometime last

night. Rigor had come and gone. Again, they'll know better after the autopsy."

I shuddered.

"Any sign that her house had been broken into?" Harvey asked. "Other than by me."

"Not as far as I know," Jack said.

Searle nodded, and took another slug of Scotch. "Was she raped?" He frowned, and added, "I mean, for *real*."

I inhaled sharply.

Jack held out his hands, palms up. "Ask the medical examiner. It didn't look like it, though, from what I understood."

"Yeah," Searle said. "Didn't look like it to me, either. I've seen dead rape victims. Usually they're missing at least some clothing, or it's torn, or disarranged, or . . . or messed up somehow."

"I've been on one or two cases where the rapist or the murderer cleaned up the body and re-dressed it," Jack said. "But, yeah, you have a point."

"So," Searle said. "What we got here is that someone walked into Yolanda's house, could have been with her permission, shot her twice, and walked out. Without stealing anything, without trashing the place, probably without sexually assaulting the victim. Why? And who?"

"Maybe it was one of her boyfriends," I offered feebly. "Or her ex-husband."

"After ten years?" Jack and Harvey asked simultaneously.

"Maybe her divorce lawyer finally caught up with him. The husband."

Harvey and Jack just looked at me.

"I guess not," I said.

Searle finished his drink and set the glass on the table between the wing chairs. Then he got up, moving, I thought, as if his muscles ached. "Gotta go," he said. "Story to write. Thanks for the booze."

"You okay to drive, Harv?" Jack asked. He glanced pointedly at the Scotch bottle.

"Sure, I'm fine," Searle said. He bent down and gave me a kiss on the cheek. "Take care, kid."

"And you."

Jack walked with him to the front door. They shook hands, and Searle left. Jack shut the door behind him. Then he came back to the living room and stood for a moment in front of my chair.

"You think Harvey'll be safe on the road?" I said.

Jack nodded. "Yeah. He was metabolizing those drinks too fast for them to go to his head."

Another shudder racked me. I'd been shivering for the past ten hours. I couldn't control it. The booze I was consuming now wasn't making me warm inside. I wondered if anything could.

Jack leaned forward, took my hands, and pulled me to my feet. "Come on," he said.

We went into the bedroom and lay down on the bed. Jack put his arms around me and gathered me in against him.

"Oh, God," I said.

One of his hands began rubbing my back in big, slow circles. "All right," he said. "It's all right." His voice was soft in my ear, and his breath stirred my hair gently.

I've heard that people confronted unexpectedly by death, particularly violent death, will react to the shock by blindly performing whatever action seems to them the most likely to affirm, even if only symbolically, life. As I pressed against Jack, listening to the slow, steady beat of his heart, what I wanted was to make love. I could feel the desire rising in me like water flowing into a pool.

I gently disengaged myself from Jack's hold, sat up, and began taking off my shirt. He lay still, one arm behind his head, watching me. I dropped my blouse and bra on the floor beside the bed and unzipped my jeans. I pushed out of them and my underpants and let both fall in a knot on top of the other discarded clothing.

I stretched across the bed and slid a hand under Jack's shirt. I could feel his skin quiver in response to the swirls I traced on it with my fingertips.

"You, too," I said.

"Oh, yes," he replied.

When we were both naked, I pulled him down on top of me. The flow had become a surge. I arched my back to increase the pressure of his chest on my breasts. I heard him breathe in, hard.

"Whatever you want," I said.

He said, "I don't need anything more than this."

A chunk of the ice inside me broke off and floated away downstream.

Sunday afternoon I was sitting at my kitchen table, making some sketchy notes for the article on the Massachusetts correctional system, when two state police detectives came to my door. I was immersed in thought, and the sound of the buzzer seemed unusually sharp and intrusive. Lucy, stretched out on the floor next to my chair, gave a single loud bark and sprang to her feet. I put down my pen and rose from the table. As I did so, I glanced automatically at the clock over the refrigerator. It read two-fourteen. The only significant thing about the time is that I should remember it so vividly.

I was neither surprised nor alarmed by the presence of the two cops on my doorstep. I had, after all, been one of the discoverers of Yolanda Sims's body, so there was nothing really unexpected in having a couple of guys from the DA's office dropping by the day after that discovery to ask some follow-up questions about it.

I knew, very slightly, one of the detectives, a sergeant named Leo McGuigan. McGuigan was a tall, heavyset man in his mid-fifties, with slouched shoulders and sleepy-looking eyes that probably missed nothing. He introduced the man with him as Trooper Michael Haslett. Haslett was much younger, perhaps in his late twenties, as tall as McGuigan but much leaner and straighter. He had the healthy color and bland blond good looks of a model for a recruiting poster.

I admitted the pair of them to the apartment and invited both to have a seat. McGuigan lowered his bulk into one corner of the sofa. Haslett perched on the edge of a straight-backed wooden occasional chair.

McGuigan glanced around the living room. "Nice place," he said.

I smiled. "Thank you." My hostess reflex came to the fore and I added, "Could I get you some coffee or anything?"

McGuigan said, "Nope; thanks, though." Haslett shook his head.

"Well, if you change your mind, let me know," I said. "You must be here about Yolanda Sims."

McGuigan smiled noncommittally. "Well, we have a few questions. First, why don't you tell us about yesterday morning?"

I did, hesitantly to begin with, not wishing to relive those events. But I realized as I spoke that they were already beginning to seem less immediate to me. Maybe because this was about the tenth time I'd had to describe them to one or another law-enforcement person.

Then, of course, there was last night.

When I finished talking, I reiterated my offer of coffee, and once more, the two detectives refused it, Haslett again with a shake of the head.

McGuigan gave me his neutral smile. Out of the corner of my eye, I noticed Haslett take out a notebook.

"Liz," McGuigan said, "can you tell us what you were doing Friday night?"

I furrowed my eyebrows at him. "Friday?"

"Yes."

"Well," I said, a little bewildered. "Nothing much, you know? I was here from about five onward. I didn't go out."

"Did you have any visitors?"

I stared at McGuigan, feeling confusion turn to unease. "Just my friend, Lieutenant Lingemann. What—could you tell me what this is about, please?"

"When did Lieutenant Lingemann arrive here?"

I kept staring at McGuigan. "About nine o'clock. A little before."

"How long did he stay?"

"Overnight," I said coldly. "He left the following morning. Also at nine."

"Was he here the entire time?"

In that moment, unease turned to cold, horrible certainty. I sat rigid, staring at McGuigan.

"Was Lieutenant Lingemann here the entire time?" McGuigan repeated.

"Yes."

"He didn't go out at any point between when he arrived here Friday night and when he left Saturday morning?"

"No." My voice sounded to me as if it were coming from a distance.

McGuigan looked at Haslett. Haslett looked at McGuigan. They rose in concert.

"Thanks for your help," McGuigan said.

I remained seated and silent. I didn't take my eyes off McGuigan's face. Again, he produced that meaningless smile.

"We'll be in touch if we need to talk to you about anything else," he said. "Have a pleasant day."

I waited until I was fairly sure they'd had enough time to get down the stairs. Then I went to the window. A brown Chevy was parked in front of the house. McGuigan got in the passenger side. Maybe Haslett was his chauffeur. I watched them drive down the street and turn left at the corner.

I ran for the phone and dialed Jack's number. No answer. Damn, damn. I replaced the receiver in the cradle with more force than was necessary.

I slumped against the closet door, rubber-limbed with anxiety. I felt sick to my stomach with the bile of my own fears. The image of McGuigan's stolid face rose up before me.

Why hadn't he acted as if he'd believed what I'd told him?

I spent the rest of the afternoon in a state of ragged distraction. Every little noise, from the creak of a branch on the oak tree outside my kitchen window to the soft rumble of the refrigerator starting up, made me jump as if I'd been lanced with a red-hot needle.

At five-thirty I made myself a drink in the hope that it would calm me down. The first sip made me gag. I poured the rest down the sink.

I kept calling Jack. I tried his number every fifteen minutes. All I got was the answering machine. I had no idea where he might be. We hadn't had any plans for this evening; I'd intended to spend the time working on my article.

The night that followed was purely awful. I didn't work. I didn't read. I barely breathed. I didn't go to bed. I finally fell asleep—or, more accurately, passed into an unconscious state—on the couch. That was at two A.M.

Six hours later, Jack was arrested and charged with the murder of Yolanda Sims.

16

"No BAIL!" I screamed.

Sam Flaherty winced and said, "Jesus, doll, keep it down, huh?"

"Why? You afraid the squirrels might hear me?"

It was late Tuesday afternoon, and Flaherty and I were seated on a bench in the little park outside the public library. We'd agreed earlier it would be a good place to meet. I had no desire whatsoever to set foot in the police station. Flaherty himself probably wanted me there even less than I wanted to be there. Given the situation.

I put my elbows on my knees and my head in my hands. Flaherty sat motionless beside me. He had been the one to call me with the news of Jack's arrest yesterday morning. Having it broken to me by Jack's partner and closest friend did not make it any easier to handle. But I understood that Flaherty hadn't wanted me to hear the news first on the radio or TV. For that I was grateful, in a numbed way.

After a moment, I raised my head and drew a long breath. "When can I see him?" I said, making an effort to at least feign composure.

"Tonight," Flaherty said. "The visiting hours are seven to nine. I'll take you."

He meant to the jail that occupied the top floor of the Middlesex County Courthouse in East Cambridge. *God.*

"I'll pick you up, oh, six-forty-five," Flaherty continued. "That okay?"

I nodded. "It's fine. Thank you."

A bent old man in a scaly cap and frayed overcoat pushed a shopping cart along the path in front of us. The cart was overflowing with plastic bags stuffed to bursting with empty bottles and soft drink and beer cans. He brought his cart to a halt beside the nearest of the wastebaskets the DPW had placed throughout the park and began rummaging through it. Flaherty watched him from beneath hooded lids.

"Why no bail?" I asked softly.

Flaherty glanced away from the treasure hunter and at me. His long, seamed face looked very tired.

"Sam," I said. "All kinds of *real* murderers get bail. Rapists get released on personal recognizance, and while they're waiting to come to trial, they rape two other people. And Jack's gonna stay locked up. For what? Why? I thought the only nonbailable offense was treason."

"Yeah, tell me about it."

I bit my lip. "I wish you would."

The old man pulled a two-liter soda bottle from the bottom of the waste bin. He yanked it free of the other debris and put it carefully into his shopping cart. Then he pushed onward, in search of another cache.

"I know the judge who was at Jack's arraignment," Flaherty said. "A real prick. He hates cops."

"What about the prosecutor?" I said. "Did *he* ask for no bail?"

Flaherty shook his head. "Naw. I think even he was surprised by the judge's decision."

"Then . . . why? Just because this judge doesn't like cops?"

"No, there's more to it than that." Flaherty massaged the side of his face. "Liz, you know the state correctional system has come in for some real heavy knocks recently."

"I'll say." I laughed sourly. "I'm supposed to be writing an article about that very thing this moment."

"Yeah, well, look at what's happened in the past few months. We're averaging one escape a week from the prisons now. We got murderers walking off work details and not coming back from furloughs."

"Yes?"

"So two of the latest escapees have been cops."

"I know. That state trooper who killed his partner and that other crud who was the brains, if you can call them that, behind that bank robbery in Melrose."

"Uh-huh."

"What does that have to do with Jack not being able to get bai—my God!" I whipped my head around to give Flaherty a saucer-eyed look. "You mean the judge—the one who was at Jack's arraignment—he's afraid that if he turns Jack loose, Jack'll disappear like those other two creeps?"

"Could be," Flaherty said.

"But Jack wouldn't—"

"I know he wouldn't," Flaherty interrupted. "You know he wouldn't. But that judge don't know he wouldn't."

I shook my head furiously. "Who is this jerk, anyway?"

"Sanger," Flaherty replied. "Judge Milton Sanger."

I repeated the name to myself, but the sound of it touched off no echo in my memory. "I don't know him," I said.

"You wouldn't want to." Flaherty took a toothpick from his jacket pocket and stuck it in his mouth. "The guy almost got censured, last year."

"For what?"

"It was sweet." Flaherty worked the toothpick around in his mouth. "Sanger was the presiding judge at the trial of this real bag of shit that had raped a couple of little kids. Took the jury about six minutes to find him guilty—it was that kind of a case, you know? So what happens? Sanger sentences the guy to five years' probation."

"Oh, God."

"Yeah. The DA was ripshit."

"I can see why. The prosecutor and the arresting officers must have been thrilled, too."

"Overjoyed," Flaherty said. "They were overjoyed." He removed the toothpick from his mouth, snapped it in two, and dropped the pieces on the grass. "My point is, Sanger got in a lot of trouble over

that episode. The parents of the victims got up a petition to have him removed from the bench."

"I don't blame them," I said. "I think I'd have shot the son-of-a-bitch. That is, after I'd shot the rapist. If those had been *my* kids."

"I bet you would have," Flaherty said. "Anyway, Sanger managed to slip and slide his way through the whole mess pretty good. Kept his seat, anyway."

"Friends in high places?"

"Probably." Flaherty scratched the back of his head. "But ever since then, old Miltie's been toeing a hard line with offenders. High bail, stiff sentences, the whole bit. He's not taking no chances unleashing any more dangerous criminals on the public."

"Which explains his treatment of that major bad guy and fiend, Lieutenant John Lingemann."

Flaherty sighed. "What can I say, Liz? It's politics. All politics."

"Sure." I nodded. "Always has been, always will be. World without end. Amen."

Just as he'd promised, Flaherty was parked outside my house in his ancient LTD at a quarter to seven that evening.

"How's it going?" he asked, as I got in his car.

"Oh, all right, I guess." I felt as if my skin were stretching to contain all the tension inside me.

"Hang tough," he advised.

"There's not much else to do, is there?"

"No," he answered. "Not a hell of a lot."

We drove out onto Cambridge Street, brightly lit and still busy at this hour.

"Sam," I said. "What kind of a case do they think they have against Jack?"

He flicked me a brief glance. "A decent one."

I made a fist and smacked my knee with it. "Oh, Christ, how can they? He didn't kill that—Yolanda Sims."

"According to the prosecutor, he had a good motive to. Look at all the trouble she was getting him into."

"Bullshit."

"Sure. But there are other things."

"Like what?"

"An eyewitness puts Jack on the scene the night Sims was murdered."

"*What?*"

Flaherty slowed the car to permit a trio of teenaged girls to cross the street. "Yolanda died somewhere between seven-thirty and ten-thirty Friday evening."

I took a deep breath. "So what? Jack was at the police station for half that time and at my house for the rest of it."

"Yeah, and when did he get there? To your place?"

"Jesus." I rolled my eyes. "About five to nine. He came straight from work."

"No, he didn't, Liz," Flaherty said. "He left the station at ten after eight. I don't care what the traffic was like; it doesn't take forty-five minutes to drive from Central Square to your place. More like ten."

I was silent as we went through the intersection of Prospect and Cambridge Streets.

"Okay," Flaherty said. "So there's this old broad lives next door to Sims. A real prune. But she's got twenty-twenty vision and all her marbles. She says she saw Jack go into Sims's house—Sims let him in the front door—at twenty-five after eight. Then she saw him leave, also by the front door, twenty to nine."

"Oh, of course," I said, my voice ragged with sarcasm. "No doubt. She saw some man go into Yolanda's house and immediately said to herself, 'Why, I know him. That's Lieutenant John Lingemann of the Cambridge Police Department.' Am I right? Is that how it went?"

Flaherty sighed. "Liz, she didn't identify him by name, she *described* him."

"Sam, at eight-twenty-five last Friday night, it was pitch dark. How could this biddy get that good a look at *anybody* going into Sims's house? Even if it was Santa Claus with his sack?"

"Yolanda had her porch light on. And the old woman who saw

. . . whoever it was . . . going in there was looking at him through
a window only fifteen feet away. The houses on that street are very
close together."

I knew that already. I'd been there.

"Well, obviously this woman is mistaken," I said.

We stopped for a light in front of the Harrington School.

"Liz," Flaherty said, his voice a deadly quiet counterpoint to my
hysterical one. "They showed the old broad a bunch of pictures. She
zeroed right in on Jack's. Then she picked him out of a lineup. It was
about as positive an ID as you can get."

"Oh, God," I said. "They did a lineup? They put Jack in a lineup?"

"Well, they had to."

I squeezed my eyes shut. Imagining Jack standing in a lineup was
as unendurable as imagining him sitting in a jail cell.

I inhaled tremulously. "Is that all they have against him? A spu-
rious motive and a mistaken identification? That's the sum total of
their case?"

"No," Flaherty said.

"What else?"

We made the turn off Cambridge Street onto Third.

"They found the gun Sims was shot with."

"Yes, and?"

Flaherty's face was nearly rigid in its blankness. "According to the
ballistics report, the gun was Jack's."

The main entrance to the Middlesex County Courthouse was on
Thorndike Street. The courthouse itself took up the entire block
between Second and Third streets. I had Flaherty drop me off at the
corner of Third and Thorndike.

"I can go in with you," he said. "Get you up there."

I shook my head. "No. I'd rather go alone. But"—I leaned across
the seat and touched his arm—"thank you for offering."

He nodded. "I'll wait for you."

"Oh, Sam. You don't have to do that."

"There's a coffee shop on First Street across from Lechmere," he said, glossing over my demurral. "I'll see you there."

"But . . . I might be a while."

"Don't matter," he said.

I was quiet for a moment. Then I said, "Okay." I opened the car door.

"Liz?"

I paused, half in and half out of the car, and glanced at him over my shoulder.

"It's gonna be all right."

"That's what you said the last time I talked to you. When all he was accused of doing was raping Yolanda Sims."

"Yeah, I know." Flaherty smiled in a tired kind of way. "Don't make what I told you any the less true, though. Just takes time to happen, that's all."

"Yes," I said. "The truth always outs eventually."

Only sometimes too late to do anybody any good whatsoever.

The main courthouse entrance had electric-eye glass doors that drew apart as you approached them. I went through the opening and up a short and shallow flight of stairs to a metal detector. I surrendered my handbag to the guard, a tall fat man in blue court officer's garb.

I cleared security and walked to the elevator bank. I had been in the courthouse many times before this. Twice I'd been here to testify, once before a grand jury and once at a criminal trial. Several times I'd accompanied Jack here while he was getting warrants. On other occasions I'd done research in the law library on the fourth floor. I'd even had lunch in the cafeteria.

I had never been here to visit a prisoner.

The jail started on the seventeenth floor. The elevator I rode up there delivered me to a room, or landing, that had three of its walls painted an eyeball-shattering electric blue. The fourth wall, to my right, was glass, a double door in its center. On one of the doors was a large decal of a Middlesex County sheriff's department star. I opened the starred door.

The jail lobby was cream-colored, with two wooden benches back-to-back in the middle of the floor and small lockers set into the far wall. To the left was a windowed guardroom. A woman in ragged jeans and a grimy sweatshirt lay on her back on one of the benches, her eyes closed and her mouth slightly open. She appeared to have no upper front teeth.

On a metal counter underneath the guardroom window was a pad of green REQUEST TO VISIT INMATE forms. I took one, filled it out, and signed it, by doing so swearing under penalty of perjury that I had never been convicted of a felony nor was I on furlough from a correctional institution. If I had felt remotely like laughing, I would have.

I passed the form by way of a Diebold tray to one of the sheriff's department officials in the guardroom. He didn't look happy that none of the pieces of photo identification I offered him was a driver's license (something I don't happen to have, although I *do* know how to drive) but finally accepted that I was, indeed, the person my various out-of-date faculty ID cards and VISA said I was. He gave me a blue-and-white visitor's pass to clip to the breast pocket of my blazer and pointed at a red steel door at the end of the guardroom wall. On it was stenciled, DO NOT TOUCH THIS DOOR. I wondered vaguely if it were electrified.

The corrections official hit an invisible button and the red metal barrier slid open. In the narrow passageway behind the door was another metal detector. This one was apparently more sensitive than that downstairs, for it registered my earrings and belt buckle. I had to remove belt and jewelry and go through the device a second time. When it had cleared me, the door at the far end of the passageway opened. I walked through it and into the visitor's area.

To my left were three narrow, windowed rooms that looked like wainscoted aquaria. The center room had no door in it on my side. Lacking any direction otherwise, I went into the nearest of the three rooms. Metal and green vinyl armchairs were lined up before the window bank on the right wall. Slumped in one of the chairs was a skinny young woman with tangled blond hair and very bad skin. As

I looked at her, she grabbed the hem of her sweater, raised it to her eyes, and wiped them. She sniffed loudly.

I knew how she felt.

I took a chair as far away as possible from the one occupied by the young woman, to afford us both some particle of privacy, and sat down in it slowly and stiffly. At the base of the window in front of me was a two- or three-inch high grille. Was that an intercom? It looked like the mesh thing that covered the exhaust vent on my kitchen stove.

I folded my hands in my lap and stared straight ahead of me.

Two men walked into the center room. One of them was Jack. The other was a guy in his middle twenties, probably, with a beard and mustache and a surly expression. His stomach protruded like an overstuffed marsupial pouch. He and Jack were wearing green shirts and green pants that looked—or would have under other circumstances—like the uniform of a grounds keeper or a custodian. Prison wear. I bit down hard on my back teeth.

Jack took the chair on the other side of the heavy window from me.

"Hi," he said. His voice came astonishingly clearly through the grille.

I nodded, unable to speak.

"Good to see you," Jack added. "Sorry about the setting." He made a deprecating face.

I shook my head dumbly.

The distraught blonde snuffled into a tissue.

I clasped my hands tighter together.

Jack was watching me very closely. He was willing me to stay composed. For both our sakes.

I lowered my head and spoke into the grille. "Well, hello," I said. "Tell me what's a nice boy like you doing in a place like this?"

"Fucked if I know," Jack replied. Then he smiled. He actually smiled. Maybe with relief that I wasn't hysterical.

"I know your accommodations here must be incredibly luxurious," I said, "but don't get spoiled by them. You aren't gonna be here long enough to take full advantage of the facilities."

"No?"

"No."

"Damn," he said. "Too bad."

"Oh, is the cooking here that much better than mine?"

He held up his right hand and flipped it back and forth. "Ah, so-so. Hard to tell. I've only had—what? Five meals? God knows what they'll dish up for dinner tomorrow night. Some gourmet treat, I'm sure."

We looked at each other. I felt a sharp sting at the base of my eyeballs. He bent forward very swiftly toward the grille.

"Don't," he said. His voice was hushed, but nonetheless urgent. My throat felt as if it were filled with cement.

Jack glanced quickly to his right, at the big-bellied prisoner. He and the messy blonde were engrossed in whispered conversation. The woman snuffled into a crumpled tissue. Her husband, or lover, or whoever, scowled at her unhappily.

Eight generations of Irish and Scots and German and Danish ancestors who *never* wept in public came to my rescue.

I cleared my throat and blinked my eyes. I smiled at Jack.

"What would you like me to bring you?" I asked.

"Oh." He sounded a little surprised by the question. "Well, I don't know."

"Other than a saw in a cake, I mean."

He laughed.

"How about some books?"

He made a thoughtful face. "That would be nice. Yeah. Something to read." He nodded.

"Anything special?"

"Oh, you pick. You know what I like."

"Gotcha."

The disheveled young woman to my left made a harsh sound that was halfway between a gag and a sob. Automatically, I glanced over at her. She pushed back in her chair and rose partially out of it, then leaned forward, bracing her thin forearms on the ledge beneath the window. "Bobby, you *gotta*," she said. "Do like the lawyer tells you, huh, honey, please? Oh, Jesus Christ, honey—"

"I ain't fuckin' takin' no plea." The fat young man virtually spat the words back at her through the grille.

The woman collapsed into her chair. I averted my eyes, very quickly, and looked back at Jack. I forced myself to smile with all the heart and animation I could muster.

He lifted his eyebrows. "Some great place, huh?" he murmured.

My throat was on the verge of clogging again. "Listen, sweetie," I said, with simulated briskness. "I should go now. But I'll be back here as soon as they'll let me."

"Thursday night," Jack said. He smiled. "I'll look forward to it."

"Me, too, love."

We got up from our chairs together. I put my right hand up to the window. He raised his and pressed it against the glass, right opposite mine. I imagined I could feel the warmth of his flesh through the heavy pane.

How can I leave you here to go back into that dreadful hole with those disgusting people?

"Good night," I said.

" 'Night," he answered.

I left the visiting room, moving rather quickly. The corrections official let me back through the entrance-exit trap. In the lobby, the woman with no upper front teeth was still reclining on her bench. As I walked past her, she opened her eyes and gave me a fey grin. She looked almost as if she knew something about me that I didn't. My skin prickled.

I took the elevator to the second floor. A ladies' room was there, I knew, adjacent to the cafeteria. On the second floor, too, were the District Attorney's office and the State Police Detectives Unit. Stepping off the elevator, I felt as if I were entering enemy territory. I'd never thought of it that way before.

I passed the entrance to the cafeteria, closed now, and pushed through a pair of swinging doors. I went into the women's bathroom. It was empty. Good. No one to observe me as I violated the tenets of my breeding.

I stood with my head against the paper-towel dispenser and cried.

17

YOU DIDN'T HAVE to pass through the metal detector in order to leave the courthouse. Evidently they didn't care what kind of armaments you walked out with, as long as you didn't bring any in.

I walked down Thorndike Street to First and then down another block to the coffee shop where Sam said he'd be waiting. He was there, at a corner table by the window. Before him were a Styrofoam cup of coffee and a foil ashtray with four crushed butts in it. I went to the counter at the rear of the shop, got a diet Coke and joined him.

"You okay?" he said, studying my flushed face.

"I'm fine."

"How's Jack?"

"Laughing. Making jokes about jailhouse cuisine."

"Christ," Flaherty said. "He's something else, that guy, isn't he?"

"Sure is."

"Man's got class."

"Yes, he does."

Flaherty and I were alone in the coffee shop, but for the counter workers. And they were too far away to overhear anything we talked about, even if we spoke in normal tones. Nonetheless, I hunched my shoulders, leaned slightly across the table, and said, in a very low voice, "Tell me the rest."

"I've already told you pretty much everything I know."

"But the gun, Sam. Jack's gun. The crime lab has to have made a mistake about that—that Yolanda Sims was shot with it."

Flaherty looked unhappy. " 'Fraid not."

"Sam, those forensic guys aren't infallible. Obviously, one of them screwed up somewhere along the line."

"Not in this case."

I bit my lower lip.

"Look," Flaherty said. "They test-fired the gun they confiscated from Jack when they arrested him. The markings on those bullets exactly matched those on the slugs they dug out of Sims. It's like fingerprints, Liz. No two people have the same prints, and no two bullets have the identical markings. Unless they're fired from the same weapon." Flaherty reached into his pocket for his cigarettes. "It was Jack's gun that was used in the murder."

"Without a doubt?"

"Without a doubt." Flaherty shook a cigarette from the pack and lit it.

The coffee-shop door banged open to admit two boys, both perhaps fifteen. They were wearing Matignon High School jackets. The taller of the two carried a hockey stick. They went to the counter and bought root beers and two bags each of potato chips and Fritos.

"Were there any fingerprints at the crime scene?" I asked.

"Plenty," Flaherty replied. "None of 'em Jack's, though."

I arched my eyebrows. "Well, that's a big point in his favor, isn't it?"

"Not necessarily," Flaherty replied. "I'm sure they'd figure he'd be smart enough not to leave any prints."

"But at the same time, stupid enough to use his own firearm to commit the murder. Jesus, Sam!"

He exhaled some smoke. "That's an interesting point."

"It's more than that," I hissed. "Even a moronic cop who set out to kill somebody would have sense enough not to use a gun that could be traced that easily to him. And Jack is about as far from moronic as it's possible to get."

"That's true," Flaherty said, stubbing out his cigarette.

I put the tip of my right thumb in my mouth and bit down on the nail, although not hard enough to shear it off. I was thinking.

"Sam?"

"Yeah?"

"Last Friday night, you said Jack didn't come straight to my place from work. Do you know where he was between ten past eight and five of nine?"

"He told the investigators he drove into Harvard Square, stopped at a newsstand, bought some magazines, then went to his place to drop off a few papers and pick up the mail."

"Right," I said, feeling a faint charge of excitement. "Let's break that story down. Okay, say it took him, oh, three minutes to get from his office to the police station parking lot. Then he had to get in the car, get it started, and get to Harvard Square. That's another five to seven minutes, minimum. Okay, for the purposes of argument, let's say he found a place to park right away. Doubtful, but possible. Okay. He gets out of his car, goes to the newsstand, picks out a couple of magazines, pays for them, and goes back to the car. Another five minutes, at least. Then he drives to his place. That could be ten minutes, especially if he hit a few red lights. It's now at least eight-thirty-three." I paused, and took in some air. "He parks his car, goes in the house, turns on a light, picks up his mail, puts his work papers away. He opens the mail and glances at it. Then maybe he uses the bathroom. Then he turns off the lights, leaves the house, locks the door, gets back in his car, starts it up. At this point, it's gotta be at least eight-forty-three. Now he has to drive to my place. That takes another ten minutes. He parks in front of my house at eight-fifty-three, and two minutes later, he's in my living room. How's that for a scenario?"

"Perfect," Flaherty said. "Too bad none of it can be verified."

"What do you *mean*? *Someone* must have seen Jack at the newsstand, at least. The clerk who took his money for the magazines, maybe."

Flaherty sighed. "Clerk can't remember one way or the other. Says he had two hundred people in and out of the stand between

eight and nine Friday night. Says he wouldn't have noticed if Ronald Reagan and Richard Nixon walked by him hand in hand."

"Damn," I said, my teeth clenched. "Well, what about when Jack went home? Did his landlord see him?"

"Landlord was out that night."

"A neighbor, then?"

Flaherty shook his head. "It's like the newsstand clerk. Nobody the investigators talked to—so far—saw anything."

"Too bad the old biddy next door to Sims's house doesn't live right by Jack, instead. *She'd* be able to tell you when he came and went."

Flaherty smiled wryly. "Yeah."

"Well," I said. "In any case, Jack can prove where he was from eight-fifty-five Friday night."

"Oh, can he?"

I scowled. "What are you talking about? Of course he can. He was with me. I said so. I told those two jerks from the state police so."

"And you think they believed you?"

I stared at Flaherty for a few seconds. Then I said, very quietly, "No. I don't think they did."

"You're Jack's girlfriend, Liz," Flaherty said. "The investigators know that."

"Which means they assume I'd lie in order to protect him."

"Uh-huh. They could."

"And probably do." I heaved a long, quavery sigh, picked up my soda, and finished it. "So Jack has no alibi for Friday night, then, has he?"

Flaherty shook his head. "No."

"Oh, God." I cupped my forehead in the palm of my right hand.

One of the counter men shoved a push broom past our table.

"I think they want to close up here," Flaherty said. "Let's go. I'll take you home."

"All right. Thank you."

The two adolescent boys preceded us out of the coffee shop. The counterman locked the door behind us and pulled down a long green shade over it.

Sam's car was a block up Third Street. When we got to it, I said, "Sam?"

He was unlocking the driver's side door. "Uh-huh?"

"You're not working on Jack's case, are you?"

He straightened up and looked at me, his gaze very level over the roof of the car. "Nope. Captain don't want me on it."

"Because you're Jack's friend?"

He shrugged. "Captain didn't give me a reason and I didn't ask for one."

"Who *is* working on it?"

"Other than the DA's office? Our internal affairs guys. Plus a couple of the detectives."

"You seem to know a lot about what's happening, though."

He opened the car door. "Not really. Just what I hear going around the department. It's not anything you won't read in the papers eventually."

I nodded.

"Whatever I learn, I'll tell you."

"Thanks." I cocked my head. "And you'll make it a point to learn as much as possible, won't you?"

"Whatever."

"Yeah, you will," I said. "You're gonna unofficially work on this case, aren't you?"

He got in the car without replying. I climbed into the front seat beside him.

"You will," I persisted. "And I know damn well why. You'll do it to clear Jack. Because you care about him as much as I do."

Flaherty put the key in the ignition and started the car.

"Sam?"

"What?"

"We're going to do this together."

He took a deep breath. "Ah, Liz—"

"No," I said, my voice hard. I could full well anticipate each and every one of his objections, and I would trample each and every one of them down flat. "You can't stop me from doing this. Damn it!"

I swiveled around in the car seat and jabbed a stiff forefinger in the direction of the courthouse. *"That* man, sitting up *there,* in *that* cell, is the best thing in my life. Do you think I'm going to sit around like some asshole wimp and let him be destroyed?"

Flaherty's hands were tight on the steering wheel. "No."

"Okay," I said. "Okay. So I'm with you on this, Sam, whether you want me to be or not."

"Liz," he said. "I understand the way you feel. Believe me, I do. But what do you think you can accomplish?"

"A lot," I said. "A lot."

18

I REALIZED as I was in bed that night trying to fall asleep that Sam was right. There *was* a limit to what I could accomplish on my own. I would need more help than even he could offer. Help familiar with the techniques of investigation. More important, help I thought I could trust.

That didn't leave me with a lot of options.

The following morning I stood in the center of my living room, hands on my hips, looking at Harvey Searle and John Ouellette.

"If I have to, I'll manage without either one of you," I said. "But I'd rather have both of you with me. You each have resources I don't. So tell me now, fellas. Are you in or are you out?"

Harvey was half-sitting, half-lying on my sofa. Today his warm-up suit was green. As I looked at him, he pulled himself upright.

"Well?" I said. "What'll it be?"

"Hell," he said. "I like Jack. I think he's being shafted. I'm in."

"Good." I turned to Ouellette. "And you?"

He hesitated, but not long enough for me to call him on it. "In."

"Why?"

Ouellette's round face looked somewhat startled. Then he shrugged. "For the same reasons as Harvey. Why else?"

I nodded. "Fine. That's what I wanted to hear. Thanks."

Harvey relaxed back into the sofa cushions. "So it's all settled," he said. "We work together."

"Uh-huh," I said. "And just think what a good story you'll get."

I was acting like a storm trooper, I knew, but I was long past caring about whether my behavior offended Ouellette and Searle. Which was, of course, a stupid way to act when you were trying to enlist someone's cooperation. Or asking them a favor.

Harvey and John exchanged a look I couldn't quite interpret.

"Liz," Ouellette said. "Go through for us what Sam told you about the investigation." He took out his notebook and smiled at me.

"And, for Christ's sake, sit down," Harvey added. "You're making me nervous standing there breathing fire all over the living room."

"Yeah," I said. "All right." I lowered myself into the rocking chair, gathered my wits, and began reciting the facts, or details anyway, of the case against Jack. I kept my voice flat and emotionless. Searle and Ouellette listened with great attention.

"The gun's the worst part," Harvey said. "It's going to be hard to find a way around that."

Ouellette nodded.

"Well, there's an explanation somewhere," I said. "We just haven't found it."

"You mean, like somebody stole the gun from Jack?" Ouellette asked. "And whoever that was used it to shoot Sims."

"Maybe. I don't know."

Harvey made a face. "You think Jack wouldn't have noticed if that had happened? If somebody'd walked up to him, yanked his gun out of the holster, and strolled off with it? You think the guy would have gotten very far?"

"Clearly," I said, "it didn't happen that way."

"Well, how then?"

"I don't *know*, Harvey. That's one of the things we're going to try to figure out, remember?"

"Okay, okay."

"Christ," John said. "If you two are going to fight, I'm bailing out right now and going off on my own."

"We are not fighting," Harvey said. "We're just bouncing ideas off

each other." He slapped both hands on his thighs. "So let's get to work, then."

"For starters," Ouellette said, looking at us both, "I suggest we talk to that old bag on Hurley Street who claims she saw Jack enter Sims's house Friday night. I take it, Harv, she's also the one you interviewed about Yolanda?"

"Who gave me the complete rundown on Sims's bedroom habits." Harvey nodded. "Yeah. It's gotta be the same one."

"What's her name?" I asked.

"Watson. Mrs. George Watson."

I didn't write it down in my notebook. There was no danger of my forgetting it.

"Well, let's go then," Ouellette said. "We can take my car."

"Boy, you really are a take-charge kind of guy, aren't you?" Harvey observed.

"Blow it out your ass, Searle," Ouellette replied, smiling.

"Is that an idea you're bouncing off him, John?" I asked.

I got Lucy a dog cookie, gave her a pat on the head, collected my jacket, and we left.

In Ouellette's car—me in the front and Harvey in the back—John said, "Liz, I almost forgot. I don't know how interested you still are in Otway Gilmore and company, but I collected a little more material. It's in a manila folder under your seat."

"God," I said. "Gilmore. I haven't thought about him in days." I smiled at Ouellette. "Thanks for going to the trouble, though, John."

"No trouble. Like I said, the stuff's there if you want it."

I fished the folder out from the cavity beneath my seat.

"It's nothing much," John Ouellette said. "Just some file photos of the principals."

The first picture was a head and shoulders shot of Otway Gilmore. It looked like a studio portrait, the kind a publicist would send out with a press release. Gilmore wasn't smiling, but his face expressed a kind of relaxed confidence that drew you. It was a compelling face, attractive.

The next picture looked like a mug shot. The subject was in his

late thirties or early forties. He had straggly dark hair that hung just below his earlobes. His eyes were small and dark and bright, with pinpoint pupils. Drug eyes. Beneath a hooked nose was a droopy *bandito* mustache. His cheeks were pitted with little craters, and a thin white scar curved down along the right corner of his mouth. He looked as if he hadn't shaved in days.

"Who's this charmer?" I asked.

John glanced at the picture. "Phillie Joyce," he said. "The guy who shot Stephen Larrain."

"Jesus," I murmured.

The third photo was of Dalton Craig. It seemed recent—probably taken when he'd made his accusations against Jack.

I stifled the impulse to rip it into tiny pieces.

The last picture featured a paunchy, middle-aged man in a plaid sport coat. He had a round face with a potato nose and a receding hairline. What hair he did have was slicked straight back, the comb tracks visible. His mouth was small and thin-lipped, and his eyes heavily pouched.

"And which one of the Seven Dwarfs is this?" I asked.

John laughed. "That's Albert Parkes."

"Oh."

"Hey, lemme take a look at those pictures when you're done," Harvey said.

I closed the folder and handed it back to him.

We drove down Cambridge Street to Sixth, turned right there, and went four blocks past Otis, Thorndike, and Spring to Hurley. John slowed to look for a parking place.

"I think there's one up there in front of that green house," I said, leaning forward and peering through the windshield.

"By God," John said. "So there is."

As we were getting out of the car, Harvey gave me back the folder of photographs. I tucked it inside the back cover of my notebook.

"Which house do we want?" John asked.

"That place with the brick front, right next door to Yolanda's," Harvey said.

We crossed the street. I looked up and to my left. The courthouse was three blocks distant in that direction. I could see its upper floors above the trees. I telegraphed a mental message to Jack.

"Are you going to pretend to be a *Herald* or a *Globe* reporter?" Harvey asked me.

"What?" I said. "Oh. Neither. I'll just be myself. Why not? This woman doesn't know my name or what my connections are."

We went up a short path to the front door of the fake brick-front house. Harvey rang the bell. He glanced at John and me. "Get ready for a real treat," he said.

The door was opened by a short, rather heavy-set woman in a flowered print housedress. She had on fuzzy slippers and support hose. Her gray hair was permed into ridgelike waves.

"Hello, Mrs. Watson," Harvey said, oozing gregarious charm. "Remember me? This is John Ouellette from the *Globe* and Liz Connors from . . . *Boston Magazine*. If it's no trouble we'd like to talk to you about what happened here last Friday night."

The woman's faded hazel eyes seemed to gleam from beneath their creased lids.

"You can come in," she said, opening the door wider.

The four of us filed down a dim and narrow hallway to a kitchen in the rear. The kitchen had windows on its back and right sides. Those on the right looked directly onto Yolanda Sims's front steps. The view of the steps, I noted, was excellent.

The four of us sat down in cast-iron chairs with plastic cushions around a round, veneer-topped table. The kitchen was sunny and immaculate. A small black-and-white television sat on the counter, tuned to a game show, volume low.

As if we'd been choreographed, Harvey and John and I took out our notebooks and set them on the table.

Harvey flashed Mrs. Watson a brilliant grin. "Been a lot of excitement in this neighborhood lately, huh?"

The chatty sociability of his tone grated on me, making my shoulders stiffen.

John noticed and shot me a brief sharp look. The look said: *Cool it. He knows what he's doing.*

"You may have witnessed something very important," Harvey said. "Can you tell us about it?"

Mrs. Watson smoothed her hands down the front of her dress. Then she placed them one atop the other on the table. "You want to know what I told the police?"

"That would be great."

She nodded. "Well, like I told them, the police that is, I was here"—she glanced around her—"in the kitchen Friday night. I was making a pie for my sodality meeting."

Harvey smiled again to encourage the flow of recollection.

"And I was standing over there," she said, pointing at the counter beneath the window that looked out onto Yolanda Sims's front steps, "rolling out the crust, and I saw this man going up the walk to *her* house."

Mrs. Watson pronounced the word "her" as if she were holding it away from us with a pair of ice tongs.

"I see," Harvey murmured, and made a scribble in his notebook.

"The man rang her doorbell," Mrs. Watson continued.

"Can you describe him?" Harvey asked. "Just as you saw him there, in that minute."

"I got a very good look at him," Mrs. Watson said, nodding. "He was tall."

"How tall?"

"Oh, very tall. Like about six-three or six-four."

"How was he built? Fat? Thin? Medium?"

"Oh, well, medium-like. He had a good build. Broad shoulders."

"Uh-huh." Harvey wrote another note. "What was he wearing?"

"Some kind of dark suit. He had a raincoat on, too."

My insides curdled. Jack had been wearing a dark-gray suit and his trenchcoat when he'd come to my house Friday night.

"How could you see that he was wearing a suit, Mrs. Watson?" Harvey asked. "If he had a coat on over it?"

Mrs. Watson smiled, and there was something very unpleasant about her face.

"One of the cops asked me that. The man was standing sort of sideways on the front steps. His coat was open."

Jack very often wore his coat unbuttoned.

"So you *did* get a good look at his clothing?" Harvey said.

"Oh, yes. He had on a dark suit, a white shirt, and a tie."

"What about his coloring, Mrs. Watson? Like his hair, for example."

"He had brown hair," the woman replied. "With a little gray in it."

"You could see that?" Harvey interrupted. "The gray?" Somehow he managed to sound curious, not inquisitorial.

"As sure as I can see you," she said.

"And this man," Harvey said. "He was white or black? Or Hispanic?"

Mrs. Watson looked startled. "He wasn't no colored. He was white."

"O-kay." Harvey scrawled again in his notebook. Then he set his pen down on the table. "You're clearly a very observant person, Mrs. Watson."

She nodded.

Harvey leaned toward her slightly. "Then give me a really *detailed* description of this man's face."

Mrs. Watson put her right hand to her chin and made a tugging gesture. "It was long, and um, sort of thin. And he had these cheekbones that stuck up a little. Like some kind of Indian, you know?"

"But he wasn't an Indian?"

"Oh, no."

"Okay." Harvey picked up his pen.

"No, he wasn't no Indian," Mrs. Watson continued, her voice flat and grim. "He was a white man, all right." Her mouth tightened. "He was some cop from right here in town."

I felt John's hand clamp down on my knee and squeeze it, hard. *Whatever she says next, Liz, you keep your mouth shut.*

"You're absolutely sure of that, Mrs. Watson?" Harvey said.

"The other cops showed me some pictures," she replied. "One of them was of *him*. I recognized it right away."

Harvey darted me a quick sideways glance. Then he said, "And it's correct that you also identified this man in a lineup?"

"As soon as I saw him."

"No doubt in your mind?"

"None," Mrs. Watson said. "That was him. The cop."

Harvey looked across the table at John. "John?" he said. "You have any questions?"

John cleared his throat. "Ma'am," he said. "Had you seen this . . . the man you saw go into Mrs. Sims's house Friday evening— had you ever seen him before that time?"

"With Yolanda?"

"Yes."

Mrs. Watson frowned, then shook her head. "No."

I removed John's restraining hand from my knee. "I have a question," I said.

Mrs. Watson looked astonished that I'd spoken. Perhaps she'd thought I was with Harvey and John to hold their pens.

I smiled at her. It took some doing. "Mrs. Watson, when Yolanda opened her door to this man, how did she react?"

Mrs. Watson looked puzzled.

"I mean," I said, "did she seem surprised to see the guy? Angry? Frightened? Was there any way you could tell?"

Harvey arched his brows at me and mouthed, *good question*.

Mrs. Watson's puzzled frown eased into one of speculation. Her eyes narrowed. A few moments passed while the three of us watched her think.

"Yolanda didn't look mad to me," Mrs. Watson said finally. "She let him, she let that cop, she let him right in the house."

"So she wasn't frightened to see him, then, either," I asked.

"Oh, no."

"What about surprised?"

Mrs. Watson hesitated, then shook her head.

"Did you have the impression that she might have been expecting the guy to come to her place that evening?"

Mrs. Watson shrugged. "I dunno. Maybe. Like I said, she let him right in."

I nodded.

" 'Course," Mrs. Watson continued, smirking, "Yolanda would do that with almost any man who came to her door. And I heard she was havin' things to do with that cop anyway. The one who shot her."

"Well, that hasn't been proven yet, has it?" I asked pleasantly.

John nudged my foot with his.

Harvey closed his notebook and slipped his pen into his inside jacket pocket. "I think that about wraps it up, Mrs. Watson," he said. "I don't have any more questions." He looked across the table at John and me. "You guys?"

"Nope," John said.

I shook my head.

"Okay." Harvey smiled at Mrs. Watson. "I guess we'll be getting along, then. Thanks very much for your time. We appreciate it." He rose, and held out his hand.

"When will this be in the paper?" Mrs. Watson asked, ignoring his hand.

Despite the way I was feeling, I had to hide a grin.

"Well, that depends on my editor," Harvey said smoothly, letting his hand drop to his side. "We have a big story here. I'll be working on it for a while. Maybe next week." He smiled again at Mrs. Watson. "Look in the paper then."

"Oh. All right."

Ouellette and I spoke our "good-byes" and "thank yous" in chorus. Mrs. Watson acknowledged them with a single nod of her head and conducted us back down the narrow dark hallway to the front door.

When we were outside, Harvey cocked his head wryly. "What did I tell you?"

I laughed.

"Sweet lady," John remarked. "Reminded me of my old grandma."

We walked to the car.

"Listen, fellas," I began.

They glanced at me.

"The way I acted this morning," I said. I made a little circular gesture with my hand. "That was completely uncalled-for. I was being a bitch. I'm sorry. And I apologize."

John was unlocking the car. "Forget it," he said. "I have."

"No," I said. "I was being a real jackass. And I don't know why." I leaned against the side of the car and stared up at the trees. "I guess maybe I was scared that you guys would think Jack was guilty, and not want to get involved with anything to do with him. Or you'd laugh at me for thinking I could help him out of this . . . mess. So I got angry. In advance. Before I even talked to you, face to face."

"And you think I didn't understand that at the time?" John asked.

I looked at Harvey. He smiled slightly. "Didn't bother me any," he said.

"You two are nice."

John rolled his eyes. "Yeah, we're swell."

When we were in the car, Harvey said to me, "Liz, that was a good question you asked the old bag. What made you think of it?"

I shrugged. "I don't know. It just seemed logical."

"How do you mean?"

"Well." I drummed my fingertips on my knees. "Yolanda was supposed to be terrified of Jack. She said so on TV. So if that were the case, doesn't it follow that she should have been freaked out of her wits by having him show up on her doorstep? A week after she publicly accused him of raping her?" I looked at them both. "But instead, she let him right into her house. Seemed strange to me."

"Maybe," John said, "this guy was pointing a gun at her, and he forced his way in."

"Oh, John. I think Mrs. Watson would have noticed that, don't you?"

He grimaced. "Yeah."

"Goddamn," Harvey said. "Goddamn. You're right. Liz. But. . ."

"But what, Harv?"

"What does it mean?"

I smiled. "I think," I said, "that it means we just found our first piece of evidence to show that whoever it was who visited Yolanda last Friday night, it wasn't Jack."

19

I GOT SAM FLAHERTY to meet me for a late lunch in a sub shop on Third Street. He was there when I arrived, working his way through a pepper steak sandwich. I bought a tuna sub and coffee and sat down across from him in a booth with cracked Leatherette-upholstered benches. He listened carefully as I described that morning's conversation with Mrs. Watson.

"You kids did a pretty good field interview," he commented, when I'd finished speaking.

A chunk of greasy pepper fell from his sandwich and landed on his tie. He picked it off and deposited it on the rim of the paper plate before him.

"So what do you think?" I said. "I mean about the business of Yolanda not being afraid of or angry at the guy who came to her door?"

"Kind of interesting."

"Oh, Sam, it's more than just that, isn't it?"

He smiled at me a little sadly. "I don't know if it would be enough to raise a reasonable doubt in the minds of a jury. A good defense attorney might be able to build it up when he cross-examined the Watson broad. Still . . ." He shrugged, and ate another bite of his sandwich.

"I think it's a significant point," I said. "If it really had been Jack there that Friday night, Yolanda should have screamed and slammed the door in his face."

"Hey, doll, you don't have to convince me of that."

I reached across the table and placed my hand on the back of his. "I know."

He turned his hand over and squeezed mine briefly. "I'll keep what you've told me in mind," he said.

He ate the rest of his pepper steak. As I drank my coffee I studied his face. The lines in it seemed more deeply grooved than they had a week ago. And his red-gray hair seemed grayer. Beneath his tweed jacket, his shoulders slumped. This was one tired man—trying not to show it.

I put my cup on the table. "What're you working on now, Sam?" I asked. "In the official sense."

He took out his cigarettes. "This and that. The Paula Young killing, for one thing."

"Oh, yes. Any progress on that front?"

He made a disgusted face. "I got shit on that front, pardon my French."

"I'm sorry. That's too bad."

"Also," Sam went on, "they stuck me with the Edward Hassler murder. The thing Jack was working on before . . ."

"Yeah. How's that one look?"

Sam smiled bleakly. "About as good as Paula Young."

I sighed. "Maybe something will break with either case."

"If it does, it better be soon." He crushed out his cigarette. "Speaking of which, I gotta get back to work."

I nodded. "Me, too."

I watched him as he left the luncheonette. No wonder he looked tired.

A great many people had apparently decided to visit their inmate brothers, husbands, fathers, lovers, or buddies that evening. I arrived at the jail at five after seven, and the lobby was already crowded. I noticed a fair number of children in the throng. But the fey, toothless woman was gone. A tubby elderly couple occupied her bench.

I had to wait until a quarter to eight before they let me through the

trap and into the visiting area. There were no free seats in the first of the three aquaria. The third had two available. I grabbed the one nearest the door, so there'd be nobody sitting down to my left. That gave me a half-private space.

About five minutes later, Jack came into the center room. He glanced around and I waved at him from my corner. He gave me a big grin. God, it was so good just to see him.

When we'd gotten settled, I said, "I brought you your books. I had to leave them out there, though. I suppose you'll get them eventually."

"Oh, sure," he replied. "So long as they're not dirty."

"Well," I said, "I *did* insert a nude photo of myself in the centerfold of *The Vision of History in Early Britain*. Think the guards'll find it?"

"Nah, those guys can't handle anything more complex than *My Weekly Reader.*"

"Then you have a treat in store for you," I said. "But, enough of this hilarity. How are you, honey?"

He held up both hands, palms out. "Oh, fine. What it is in here, mostly, is just boring." He smiled. "The books'll help with that."

"And the nude photo. Don't forget about that."

He tilted his head. "You know, Liz, I'm almost beginning to think you *did* put a picture of yourself in that book."

"Well, you'll just have to wait and see."

We looked at each other for several seconds.

"I miss you," I said, softly. "I think about you all the time."

"I think about you, too," he replied.

"We're going to have such a great party, just you and me, when you get out of this place."

He took a deep breath. "*If* I get out of this place."

"Oh, Jack, don't say that."

"Honey, do you know what kind of a case they have against me?"

"Sam told me the outlines."

"It's not good, cookie. They got motive, opportunity, method, and an unshakable eyewitness. Hell, *I* almost think I'm guilty."

"Don't say that," I repeated, more sharply this time. I shook my head. "It's not a case. It's a house of cards that's going to collapse the first time anyone breathes on it."

"Liz, Yolanda Sims was shot with my gun. *My gun.*"

"All right," I said. "That's the part I don't understand. Jack, how on earth did whoever killed Yolanda manage to get your gun away from you?"

He gave me an odd look. "It was stolen from my apartment. And returned afterward. Sometime that Friday night, so far as I can tell."

I pushed back in my seat and scowled at him in bewilderment. "What are you talking about, Jack? You had your gun on when you came to my place. And you took it off, and you unloaded it, and you put it in the drawer of my night table. I *saw* you do that."

For a moment, the expression on his face mirrored my own confusion. Then it cleared. "You're missing a piece," he said. "I guess Sam forgot to tell you. Or maybe he assumed you'd figure it out."

"Figure what out?" I leaned toward the speaking grille.

"The gun that was used on Yolanda wasn't the one I carry every day," he said. "It was the other. The one I keep cuffed to the pipe underneath the kitchen sink."

"Oh, my God," I said. "Of course. That thirty-eight you had when you were a patrolman."

He nodded.

"You haven't carried that in—what? Fifteen years?"

"Longer than that. But I keep it cleaned and oiled and in working order."

I was silent, turning over this new information in my mind.

"Jack," I said. "When did you last check to see if that gun was still in its proper place?"

"Oh, Christ, sweetie, I don't know. Maybe a few months ago, when I took it out to oil it."

"But not since then?"

He shook his head.

I smiled at him. "This is really wonderful news. It just makes the prosecutor's case that much weaker. The damn thirty-eight could

have been stolen any time and you wouldn't have known it was gone. And put back in place equally without your knowing."

"Risky," Jack said.

"Not for someone who knows something about your habits, Jack," I argued. "You spend half your nights at my house. You've been doing that for years now. Your apartment is left untended all day long, too."

"I have good locks," he said, drily.

"Oh, honey. How often have you yourself told me that almost anyone can break in almost anywhere any time? Besides, Cambridge is Burglary City."

"I'm not disagreeing," Jack said. "I think you're right. It probably happened exactly the way you described it. But tell that to the prosecutor."

"Why doesn't your lawyer do that very thing?"

Jack gave me a faint smile. "You know what the prosecutor's answer would be?"

"Tell me."

"He'd say, 'Fine. Now *you*, sir, explain to me why this *alleged* person whom you claim knew your client's schedule so well—you, sir, explain to me why this alleged person should have broken into *your* client's apartment, stolen *your* client's gun, and used it to shoot Mrs. Sims.' "

I waved my hands. "Oh, that's crap."

"No, it isn't." Jack's voice was gentle. "Honey, I'm the only one they've found who had any reason to want Yolanda Sims dead."

"But you didn't want her dead."

"That's a matter of opinion."

"Oh, God." I closed my eyes. When I opened them, Jack was gazing at me, his face quite serious and a little sad. Sad for me, not for himself.

"Okay," I said. "If we're going to talk about opinions, you might like to know that in the opinion of Harvey Searle and John Ouellette, you're really being screwed in this deal."

He smiled. "That's nice to hear. Always good to have the press on your side."

"Jack, I'm sure a lot of people are on your side."

"Well, you are. That's all that counts."

I felt my throat tighten.

"You know, honey," Jack said, "if you're going to be a regular visitor of mine—"

"You know I am."

"You can apply to make what they call 'contact' visits."

I cleared my throat and tried to assume a jocular tone. "Contact? I could use some contact with you."

"You're confusing *contact* with *conjugal*, sweetie," Jack said. "I'm afraid we don't rate conjugal. For that, you gotta be married."

"So what's a contact visit, then?"

Jack pointed at a big open space that had in its center a row of library-carrellike desks and some vinyl and metal chairs much like the ones we were using. "We can sit out there and talk to each other without a sheet of glass between us," he said. "Maybe even hold hands." He grinned. "It's better than nothing, I suppose."

"I'll take what I can get," I said. "When can I make my first contact visit?"

"Sunday afternoon," he said. "And Monday night."

"I gotta wait that long?"

"Those are the rules."

"The rules suck."

He laughed.

It was, according to my watch, three minutes to nine. Visiting hours were ending.

"If I kept sitting here," I mused, "would the guards—excuse me, the corrections officials—would they come in and drag me out?"

"I don't know," Jack said. "It's not something I want to leave to chance, though. I'd break through this glass"—he tapped the window with his forefinger—"and kill anyone who touched you."

"In that case, I'll go quietly." I rose, and smiled at him. "Until Sunday, then, love. And the heavy hand-holding."

"Exactly."

20

THE NEXT MORNING, I let myself into Jack's apartment with the key he'd given me long ago. His house was quiet and orderly. If the cops who'd searched the place had ripped it apart, at least they'd had the grace to restore everything to the proper position. Professional courtesy. Or perhaps Jack's cleaning woman had made her regular Wednesday visit, despite the fact that her employer was in jail.

I walked into the living room and pushed aside the draperies over the front window. The windowpanes were intact. Nor was there any sign, to my untrained eye, that the lock had been jimmied or in any manner broken or disengaged. The other window, on the north side of the room, appeared similarly undisturbed.

I made a check of all the windows—kitchen, bathroom, bedroom, and little combination guest room-study-library. All solid. So was the kitchen door, with its double-keyed deadbolt. Of course the front door had been as tight as a drum.

There was another door in the kitchen, though, leading down to the cellar. It had a button-depressed lock. I grabbed the knob and twisted it back and forth, then pushed and pulled on it. There was virtually no give. The door was a two-inch-thick slab of oak, not hollow core, six-and-a-half feet high and three feet wide. Pretty hard to bust open, unless you went at it with a chain saw or something.

Still, button locks were notoriously easy to pry. You could do it

with a credit card or a paring knife. Someone could have gotten into
Jack's apartment this way, through this door.

Yes, and who? A troll who lived under the furnace?

I got out my keys and unlocked the other kitchen door, the one
going out to the back yard.

A bulkhead was set into the rear wall of the house. I grabbed the
handle and yanked. The hatch came up with surprising ease.

Jack would be positively thrilled when I told him that his landlord
was neglecting to keep the bulkhead latched from within.

I went down the steps into the cellar. It was musty, dim, and tidy.
A workshop in one corner. Boxes and trunks neatly aligned along the
walls. A bicycle and some skis. No trolls, though.

I went up another flight of wooden stairs to Jack's kitchen door. I
snapped on the light switch just above the railing. Then I reached
into my wallet for one of my laminated faculty ID cards. It was just
slightly too thick to insert in the hairline crack between the door and
the door frame. My nail file wasn't. In under fifteen seconds, I
managed to pop the lock. And in so doing, I noted, left no scratch
or abrasion marks on the door itself. I stepped up into the kitchen.

I shut and relocked the door behind me, then went out into the
back yard again and closed the bulkhead. I returned to the kitchen,
savoring the knowledge that I had just proved that any dimwit could
break into Jack's apartment in no time flat.

So what?

I wandered into the living room and dropped down on the couch.
It was a nice couch, strongly built but soft and cozy. It had been one
of Jack and Diana's first purchases after their marriage, I recalled.
Jack and I had sat on it countless times to have a drink, read, talk,
or watch television. We'd even made love on it.

That latter remembrance hurt. Actually, it hurt a lot. I rubbed my
hand on the cushion beside me, letting the nap of the fabric tickle
my palm.

I got up quickly and left the living room. I walked into the little
study. Underneath the window was a desk. I pulled open the top
right-hand drawer. At the bottom, covered by some file folders, was

a large manila envelope. Inside the envelope, I knew, was an eight-by-ten color photograph in a wooden frame. I'd seen it before.

I hesitated, then opened the envelope and took out the photograph. I turned it right side up and stared at it.

It was a picture of Diana, a close-up head and shoulders shot taken against a backdrop of extravagantly blossoming forsythias. She had short brown hair and large blue eyes, and she seemed to be laughing uproariously. The face wasn't beautiful in a classic sense, or more accurately, a commercial one, but it radiated intelligence and good humor.

As I gazed at it, I thought, what would *you* be doing now? Here, in my place?

I had never quite understood why Jack kept this picture hidden away. It wouldn't have bothered me to see it on the mantel. Maybe it would have bothered *him*, though.

"She must have been an incredibly nice person," I'd told Jack. He'd replied, "She was."

I put the picture back in its envelope and returned it to the drawer. Then I went back to the living room and sat down again. I put my feet up on the coffee table, alongside a small stack of magazines.

I glanced down at them automatically. The uppermost one had a current date. Probably it and the three underneath were the ones Jack had bought before coming to my house last Friday night. Maybe I should bring them to him so he could read them.

The magazine on top of the pile had a small, raggedy-edged piece of paper tucked inside its front cover, next to the binding and protruding slightly. The receipt for its and the others' purchase, I guessed.

I sat very still.

The receipt.

Jesus Christ. The receipt.

Most cash registers were semicomputerized now, for inventory purposes. The receipts they gave recorded not only prices for each individual item, sales taxes, and final totals, but stock numbers and the time and date of the transaction as well.

Hi-tech had its uses.

I got my nail file from my purse. Then I leaned forward and slid the blade beneath the front cover of the magazine. I flipped it back. With the point of the file, I drew the register receipt toward me. I bent down further and peered at it.

The print was light blue, but quite readable. At the very top of the strip of paper, below the name of the newsstand, was stamped a date.

It was last Friday's.

Beneath the date was stamped the time.

The print read: 8:26 P.M.

Jack had been in Harvard Square paying for these four magazines one minute *after* Mrs. George Watson had seen him being admitted to Yolanda Sims's house in East Cambridge.

Two-and-a-half miles distant.

I very delicately tucked the register slip back into place and shut the magazine. Then I sagged back into the couch. I looked up at the ceiling and said, "Thank you."

21

"I LEFT the magazines right there on the coffee table," I said. "I didn't even touch them with my hands. I didn't want to screw up the—what do you call it? Chain of evidence?"

"Yeah, that's right." Sam gave me a broad smile. "You done good on this one, doll. Real good."

"You think it'll help Jack's case?"

"Well, it sure as hell won't hurt it, I can tell you that."

"So the receipt counts as genuine physical evidence?"

"Uh-huh. First piece of it for our side."

It was early that afternoon. We were walking down Green Street, away from the police station. I still didn't want to go in there, and wouldn't until Jack had been restored to his office on the third floor. What had once been so familiar and comfortable now seemed alien and hostile.

"By the way," I said, "I think I also proved how easy it would be for someone to break into Jack's apartment. Without leaving any sign of a break. Is that also useful for you to know?"

"Showing that somebody *could* burglarize a place ain't quite the same as showing somebody *did* burglarize a place."

"No, I know that."

"It's sort of negative evidence," Sam said. "Which don't mean, of course, that I'll just forget about it."

"It's a tiny little piece of a much bigger picture."

"Uh-huh. The big picture. Right."

Something occurred to me that hadn't before. My stride lagged a bit. "Sam?"

"Yup?"

"I was just thinking that it might not have been necessary for someone to break into Jack's house to get the gun."

"How's that?"

"Well, Jack has a cleaning lady. She has a key."

Sam smiled. "And you think she might have swiped the thirty-eight?"

I laughed. "No. Not really. She's been with Jack for something like seven years now. If her fingers were light, he'd have noticed it before this. But she might have accidentally left a door or a window unlocked or the burglar alarm off and whoever *did* take the gun just strolled in."

"She ever do that before? Leave a window or whatever open?"

"Not to my knowledge," I replied. "But it could happen."

Sam made a noncommittal sound.

We walked behind the post office. Some guys on the loading dock were heaving great sacks of mail into the red, white, and blue trucks.

"Jack's gun," I said. "Was it tested for fingerprints?"

"Naturally," Sam replied. "Nothing. Zero, zip. Big surprise, huh?" He made a face. "Those kind of guns don't take a good print or even a smudge, anyway."

"More negative evidence," I said.

"That's right."

A police cruiser went by us. The driver tapped the horn. Sam and I waved.

We turned right onto Sellers Street and trudged up the slight hill to Mass. Avenue.

"Let's get some coffee," Sam said.

"Okay."

Sam and I went another block down Mass. Avenue and into a lunchroom. It occurred to me, as we took our seats at a chipped Formica table, that Sam and I were spending practically all of our

time together in Cambridge's premier bastions of *bas cuisine*. The waitress brought us coffee. It was served in those thick white mugs that have an almost porous look from having been through a dishwasher ten times a day.

"You're the big writing brain," Sam said. "Tell me what you make of this." He reached into the inner pocket of his rumpled tweed coat. From it he removed a white, legal-sized envelope and tossed it across the table at me.

I caught the envelope in both hands and turned it right side up. It was addressed to Sgt. S. Flaherty of the Cambridge Police Department. In the upper left-hand corner was typed the name Pamela Justine, and beneath that a return address in Morristown, New Jersey.

The envelope was slit down its top seam. I rubbed it tentatively between my thumbs and forefingers. Reading other people's mail appealed to me about as much as crying in public did.

"Go ahead," Sam said.

I reached in and withdrew a single sheet of white bond. I unfolded it. It was a letter, typed, single-spaced. It read:

> Dear Sergeant Flaherty:
> I understand you are investigating the murder of my sister, Paula Young.
> Your department has informed me that Paula was most likely the victim of a random street attack. Given the circumstances of her death, this is probably true. One of your colleagues, however, a Detective Capuano, told me that the police would not rule out the possibility that Paula could have been killed for other reasons. He also urged me to get in touch with you if I could remember Paula mentioning to me some particular concern or personal or professional problem. As you can imagine, I have spent a great deal of time thinking about this.
> All I can tell you is that, two weeks before she died, Paula came down to New Jersey to visit me and my family. She arrived at my house on a Friday night and left for Cambridge Sunday afternoon. I didn't really get a chance to talk to her because we had other guests. But I could see from the way she

acted that she *was* bothered about something. She was quiet and tense the whole weekend, which I can assure you was not her normal behavior.

I got the sense that whatever was bothering her had something to do with her job. Come to think of it, she did say there was a "problem at work." Beyond that, though she wouldn't say anything. I should have kept after her, but I didn't.

I'm sure Paula's problem had no bearing whatsoever on her murder. But I thought you would like to know that she was troubled about something before her death.

Please let me know if I can be of any further help in bringing my sister's killer to justice.

Yours very truly,

Pamela Young Justine (Mrs. William)
201-555-7673

I let the letter drop on the table.

"Well?" Sam said.

I sighed. "I think that's one of the saddest things I've ever read."

He gave me a quizzical look. "In what way?"

I shook my head. "The whole tone of it. So stiff and controlled on the surface, and beneath that, so much pain."

He frowned thoughtfully. "Yeah, right. I guess I was thinking of it only as a piece of information."

I refolded the letter and tucked it back into its envelope. "When did you get this?"

"Came in today's mail."

"Have you spoken to her yet?"

"Yeah. I called her this morning."

"Well? Was she able to be more specific? About Paula's problem at work? Did she remember anything else between the time she wrote you and the time you called?"

"Nope."

"Damn." I picked up the envelope and handed it back to him. He put it back in his jacket.

"Well, Sam, I don't know what to tell you." I put my elbow on the

table and rested my chin on my fist. "Paula was worried about work. Is there a connection between that and her getting beaten to a pulp on Trowbridge Street?"

"Hard to see one."

"But you'll check to see if there is."

He grinned at me. "I'm not that bad of a detective that I wouldn't. I talked to her boss today."

I raised my eyebrows. "And?"

Sam shrugged. "Far as he knew, Paula was fine. Doing good work, getting along with the other people in the company."

"And you took his word for that?"

Sam gave me a look. I laughed.

"You want some more coffee?" he asked.

"Sure."

He signaled the waitress and pointed at our cups.

"I gotta fresh pot working," she yelled. "You wanna wait for that?"

"Yeah, fine, Mattie," Sam said. He leaned back in his chair and took out a cigarette.

I tapped my spoon lightly on the Formica surface of the table. "Sam?"

"Yeah?"

"Do you have any idea of what Paula was working on before she died? I mean, was she involved in some kind of special project?"

Sam lit his cigarette. "Her boss told me she just finished an external audit of some venture capital firm."

"Anything out of the ordinary with that?"

"With her doing an audit? No. That was her job."

I shook my head. "That wasn't what I meant. Was there anything funny going on with the venture capital outfit?"

"Not that I've found out, so far."

"So far."

He smiled.

The waitress approached our table with the coffee pot and a saucer piled with plastic containers of half-and-half. "Thanks, Mattie," Sam said.

I ripped the lid off one of the cream pails and dumped its contents into my coffee. "So what's the name of this place?"

"The venture capital company? Barrow, Showalter, and Stevens."

I wrinkled my forehead. "Sounds vaguely familiar."

Sam put out his cigarette.

"Maybe I read about them someplace," I continued. "Although I usually never do anything more than glance at the business pages of the papers." I picked up my cup.

"You mean you're not interested in high finance?"

"Naw. The only kind I can relate to is low."

"Yeah," Sam sighed. "Tell me about it."

We finished our coffee. Mattie brought the check.

"I'll get this," he said. "Your finances gotta be lower than mine."

"I may be poor," I replied. "But at least I'm happy." I shrugged into my wool blazer. "And I'll be euphoric when we get Jack out of the slam."

"You're doing better at that than I am."

"Well, *I* can give it my undivided attention." I shook my head. "Is Paula Young's sister your only lead?"

He held the door of the lunchroom open for me. "At this point, Liz, I'll take what I can get."

Outside, he said, "When you gonna see Jack again?"

"Sunday afternoon. For a contact visit. We get to hold hands."

"Well, jeez, don't get carried away."

"I think the guards would probably object. Spoilsports."

"More likely," Sam said, "just jealous."

He leaned forward and gave me a quick, awkward, one-armed hug. I was a little surprised, and more than a little touched.

"Stay outa trouble," he said.

"Don't worry, Sam," I replied. "We're already in enough as it is."

Rosa Dominguez, the woman who cleaned Jack's apartment, lived on Day Street off Davis Square in Somerville. I took the subway out there from Central Square.

I had once lived just outside Davis Square myself. Ten years ago, it had been a shabby agglomeration of dingy little Mom-and-Pop tobacconists, variety stores, newsstands, and the kind of bars where the waitress runs a dustcloth over the customers every month or so.

Now it had its own subway station, a renovated Art-Deco theater, a bookstore, and a barbecue joint that required reservations. There was also a deli that sold the best prosciutto in all of Boston, and even a mini-mall. What had been in my time a fruit-and-vegetable store run by a large, cheerful Italian family was now a combination computer-video rental place.

Sometimes I thought the entire United States was in the process of becoming the Upper West Side.

Day Street, though, looked pretty much as it always had, a brick-and-frame mixture of apartment buildings and one-, two-, and three-family houses. The Dominguezes lived on the bottom floor of a gray double-decker. I went up the steps and rang the bell.

Rosa came to the door almost immediately. She was perhaps four years younger than I was, brown-haired, olive-skinned, and slim in tight, faded jeans and a baggy pink sweatshirt. She and her husband owned a bar in Medford. Rosa did housework for pin money and to help with the mortgage on their summer home on the Cape.

If you think it's odd that a cleaning person should be so upscale, then you don't know Cambridge. The guy who washed the hallway floors, the windows, polished the banisters, and did repair jobs in my apartment building had a degree from Antioch. He was an aging hippie whose politics prevented him from taking on almost any other kind of work, and he still lived in what must have been one of the few remaining communes in the country. Rosa wasn't similarly motivated to clean houses. She just liked working for herself. And she was highly selective of her clientele, limiting it strictly to people she liked. Jack was number one on her list. They were on a first-name basis.

Rosa and I had gotten to know each other fairly well from all the times she'd let herself into Jack's apartment on a Wednesday morning and found me there in my bathrobe.

Rosa's eyes, already large, widened at the sight of me on her doorstep.

"Hi," I said. "Talk to you for a minute?"

She pulled the door back. "Come in."

We went into the living room. The Dominguez's two-year-old son, Fabian, was sitting in the middle of the floor, amusing himself with a set of large, foam-rubber alphabet blocks. As I walked into the room, he stopped what he was doing and gave me that intent owl-eyed stare all toddlers have mastered. I grinned at him and he ducked his head coyly.

"Coffee?" Rosa asked.

"That would be great," I said.

I didn't really want the coffee, but I did need some time to think. There had to be a tactful way to phrase the questions I wanted to ask Rosa.

I squatted on the floor beside Fabian and picked up one of the blocks he was playing with. He gave me a wary look.

We were having a good time building a very leaning foam-rubber Leaning Tower of Pisa, and an even better time knocking it down, when Rosa came in from the kitchen with a tray. She glanced at the two of us, rolled her eyes, and set the tray on the coffee table.

"Just a child at heart," I said. I tickled Fabian under the chin, rose stiffly, and went to sit on the couch. Rosa handed me my coffee.

"Tell me about Jack," she said.

I shrugged. "He's okay, given the circumstances. I guess you could say he's fine."

She nodded. "When I saw on the news that he'd been arrested for *murder*, I . . ." She gave me an intent look. "This must be terrible for you."

"Well," I said, "I'll manage." I hoped my reserve didn't strike her as standoffishness. I was here to gain Rosa's confidence, but I couldn't shake the feeling that I was here as a spy.

We drank our coffee and watched Fabian, who was lining up his blocks very precisely on the carpet. His little face was puckered with concentration.

The silence seemed to go on for a long time, and just as I was

about to say something, Rosa said, "How could they think somebody like Jack would . . ."

"Commit a murder?" I said bluntly. "Kill a woman?"

Rosa winced. I pressed my advantage.

"She was shot with Jack's gun," I added.

Rosa gave me a saucer-eyed look of incredulity. "How on earth could that happen?" The words blew from her mouth like a tiny explosion.

"Somebody stole it from his apartment." Either broke in or walked in, I was thinking. Walked in if someone had been careless and left the door open. But I couldn't say it.

I told Rosa how I'd popped the lock on Jack's kitchen door, the one that led to the basement. "Anyone could get in that way," I concluded.

Rosa frowned. "It could be," she said finally. "I don't know. I don't use that door. I never have any reason to go down to the cellar." She looked up at me. "I guess," she said slowly, "if somebody *was* going to break into Jack's place, it would have to be that way." She sat up straight. "But I always check all the windows and both outside doors before I leave, just to make sure they're locked. And I turn on the burglar alarm."

I thanked Rosa silently for answering the question I hadn't asked.

"I've also *never* let anyone into the house while I've been there," Rosa said. "But I do see workmen around the place sometimes. And the meter readers."

I looked at her. "Who lets them in, then? If you don't?"

She shrugged. "I don't know. Maybe the landlord? Or another tenant? I never thought about it."

"Do they come in the house the front way, or through the back?"

"Well, the gas and electric guys would go down the cellar by way of the bulkhead, I guess."

"That makes sense," I said. "It also proves my point about easy access to the house."

Fabian pitched a blue block at me. I caught it and tossed it back.

Rosa's hands were folded in her lap. She was looking not at me,

nor at her son, but at the wall opposite. A tiny frown creased her forehead.

"What is it?" I said.

She gave her head a slight shake. "Oh, nothing. It's just . . . there was a workman around the place the last time I was there."

I looked hard at her, trying to remain calm.

"When was that?"

"The Wednesday before Jack was arrested."

"What was he doing?"

She shrugged again. "He went down the basement through the bulkhead."

"Yes, and?" A tiny jolt of excitement shot through me; I felt myself leaning toward Rosa.

"I don't know. I guess I figured he was there to read the meters. He had on those gray work clothes, you know? Like the gas company guys wear?"

"What did he look like?"

Rosa laughed in a self-deprecating way, and held out her hands. "Oh, Liz. He was a guy in uniform. Beyond that, I didn't pay any attention."

I felt my shoulders drop back to their usual position. "Yeah, who ever does?" I got up to leave. "Thanks, Rosa. For the coffee and the information."

She walked with me to the front door, Fabian lurching after us. "You give my best to Jack, Liz, when you see him. All right?"

"Yes."

"Tell him . . ." Her voice trailed off, and she looked pained.

I nodded. I knew what she wanted to say.

I walked back to the Davis Square subway. I was nearly home before I realized that whoever Rosa had seen, he hadn't been a representative of one of the utilities companies. They read the meter on the first day of the month. And the Wednesday before Jack's arrest was the tenth.

22

"OKAY, so it wasn't the gas man, like Rosa thought," John Ouellette said. "It could have been the plumber. Or a carpenter. An exterminator." He drank some beer. "The point is, the man Rosa saw wasn't necessarily the guy who stole Jack's gun."

"Yeah, I know," I said, picking up another slice of pizza. "But he could have been, which just goes to prove my point that anyone who wanted to get into Jack's house could have done so, right?"

"All right," John agreed. He finished his beer and pushed the bottle aside.

"And," I said, "what better way to get in is there than posing as a workman?"

"I'm not arguing with you there, either," John said.

"I know, I know. It doesn't prove that it did happen."

John got up and went to the fridge for a second beer.

John and Harvey had come to my place so we could pool the information we'd all gathered over the past few days. So far, I was the heaviest contributor. But that wasn't surprising. Much as Harvey and John might want to get Jack out of jail, they had other things to do. I didn't. And even if I had, I'd have set them aside.

"The stuff about the receipt for the magazines," Harvey said. "That's really good, Liz."

"Thanks." I reached over and patted his hair. He scowled and jerked his head away.

John returned to the table with his beer. "With respect to that," he said, "the prosecution could always claim that you"—he tilted the bottle at me—"planted the receipt there in Jack's apartment. That *you* and not he bought those magazines the night he was supposed to be off shooting Sims."

I let the pizza drop onto my plate. "Christ," I said, "that's a little farfetched, isn't it?"

John shrugged and took a gulp of beer. "No more farfetched than an exterminator stealing Jack's gun."

"John likes to play devil's advocate," Harvey said.

"No shit."

"All right." John said. "I'll check out the business about the *alleged* workman Rosa *allegedly* saw. Maybe I can find out what the guy was doing there. Who let him in. Maybe even get some kind of description of him."

"I was going to do that myself," I said, pulling bits of crust off my pizza. "Tonight. After you guys leave."

"A little late, don't you think?" Harvey asked, looking at the clock. It was nine-fifteen.

"That means all the people in Jack's building might be home."

"Sure. But tomorrow's Saturday, and it's even more likely they'll be there in the morning."

"Either way," I said. "I'll take care of it."

John smiled. "Let me ask you a question, Liz."

"Yes?"

"Are you friendly with Jack's neighbors?"

I was puzzled. "Well . . . I know them to say 'hi' to. Yeah, I guess so."

"In view of that, when you go talk to them, do you think you'll be able to stay objective?"

I scowled. "Of course."

"Will they?"

I went back to being puzzled. "Why shouldn't they?"

"Come on, Liz. You're his girlfriend. Don't you think when you question them, they might just answer what they think you want to hear? Or be too uncomfortable to say anything?"

"Just because I'm friendly with them?"

"It happens."

"Oh, John."

"Look, let me do it," he said. He paused a moment, and a serious look crossed his pale-skinned moon face. "I haven't been able to do much else, so far."

I felt myself softening toward him. "That's the real reason, isn't it?"

He smiled.

"Okay," I said. "If that's the case, then go for it."

We finished the pizza. The last time I'd split one with somebody, the somebody had been Jack. I balled up my paper napkin and tossed it into the empty box.

"What are your plans?" Harvey asked me.

I drank the lukewarm remains of my diet ginger ale. "Well, Sunday I get my first contact visit with Jack. Then I'm going to talk with Mrs. Watson again."

Harvey stared at me.

"I want to pin down exactly when she *allegedly* saw Jack going into Yolanda's."

Harvey nodded. John laughed.

"What about you?" I asked.

"Gonna backtrack Yolanda," he said.

"Oh?"

He slumped back in his chair. "Yeah, well, it would be interesting to know a bit more about her past, don't you think?"

"Like what?" John said.

"Why should I tell you? So you can steal my idea?"

"Oh, fuck," I said.

They both laughed.

"Just joking," Harvey said. He folded his hands over his stomach. "I just want to find out something more about her employment history. And other things besides her bedroom habits."

"Yeah?"

Harvey ran a hand through his dark hair. "Look," he said. "The woman pulled a giant scam on Jack, with the bullshit rape charge and all." He let his hand drop to his lap. "Be interesting to know if she was ever involved in any other kind of similar deal, that's all."

We were silent for a moment. Then I said, "Insurance fraud? Perjury? Something like that?"

"Whatever," Harvey replied. "We'll see."

"It couldn't not help Jack's case," I said. "Especially if it could be demonstrated that Yolanda had a record of, or at least a prior incidence of . . . what shall I call it?"

"Bearing false witness?" John suggested. "To put it Biblically?"

"That'll do," I said. "Very nicely."

Jack and I sat across from each other in green vinyl armchairs, in a big open space to the right of the three aquaria. I kept bending forward to touch him, patting a knee or putting my hand over his, as if I had to assure myself he was there in the flesh.

"You look good," I said. "How are you?"

He smiled. "Fine. Still bored. I enjoyed the books you brought, though."

"What a pity I didn't really slip you a nude photo."

"I'm glad you didn't. It would have made me crazy."

"Well, I can understand that."

We both laughed, although in a hushed and guarded sort of way.

I glanced around quickly, double-checking that no one was within earshot, and murmured, "Has your lawyer been in?"

"Oh, yeah. Almost as much as you have."

"And what's he doing?"

"Running around trying to get me bail."

"Is he making headway?"

Jack shrugged.

"I have something to tell you," I said.

His face grew wary. I pressed my hand harder on his knee.

"It's not bad news," I said hastily. "Far from it, in fact."

I told him about the magazine receipt. When I finished, he leaned over and kissed me on the mouth, hard. Then he pulled back and said, "Jesus Christ, Liz, you are wonderful. I love you."

"Well, the first pretty much presupposes the second, doesn't it?"

He shook his head slowly. "Fantastic," he said. "In-fucking-credible."

"Aw, shucks," I said.

"Goddamn evidence right there in my own living room," Jack said. "And I never even thought of it. Some detective, huh?"

"Oh, sweetie. Come on. I only discovered it by accident. Who the hell would think of getting a receipt from a newsstand? It's like remembering to get a sales slip from a gum machine."

"Honey, you really don't have to be so careful of my ego."

I stroked his hand. "I know I don't. Anyway, I told Sam about the receipt."

"Good. And I'll tell my lawyer."

I hadn't mentioned to Jack that Flaherty was working in whatever way he could to get Jack out of this trouble—because I knew I didn't need to. Jack would have done the same for Sam, without question or comment. There were things you could take for granted, and this was one of them.

We smiled at each other. He squeezed my fingers tightly, then loosened his grip just enough for me to withdraw my hand.

"Okay," I said. "Now I have to tell you something a little less swell."

His face got that cool, watchful expression again.

"It's the door in your kitchen. The one that leads down to the cellar."

"What about it?"

I explained.

Jack didn't reply when I finished speaking. He looked away from me and at the aquaria to his right. After a moment, I nudged his foot with mine.

"What's the matter?" I said.

"Christ, this is embarrassing."

"What is?"

"I've got Fort Knox locks on the front and back outside doors," he said sourly. "I always meant to get that thing in the kitchen changed. Plus hook it up to the burglar alarm on the other two doors."

"In a way, it's good you didn't do either," I said, briskly. "Now we know how the son-of-a-bitch who stole the gun got into your place."

"Yeah." His face was twisted with self-disgust. "That'll be a nice thing to have brought up in court, won't it?"

"Oh, Jack. Stop it. Look at all the other cops in town who've had their houses broken into. Or even their cruisers stolen from underneath their noses."

This latter, actually, had happened several times. A lot of patrol officers, when they answered a call, not only left the radio cars unlocked, but the keys in the ignition and the motor running. If the car itself wasn't taken, its contents were.

I could also have reminded him that the chief of police's house had been burglarized at least twice in my memory, but I decided not to. Instead I changed the subject.

"Whoever took your gun," I said, "I bet it was somebody pretending to be a workman."

"Why?"

"Rosa says she sees them every so often around the house."

"You talked to Rosa?"

I nodded. "She told me she's never let anyone into your place."

"Yeah, I believe that." He frowned.

"What is it?"

He was silent for a few seconds. Then he said, "I'm sure it's *possible* that whoever stole my thirty-eight was dressed as a workman."

"Sure."

"Or dressed up as Bozo the Clown."

I snickered. "Of course. In Cambridge, who'd know the difference?"

"No one. But that's not the point."

"Huh?"

"Something I keep thinking is . . . the person who used my gun to shoot Yolanda was someone who wanted to get her dead as much as to get me in trouble."

"You mean, like a two-for-the-price-of-one deal?"

"Uh-huh." Jack sucked in his lower lip. "Be interesting to know what the order of priority was, wouldn't it?"

I stared at him. "Yes, it would."

Leaving Jack behind in the jail hurt no less the third time than it had the first two. I could feel my eyes stinging as I went through the entrance/exit trap. The lobby was crowded with those still waiting to be admitted for their contact visits. I made my way through the throng as quickly as possible.

In the elevator, I blew my nose and blinked hard several times, to clear the moisture from my eyes.

Now I had to pay a call on the ineffably charming Mrs. George Watson.

I got off the elevator on the ground floor of the courthouse, and went to the public phone there. I wanted to check the messages on my answering machine. I dialed my own number, listened to my recording, then went into the little numerical recitation that would activate the message replay. Ah, the joys of beeperless remote and automatic retrieval. I heard a click, and then John Ouellette's voice.

"Hi. Just wanted to let you know that I talked to the people in Jack's house. None of them was home the day Rosa saw the gas company guy, or whoever."

"Shit," I mumbled.

"But," John's voice continued, "I talked to some people in the houses around his. One guy *thinks* he saw a workman in the back of Jack's place Friday afternoon. No particular description. Whoever it was came and went pretty quickly. Guy who saw him didn't think much of it. Says a couple of people on the street are having their houses renovated, and there're always construction crews and like that around the neighborhood. I don't know what this means. Probably nothing. Anyway, talk to you later. 'Bye."

I heard a beep, indicating that there were no other messages, and then the sound of the tape rewinding. I hung up the phone.

I left the courthouse and walked the two blocks down Third Street to Hurley.

Mrs. Watson remembered my face, but not my name.

"Liz Connors," I said, smiling mightily. "From *Boston Magazine*. I was here the other day with the two guys from the *Globe* and the *Herald*. If you could be so kind as to answer just one or two more questions?"

I could tell, by her expression, that she'd have liked me better if I'd been Harvey Searle or John Ouellette. But maybe she figured a girl reporter was better to talk trash to than no reporter at all. In any case, she let me into the house, and into a small, dim, overfurnished chamber that she called the "parlor." I sat down in a Naugahyde armchair of considerable slipperiness and opened my notebook. Mrs. Watson settled on the edge of a flowered loveseat and smoothed her dress.

I smiled at her. God, she made me uncomfortable. I had a sense of something sly and nasty peeping out at me from behind the grim blank mask of her features.

Prurient. That was the word I wanted.

"Mrs. Watson, you were quite sure what time it was that Friday night when you saw the, uh, man going into Mrs. Sims's house."

"You mean the cop?"

I could feel my jaw muscles stiffen. "Well, whoever it was."

"It was that cop, all right."

I bent my head and pretended to check my notebook so that she wouldn't see my face.

"Okay," I said. "The cop. The point is, Mrs. Watson, how could you be so sure of the time you saw him? Eight twenty-five, I think you said?"

"That's what I said."

"Well, is there any possibility it could have been a bit earlier? Or even later?"

She shook her head, very decidedly.

"How can you be certain?"

"I was timing my pies. The pies I was making for my sodality meeting."

"I see."

"I had to keep an eye on the clock."

The one that wasn't fixed on Yolanda Sims's doorstep, I assumed.

But I wasn't displeased by her certitude. I now had no doubt she'd seen a man going into Yolanda's house exactly when she claimed she had. She simply hadn't seen Jack.

I squeezed out another smile, this one more sincere than its predecessor. "Well, thanks for being so helpful, Mrs. Watson. I won't keep you any longer."

She nodded.

I was eager to get out of this house, and rose too quickly from the armchair. As I did so, my notebook slid from my lap and tumbled to the floor. A few loose pages fanned across the carpet, along with the set of photographs John Ouellette had given me.

I sighed, and knelt to retrieve them. Mrs. Watson peered closely at the disarray.

I shoved the papers back into the notebook and began gathering up the photographs. She leaned forward and snatched one of them from my hand. I sat back on my haunches and stared at her.

"I seen this guy before," she said.

"You have?"

"Sure." She took a final look at the picture and smirked. "Seen him at Yolanda's. One of her boyfriends."

The final word was pronounced with great scorn.

She handed the photograph back to me. It was a picture of Dalton Craig.

23

By six o'clock Sunday evening I had Harvey and John assembled in my living room. Sam Flaherty was on his way over. The two reporters were discussing what I'd told them, and making vast inroads into the spread of nuts and cheese and crackers that I'd set out for them, good little hostess that I was. Too keyed-up to snack myself, I paced around the room, martini in hand, trying to calm my brain and body. Lucy, keenly sensitive to my emotions, followed me, wagging her tail and panting gently. Perhaps she also had some dim canine awareness of what was at stake here.

The doorbell rang and I jumped slightly. Lucy let out a loud bark and ran to the door.

"That must be Sam," I said, setting my glass on top of the television. I followed Lucy, punched the intercom button, and said into the speaker, "Sam?"

"Yup."

A moment later Sam appeared at the head of the stairs. Behind him was Joanne DeMarco, the narcotics detective I'd seen the last time I was in the police station. I gave Sam a questioning stare. He shot me a half-smile; his face looked worn, and the circles under his eyes seemed larger, darker.

I let them both into the apartment. Lucy went sniffing along after them. Joanne bent to give her a scratch behind the ears and Lucy licked her hand.

"Please sit down," I said. "Get you a drink?"

I looked first at Joanne. She straightened up and began unzipping her jacket. "Oh, don't go to any trouble."

"No trouble."

She smoothed her shoulder-length black hair, ruffled from the wind. Her nails, I noticed, were long and scarlet. "All right, then . . . a glass of wine, if you have any," she said.

"Sam?" I looked over at him. He was draping his coat over the back of the rocking chair.

"Beer?" he asked hopefully.

"Plenty of that. Harvey brought two six-packs."

The cheese and crackers were almost gone. I picked up the plate and went to the kitchen, Lucy in tow. Joanne followed me, hands in the pockets of her jacket, and stood in the kitchen door as I opened the refrigerator.

"You're surprised to see me," she remarked.

I looked at her over my shoulder. "A bit."

Her large brown eyes were wary. "Why?"

I shut the refrigerator door a little more firmly than was necessary. "To be blunt," I said, uncorking the wine, "I'm not sure who I trust in the Cambridge Police Department any longer. With the exception of Sam."

Her face flushed slightly beneath its normal olive tone and tightened as if I'd slapped her. "Liz—"

"Well, why the hell should I? Who among you has leapt to Jack's defense? Except"—I nodded in the direction of the living room—"for Flaherty?"

"Well, shit, why do you think I'm here tonight?" She took a step into the kitchen.

"I don't know," I said, getting a wineglass from the cabinet over the sink. "Tell me."

She sighed, walked over to the table, yanked out a chair, and plunked down into it. I handed her her wine.

" 'Scuse me a second," I said. "I have to take Sam his beer."

When I came back to the kitchen, Joanne was holding her glass by

the stem, turning it slowly around on the tabletop. She looked up at
me as I walked into the room.

"I know how it must seem to you," she said.

"Do you?"

"Yeah." She sipped her wine. "Liz, most of—all of the guys are
behind Jack on this."

"Uh-huh." I opened a box of crackers. "The cards and letters of
support have really been flowing in."

She was quiet.

I turned to face her, resting my hips against the counter. "Joanne,"
I said. "I'm sure you're right. They *are* with him, in their way. By
which I mean, when he's released, or acquitted, or the charges
are dropped, or whatever, they'll welcome him back to the department with open arms. And slap him on the back and tell him how
they were on his side all along." I drew a deep, ragged breath. "But
until that time, they're not going to commit themselves, are they? For
fear of—what? The contagion? The contamination?" I turned back to
the counter to unwrap the cheese. The silence in the kitchen was
thick.

"Okay, you're right about that," Joanne said, a kind of weary anger
in her voice. "But don't put me in the same category with them,
huh? I'm here. They're not."

My back to her, I stood motionless for a moment. Then I said,
"Yes, you are. And you were going to tell me why."

"If you'll give me a chance." She pushed back her chair, rose, and
crossed the room. She leaned against the refrigerator door and stared
at me.

"I'm thirty-three years old," she said. "I got out of the police
academy two years ago. I was on patrol for six months. Then they put
me in plainclothes and transferred me to narcotics. Which I thought
was great at the time, you know?" She clenched her right hand and
thumped the fist into her left palm. "I was gonna get out there and
do stakeouts and bust all the dope dealers and . . . like, clean up the
town, right?"

I figured it was a rhetorical question.

"So, okay, there I was, all gung-ho," she continued. "I went bouncing into the vice-narcotic squad room, all ready to go out and make the big pinch, huh? And you know what those assholes did, my first day?" She leaned toward me, as if to emphasize her words. "They left me a package wrapped in nice paper with a bow on it." Her mouth twisted. "I figured it was some kind of little joke present, right? To welcome me to the team? So I opened it. It was a joke, all right. You know what was in that fucking box?"

I shook my head.

"A douche bag with a hypodermic stuck through it."

I winced.

"That's how they felt about having a broad on their team." She went to the table and picked up her wine.

"Shit," I said. "I'm sorry, Joanne."

She nodded.

"You've done some wonderful work while you've been in narcotics, though," I said. "Jack told me about that bust you made in Inman Square last summer. He was very impressed."

Joanne glanced at me. "He was the only one who ever said anything to me about it." She shook her head quickly. "Not that I expect the whole department to tell me how terrific I am every day I walk in the place. I mean, I do what they pay me for."

"Still, it's nice to get credit for making a good arrest, once in a while."

"Yeah." She drank some wine, and pressed the rim of the glass against her lower lip. Her face grew thoughtful. "Anyway, I came to work the next morning after that bust in Inman Square. And, first thing, Jack came down to the narcotics office. And in front of all the guys, he put his arms around me and gave me a kiss on the cheek, and congratulated me." Joanne raised her head and gave me a straight, steady look. "That's why I'm here tonight."

My throat felt hard. I closed my eyes and nodded. "Okay," I said. "Okay."

Joanne lifted her glass to me and produced a one-sided smile. "Maybe we should get back to the living room and see what the boys are up to, huh?"

"I guess we better." I picked up the plate of cheese and crackers and followed her out of the kitchen.

24

FOR SAM AND JOANNE'S benefit, I gave a detailed account of my experience that afternoon with Mrs. Watson. And, surprisingly, I did so without having to backtrack or correct myself once. When I'm agitated, I usually yammer, but my conversation with Joanne had calmed me. Made me articulate. Lucy lay at my feet, muzzle on forepaws, eyes half-closed.

"I think we all know what the next step is," I said. "I vote we do it tonight."

John reached for a handful of peanuts and started popping them serially into his mouth. "Not meaning to be a wet blanket," he began, "but . . ."

"Yes?"

"Liz." He paused a moment, grimacing. "There is one little problem."

"What's that?"

"If Mrs. Watson could misidentify Jack as the guy who went into Yolanda's house that Friday night, how can we be sure she hasn't confused Craig with someone else too?"

That thought had occurred to me earlier. I'd had sufficient time to deal with it so that I wouldn't grow testy at anyone else's mentioning it.

"I know, John," I said. "That's certainly possible. But we still have to check it out."

"Oh, I agree." He popped more peanuts.

I looked at Harvey. "I'm up for anything," he said.

I looked at Joanne. She nodded.

I looked at Sam.

"Let's take my car," he said. "It's the only one big enough for all of us to fit into."

Joanne and John and Harvey scrunched into the backseat of Sam's old LTD. I joined Sam in the front.

"I got an address from the phone book this afternoon," I said. "Nineteen Cotuit Street."

"I know it," Sam said.

I glanced at him out of the corners of my eyes. "Of course you do."

"We all do," Harvey said.

The traffic on Sunday evening at six-thirty was light, and we made good time getting out of Cambridge and onto the turnpike and from there to Route Nine.

We talked only briefly during the ride, just enough to arrange and agree on what we were all going to do. There was no argument, and very little debate.

I felt as if every corpuscle in my system were rushing toward its own individual battle station.

Sam pulled the car to a quiet stop in front of Nineteen Cotuit Street. I peered at the house. A well-kept ranch, just as it had appeared to be on the six o'clock news. There were lights on over the garage and over the door. Several front windows were less brightly illumined from within.

Harvey got out of the car and went up the path to the door. After a moment, during which he presumably rang a bell, it was opened by a woman. She and Harvey spoke briefly. Then the door shut and Harvey came back down the path to the car.

"Out," he said, climbing into the backseat next to Joanne. "Wife thinks he'll be back around eight. Guess we go to Plan B."

Sam started the car.

"Aren't we going to wait for him?" I asked nervously.

"Sure," Sam said. "First we're going to pretend to leave, though."

"Oh. Gotcha."

We drove around the block. Sam parked the car again on Cotuit Street, this time about a hundred yards up from the ranch, in the shadow of an enormous white oak. The house on that lot and the one across from it were dark.

"Jeez, I hope no cops come along," Joanne said.

I laughed, a little hysterically.

"Wake me when it's time to move," John said.

"You got a deck of cards in the glove compartment?" Harvey asked.

"Sorry," Sam replied.

I leaned back against the seat and folded my arms across my chest, holding in the tension.

At a quarter to eight, by the dashboard clock, Sam raised his right hand. The five of us got out of the car, shutting the doors behind us as quietly as possible, and walked in silent Indian file down Cotuit Street. Harvey went up the path of the ranch house to the front steps. John, Joanne, Sam, and I split up, Sam and I heading to the left of the house and Joanne and John to the right.

About five minutes later, a black Trans Am turned into the driveway. The garage door, controlled apparently by a remote device, slid upward to admit the car to the bay.

As we'd figured he would, the driver of the Trans Am had noticed Harvey standing on his doorstep. He emerged from the garage, pulling the door down behind him, and walked toward the entrance to the house.

"You looking for someone?" he said.

"You're Dalton Craig and I'd like to talk to you for a moment," Harvey replied. "I'm Harvey Searle, from the *Boston Herald*. Maybe you remember me. I interviewed you for my paper a few weeks ago."

Craig stood still, peering at him. "What you want?"

John stepped out from behind a rhododendron. "John Ouellette," he announced. "*Boston Globe*. I'd like to talk to you, too."

Craig jerked his head around to stare at John.

Joanne walked around the corner of the house to the front steps.

"Joanne DeMarco," she said. "Cambridge Police Department. And *I* want to talk to you."

Craig took a step backward. "What the fuck is this?"

I emerged from the shadows and paced toward Craig. I stopped fifteen feet away from him. "Elizabeth Connors," I said. "From no place special. But I have a very good friend named John Lingemann, and I'd really *love* to talk to you about him."

"Even more than I would." Sam moved into the apron of light cast by the fixture over the garage door.

Craig spun in a half-circle at the sound of the voice behind him.

Sam stood with his hands on his hips, grinning.

"No need for me to introduce myself, is there, asshole?" he said.

25

CRAIG TRIED to run. As he pounded down the sloping lawn I sprang at him, my right shoulder lowered. I didn't slam into him head-on, as I'd intended, but caught his side with my shoulder. Not enough to crack his ribs, but enough to knock him off balance. I swung my leg up and kicked him in the groin. He let out a muted, choky scream and fell back onto the grass, clutching at himself.

There was a kind of fuming red haze inside my head.

I dropped to my knees beside Craig and raised my fist. I was about to pound it into his face when somebody grabbed my wrist.

"For Christ's sake, Liz, don't kill him." Harvey clamped my shoulder with his other hand. "Jesus!"

Craig continued to writhe, moaning and gasping.

"I know he's a piece of shit," Harvey said. "But we need him."

I got up slowly; looking down at Craig, I stifled the impulse to spit in his face.

"Sure," I said. "Okay."

The door to the ranch house opened. A woman's voice, high and nervous, trembled into the darkness. "Dalton? Is that you?"

Joanne and John moved quickly to block her view.

"Oh, swell," Sam muttered. He put a foot on Craig's left ankle. "Open your mouth, asshole, and you spend the rest of your life limping."

"Who's there?" the woman called, her voice ragged with alarm. "Who are you?"

Craig was breathing heavily. Apart from that, he was silent.

"I'm calling the police," the woman said. She slammed the door.

"Just what we need," Sam said. He gestured sharply at Harvey and John. "Help me get him up. Quick."

The three of them reached down and hauled Craig, not tenderly, to his feet. They half dragged, half walked him toward Sam's car. Joanne and I followed.

"Holy Christ, Liz," Joanne whispered to me. "I never knew you were such a savage."

I looked at her. "Is that a compliment or a criticism?"

"Coming from me?" She grinned. "Guess."

Harvey and John loaded Craig into the back of the LTD. Joanne and I got in the front with Sam. He made a U-turn, drove down to the end of Cotuit, then onto another quiet street. As we left it and hit the main road, a Framingham police cruiser passed us, going in the opposite direction.

I looked over at Craig, huddled between Harvey and John; his chin was pressed against his collarbone.

"Jesus Christ," Joanne said, "this is kidnapping."

"Yeah," Sam replied. "Know any good defense lawyers?"

She laughed shortly.

"What now?" I said.

"We'll ride Dalton around till he recovers the power of speech," Sam said, "then we'll find a place to chat."

We went to a sort of roadhouse on Route Nine. Judging from the exterior, it wasn't the place where the Framingham elite would dine. On the other hand, it didn't look like the cops were in there breaking up knife fights every fifteen minutes. Which made it perfect for our purposes.

The interior was almost as dark as Plato's cave, lit only by one small lamp over the bar and the lurid neon tubing of the jukebox. Tammy Wynette was singing about standing by your man. Several

people were mooching around by the bar, and others, in groups of twos and threes, sat at tables near the door.

We took a booth at the back, which offered privacy.

As we seated ourselves, I glanced at Craig. He was pale and sick-looking, but moving of his own volition.

A painfully thin waitress with a yellowing bruise on her left cheek-bone and hair moussed into the stratosphere approached us.

Flaherty nudged Craig with his elbow. "What'll it be, buddy boy?" he said. "My treat."

"Scotch," Craig mumbled.

"Double Scotch for my pal here," Sam said. "Gimme whatever you got on draft."

"Glass of red wine," Joanne said.

"Vodka," I said. "Rocks."

Harvey and John ordered beers.

Craig put his elbows on the table and his head in his hands.

"Do you think we can get him to talk?" I whispered to Harvey.

"No problem," he murmured back to me. "We'll just threaten to turn you loose on him again."

The waitress brought the drinks. The sight of Dalton half lying on the table didn't seem to disturb her. She looked as if she'd seen it all before anyway. Going by the mark on her face, she'd had some of it done to her.

Craig grabbed his drink and slurped at it. He set the glass back down on the table, coughed, and gasped.

"Down the wrong tube?" Sam asked solicitously.

John rested his chin on his palm and looked at Craig. "Whenever you're ready, we have some questions for you."

Craig swiped at his mouth with the back of his hand. "I got nothing to say to any of you."

"Sure you do," John said, his voice mild, almost friendly. "It's very simple: You answer the questions, or we take you out in the parking lot and maim you."

I widened my eyes at him. This was a side of John I hadn't seen before.

"Fuck you," Craig said.

Sam grabbed Craig's right arm, raised it, and slammed it down at such an angle that Craig's elbow hit the sharp edge of the tabletop. Craig's face turned a shade paler.

"I'll be happy to keep on doing that all night," Sam said. And he did it again, just to emphasize the point.

Craig's eyes were squeezed shut.

I glanced around the bar, a bit nervously. I'd be perfectly happy to sit and watch Sam disassemble Craig piece by slow piece. But I didn't want him to attract any attention while he did it.

Nobody was looking at us.

Craig blinked, and then opened his eyes fully. They glittered with tears of intense pain.

Sam let Craig's arm drop. With his working hand, Craig picked up his glass and drank about half the contents.

"Dalton," Harvey said. "You're outnumbered pretty heavily. And you're not going to go anywhere until we let you. We know you knew Yolanda Sims. Why don't you just tell us about it?"

"We have a witness who saw you going into Yolanda's house on several occasions," Joanne added.

"Big fuckin' deal," Craig said.

I put my hands on my thighs and leaned across the table. "The deal is this, shithead," I said. "A month ago, you went to the press with some bullshit story about how Sam"—I nodded at Flaherty—"and your former brother-in-law, John Lingemann, belonged to some secret police spy unit. And how the three of you conspired to frame Albert Parkes for murder. How does that connect up with you being tight with Yolanda Sims?" I grinned. "Because it does, doesn't it?"

Craig finished his drink. He put his head back and looked at the ceiling.

"Answers, Dalton," Flaherty said. "We want answers."

"Fuck you," Craig replied. He certainly had an extensive repertoire of original insults.

Flaherty sighed. He grabbed Craig's arm and smashed his elbow

again. Craig's face stiffened, but he remained silent. For a slimy weasel, Craig had guts.

The bartender appeared beside the booth, wiping his hands on a white cloth. He was a tall, beefy man with a paunch and slow, suspicious eyes.

"Everything okay here?" he said.

Sam smiled at him. "Dandy. My buddy here'll have another Scotch, though."

The bartender looked at us all very carefully. I sipped my vodka. Joanne toyed with her wineglass. Craig stayed mute.

The bartender left us.

"He'll remember our faces," I muttered to Harvey.

Harvey shrugged. "At this point, does it matter?"

I shook my head.

The skinny waitress delivered a second Scotch to Craig and retreated without asking the rest of us if we wanted our drinks renewed.

I glanced over my shoulder. The bartender was at his post, swiping his rag up and down the wooden counter before him. Every moment or so, he'd glance in our direction. It would be wise if we got this business over with as quickly as possible.

I took a gulp of my drink. "Dalton," I said. "You're out to get Jack. That much is clear. You wanna tell us why?"

Craig gave me a heavy-lidded stare that lasted for perhaps half a minute. I returned it as steadily as I could. His eyes were hard, but deep within them something burned and shimmered, like a candle flame seen from a distance.

"Sure," he said. "I can tell you that."

I waited. It was just him and me now.

"He killed my sister," Craig said.

I inhaled sharply. John and Harvey stared at me, their faces question marks. Joanne put her hand to her forehead. Sam was motionless, silent.

The corners of Craig's mouth lifted a bit. "You're his latest cunt, aren't you?"

John leaned across the table and drove the side of his hand into

Craig's throat, just above the Adam's apple. "Shut your filthy garbage mouth," he said softly.

Craig sagged against the back of the booth, retching.

"Oh, Christ, he's gonna puke," Harvey muttered. He pushed
against me and I slid out of the booth. Joanne, sitting opposite us on
Craig's left, did the same.

"Lemme get him to the men's room," Harvey said.

"Want help?" John asked.

"No." Harvey shook his head. "We're attracting too much attention as it is." He leaned down and hauled Craig, limp and unresist-
ing, from the booth.

"Upsy-daisy, scumbag," he said, bracing Craig against him.

I glanced back at the bar, making eye contact with the bartender.

"I'll pay the check," Sam said. "Then let's get the hell out of
here."

"Good idea," Joanne said.

Flaherty reached the bar just as the bartender was emerging from
behind it.

I finished my drink.

"Liz?" John said.

"Yes?"

"What was that stuff Craig said about . . . ?"

"Oh, God." I put down my glass. "You mean about Jack killing
his sister?"

"Yeah."

I told him. *Sorry, Jack. I had to.*

"I see," was all he replied, when I'd finished. He looked thoughtful.

Sam settled the bill. Then he went into the men's room.

"I hope you and Sam don't get into any trouble over this," I
murmured to Joanne.

She shrugged. "If we do, we do." Then she grinned. "Tell you
one thing, though. If we do, it'll have been worth it."

Sam and Harvey came out of the men's room. Craig wasn't with
them. I craned my neck. He wasn't behind them either.

I stared. "What—"

Sam made a violent hushing gesture at me with his left hand. "Come on," he said. "Let's go."

Harvey's face was pale and a little damp.

We followed them out to the parking lot.

"What happened?" I hissed. "Where's Craig?"

Harvey leaned against the front fender of the LTD, arms crossed over his stomach, breathing heavily.

"Harvey?" I said. "What's wrong?"

"Son-of-a-bitch kicked me in the gut," he mumbled.

"Jesus," Joanne said.

"So where the hell's he gone?" John asked.

"Out," Sam said, sourly. "Through the window in the crapper."

"Oh, God."

Harvey closed his eyes and rubbed his stomach. I moved up next to him and patted his back. It probably didn't help, but I couldn't think what else to do.

"The bastard conned us," Harvey said. "Conned me, anyway. Soon's we get into the men's room. I shut the door, and next thing I know I'm on the floor with my head under a urinal."

John snorted.

"Go ahead and laugh," Harvey said.

"Then what happened?" I asked, scowling at John.

"Like Sam said, he went out the goddamn window."

"Should we look for him?"

"What's the point?" Flaherty said. "He's long gone."

I nodded.

"Harvey?" Joanne looked worried. "You gonna be okay?"

"Yeah, yeah, I'm fine." He rubbed his stomach gingerly.

"Well, now what? Have we had enough for one night?"

"No, John," I said. "We haven't. If you'll all come back with me, I'll tell you why."

"Can't you tell us now?"

I shook my head. "I need to think a little more."

26

WE WERE AS QUIET on the ride home as on the ride down, but for different reasons. Harvey was slumped beside me in the rear seat, nursing his gut. John just gazed out of the window at the darkened turnpike and drummed his fingers on his knees. Joanne drove. Sam seemed to be asleep—at least, his head lolled back against the front seat and his eyes were closed. He probably needed what rest he could get.

I sat with my hands pressed tightly together in my lap, holding in the excitement that was mounting as I organized my thoughts. What I'd figured out was stuck together pretty precariously with speculation and supposition, but I thought it would bear up under scrutiny.

When we reached Cambridge, the color had returned to Harvey's face. Joanne parked the car in front of my house, and leaned across the seat to give Sam's shoulder a gentle shake. He awoke with a slight start.

"Come on," I said. "I'll make us something to eat."

There was some sliced Genoa salami, boiled ham, and Swiss cheese in the fridge, and an untouched loaf of light rye in the breadbox. I waited till everyone had settled down with food and drink before I began.

"Dalton Craig stole Jack's gun."

Four heads lifted simultaneously.

"Oh?" John said. "How do you figure that?"

Sam smiled. He knew.

I stood up and started pacing. "That thirty-eight was kept unloaded, handcuffed securely to a pipe beneath Jack's kitchen sink."

"Standard procedure for a cop," Sam said. "Especially if he has kids."

"Or if he doesn't want some burglar to nab his gun."

"Uh-huh."

"But," I said, "if the burglar happened to be an ex-cop, he'd know exactly how to deal with such a situation, right?"

Joanne nodded.

"So?" Harvey asked.

"Look," I said, "it isn't just that Craig's an ex-cop familiar with cop gun-concealment tricks. He's also Jack's brother-in-law. The apartment Jack has now is the same one in which he and Diana lived while they were married. Don't you think Craig visited them there? And knew the layout. And know exactly where Jack would stash his extra gun."

"Christ," John said. "You're right."

"So how'd he get the gun off the pipe without unlocking the cuffs?" Harvey asked.

I shrugged. "Hacksaw." I glanced at Sam, my eyebrows raised. "Could be."

"Then," I continued, "when Craig brought the gun back to Jack's apartment, he simply locked it back in its place with another pair of cuffs. Sam?"

"It listens."

"Okay. Now Craig, because he knew Jack, would find it easy to map out Jack's habits—when he was likely to be home, and so on. And as an ex-cop, he'd know how to do stakeouts and such unobtrusively." I smiled. "He might even have masqueraded as a workman and let himself into Jack's place. Why shouldn't a workman carry a hacksaw?"

Joanne sipped her wine. "You know, I once dressed up as a plumber's assistant to make a drug bust."

"Exactly."

We were all silent for a moment. Lucy edged up to the platter of cold cuts on the table. I nudged her away with my foot.

"You think Craig shot Sims?" Harvey asked.

"No," I said. "The Jack clone did that with the gun Craig stole and gave him. That was the whole point—to have the murder committed by someone the watchful Mrs. Watson would take for Jack." I paused, remembering the conversation I'd had with Jack in jail this afternoon. "Of course, they probably had good reason to get rid of Yolanda as well."

"Yeah?" Harvey said. He was leaning forward slightly, listening intently, the injury to his stomach apparently forgotten. "What reason?"

I bit my lip. "Her instability? Unreliability? They probably bribed her to accuse Jack of raping her. Which, as we know, she did. But then she may have decided not to press the charges unless they offered her still more money. Look, we know Yolanda needed money. Her ex-husband had defaulted on his alimony and child-support payments, so she probably saw this as a golden opportunity to lay her hands on some major bucks, along with those she'd get when she sued the city. Plus it'd be a way to avenge herself against Jack for putting her punk kid in the slammer."

"But she ended up screwing herself," John remarked.

"Sure," I said. "She gave *them* a good reason to get rid of her, and, in so doing, the chance to get Jack in even bigger trouble than he was already. Kill Sims and make it look as if he did it to shut her up."

Harvey was looking very hard at me. "Who's *them?*"

I took a deep breath. "I don't know who all of *them* are, or how many of *them* there are. But one of *them* is certainly Albert Parkes. It was he who started this whole thing, not Dalton Craig. I bet Parkes went to Craig and hired him to go on TV with that story about the spy unit. You gave me that idea, John, about a million years ago."

"Wait a minute," Joanne said. "How would Parkes have known to go to Craig for something like that?"

"Craig was one of the cops who investigated him for the Larrain murder."

"And Parkes would just assume that Craig could be bought?"

"He would have known he was a scumbag," Sam said. "Every-

body else did. Hell, you don't know, maybe way back when, when Parkes was first arrested, Craig offered to try to fix the case for him. He knew Parkes had the money for a decent payoff."

"Sure did a hell of a fixing job," Joanne said. "Parkes went to prison. But, yeah, even if the deal fell through, it could have planted a seed in Parkes's brain."

"All right," Harvey said. "Where does Yolanda come into the picture?"

I looked at him. "I thought she was just jumping on the band-wagon with her rape story." I shook my head. "Stupid. I should have put it together before this, that there was probably a connection between Parkes and Craig and Sims, as well as Parkes and Craig."

"Well," Sam said. "You didn't have no reason to, doll, until the Watson broad saw Dalton's picture and fingered him for you." He grimaced. "Me, neither. Speaking of Sims, I got a little bad news on that front."

I sat down heavily on the floor. "Tell me."

"Ah, it's stupid. It's just that Yolanda's kid Joey says the last time his mom visited him in Walpole, she was telling him how she received these threatening phone calls from Jack."

"Oh, Christ," I said. I leaned forward and pressed my forehead against my right knee, then looked up at Sam. "When did he come out with that tidbit?"

Sam grinned his horse-toothed grin. "Day before yesterday."

"I'm surprised it took him that long," Harvey remarked.

"Yeah," Sam said. "Well, Joey's not the swiftest of the swift."

"Uh-huh," John said. "Does Joey have a specific date and time for when Yolanda told him this?"

"Not that I heard," Sam replied.

"I'm sure he'll think of one," Joanne said. She filled her glass and drank the last few drops of her wine.

"No kidding," I said. "But surely no one with half a brain would believe a bag of dirt like Joey, would they?"

Flaherty shrugged. "You can never tell what a jury will take se-riously."

"What was the content of these *alleged* threats?" I asked.

"You can guess," Flaherty replied. "A lot of horseshit about how Jack told Yolanda he'd take care of her or get her, if she didn't drop the rape charge against him."

"Uh-huh," I said. "And there's probably somebody out there moronic enough to think Jack would do something like that."

"Well," John said, "it *does* gibe with the first story Yolanda told about Jack threatening to get Joey in trouble if she didn't sleep with him. Fits the pattern, you know."

I looked at him. "Yeah. I know."

Joanne went to the kitchen for more wine. I had no appetite, but I made myself half a ham and Swiss on rye anyway. The bread stuck to the roof of my mouth. I took a sip of vodka to wash it down.

"Harvey?"

He glanced up from his plate. "Hmm?"

"Have you done your backtracking on Yolanda yet?"

He shook his head. "Haven't had time."

"Well, when you do, I bet you'll find out she worked for Parkes."

Harvey gave me a questioning look; so did John. Sam was smiling again.

"If, as we're assuming, she was hooked up with Parkes and Craig in some kind of conspiracy to frame Jack, then one of them had to have known her, right?"

"I'm with you," Harvey said. "But why do you think it was Parkes and not Craig?"

"It's just a feeling. But also, how would Craig have known about Jack arresting Joey? He left the police department and Cambridge long before that happened." I sipped my vodka. "But if Yolanda had worked for Parkes at some point, as a secretary or a receptionist or something, he'd probably have heard that her kid was in trouble. Stuff like that gets around. Even to the boss." I put my glass down. "Parkes could have gotten in touch with Yolanda with a nice little proposition—something like, 'Hey, honey, I know how you can fuck over the cop who busted your kid *and* get your hands on some big money.'"

"Refresh me," John said. "When *did* Jack bust Joey?"

"Three years ago."

"All right. I'll look into it," Harvey said. "Tomorrow morning, first thing."

"Actually," I said, "it doesn't really matter whether it was Parkes or Craig who hit on Yolanda. Not in the grand scheme of things."

"Still," John said, "it would be good to know."

John picked up a slice of salami, rolled it into a cylinder, and chewed it down like a strand of spaghetti. Then he said, "You know, I'm famous for asking obnoxious questions."

"Your job," I said.

He smiled. "I have another one."

"Go ahead."

"Anybody ever figure out *why* Parkes is after Jack?"

"I think he wants to sue and make a pile of money quickly, dear," I said. "At least, that's my interpretation."

"Yeah, sure, I know about the money."

"I'm afraid I don't get your point."

John wiped his hands on a paper napkin. "Parkes wasn't acquitted of the charge of conspiring to kill Stephen Larrain, was he?"

"No."

"But the charge against him could be refiled at any point, John," Sam added.

"Right." John nodded. "So why the fuck does Parkes want to stir up the hornet's nest? Sure, he might make some money on the deal, but hell, he'd just be opening himself up for trouble. Maybe the cops and the DA's office would reopen the investigation into his role in the Larrain murder? And maybe this time they'd find something really heavy." John reached for the platter of cold cuts again. "Would that be worth it to Parkes? Why doesn't he just leave well enough alone? He certainly doesn't need the money. He's already loaded."

Sam, Harvey, and I were silent. John, paying great attention to what he was doing, prepared himself a salami and cheese on rye.

Joanne came back into the room carrying a full glass of wine.

"Did I miss something?" she asked.

27

I SPENT the next morning trudging up one side of Hurley Street and down the other, knocking on every door. Anybody who answered got photos of Dalton Craig and Albert Parkes shoved under his or her nose and was asked if either face were familiar. I didn't bother to give them my song and dance about being a magazine writer doing a story on the murder of Yolanda Sims. That, and the explanation it almost always entailed, would have taken too long. And to have to repeat the same thing twenty or thirty times . . .

So I said, civilly enough but very curtly, that I was a detective. Not a Cambridge police detective, mind you. Just a detective. A detective looking for the two men in the pictures. Let those I introduced myself to as such assume what they wished. And no one challenged me.

But no one recognized the faces of Albert Parkes or Dalton Craig, either.

Rosa Dominguez was at her front door. She and Fabian had just returned from getting groceries at the Star Market in Porter Square. I held her shopping bags while she let us all in.

"What can I do for you?" she asked somewhat wearily.

I slipped the photograph of Craig from the folder and held it out to her. She took it, eyebrows raised.

"Is this the workman you saw around Jack's house?" I said. "The Wednesday before he was arrested?"

She stared at me and then at the picture. I saw her eyes narrow.
"Rosa?"

She handed the photo back. "I don't know."

I felt my insides sag. Rosa must have seen the disappointment
on my face. At any rate, she repeated, "I'm sorry, Liz. I just don't
know."

I smiled. "It's all right."

She nodded at the photograph in my hand. "You think he was the
one who stole Jack's gun?"

"Yup."

"Well, I hope they nail him."

"Yeah, me too."

That afternoon, I canvassed Jack's street. John had given me the
name and address of the guy who'd seen a workman hanging around
Jack's building. When I showed him the picture he shook his head.
Like Rosa, he couldn't commit himself either way. I went to two
more houses—at one, the woman who answered the door said she
didn't want to get involved; and at the other, the old man who lived
there was legally blind.

I hit pay dirt at a vine-covered stucco house a few numbers up
from Jack's place. A trim, balding middle-aged man with a goatee
and mustache was mulching a patch of sere earth that in a greener
season must have been a flower bed. He gave me a look of pleasant
inquiry as I approached him. I didn't bother to use my phony detective routine on him. He didn't, somehow, look as if he'd buy it.
I resumed, instead, my true identity as Ms. Intrepid Crime Writer
doing a story on the Cambridge cop accused of rape and murder.
That would elicit a better response here.

This was a *very* liberal section of Cambridge.

"Do you know Lieutenant Lingemann?" I asked.

The goateed man shrugged. "Not really. I know him by
sight, certainly. We've spoken briefly once or twice. He *seemed* like
a pleasant person." There was a lot of emphasis on the word
"seemed."

I nodded neutrally and took out the picture of Dalton Craig. "Have you ever seen him in this neighborhood?"

He accepted the photo and peered at it.

"I'm not asking you to finger anyone," I added reassuringly. "This is purely background."

Ho-ho.

"I assume this person has some relevance to your story about the police officer."

"That's correct."

He nodded and looked again at the picture. "Not a very memorable face, is it?"

"No. He's pretty nondescript."

The goateed man tilted his head. "Actually, though, I believe I *may* have seen him."

"Oh?"

"As far as I can tell, he's part of the construction crew working on the Sullivan house." The man pointed down the street, toward but not at Jack's building. "They're renovating, like everyone else around here."

"So there are a lot of workmen around, then."

The man grimaced. "And they all seem to start work at seven A.M. The noise"—he rolled his eyes. "God."

I didn't have to feign a sympathetic shudder.

The man laughed. "And I don't have to get up to teach until eleven."

"Oh? Where?"

"Tufts. In the philosophy department."

I nodded. "I once taught college English myself."

That small bond of collegiality established, I could question the goateed man further.

"Getting back to the guy in the photograph," I said. "Do you really recall having seen him recently?"

The man frowned, and then shrugged slightly. "Well, in the first place, I can't really swear it's him, of course."

"No, no, I understand."

"But . . ." He shrugged again. "I suppose I've noticed him—if it is indeed him—a few times in the past few weeks."

"I see."

"I can't be any more specific than that."

"I understand." I took back the photo and slipped it into my notebook. "It's not," I added, "a matter of grave importance."

The man nodded. "Well, good luck with your article. Who's publishing it?"

"*Boston Magazine.*"

"I'll look forward to reading it."

I smiled. "Thanks."

"I thought prisoners were supposed to be all pasty and pallid," I said. "But I swear your face looks tan. Got a sunlamp in your cell or something?"

Jack pointed at the ceiling with his thumb. "There's an exercise area on the roof. They let us out for fifteen minutes every day, weather permitting."

"Oh, like recess."

"Yeah, and when it rains we stay in homeroom and finger paint."

I laughed, leaned forward, and kissed him on the mouth. I was getting used to doing that in the presence of twenty or thirty other people. I had to get used to it.

"Well," I said. "It was a sunny day today."

He nodded. "I shot baskets with a couple of other guys."

"Yes? Who?"

He smiled. "A bank robber and a car thief."

"Jesus," I said. "Were either of them anyone you'd ever arrested?"

"Nope."

"Oh, good. Could be awkward otherwise, I suppose."

"Ah, probably not. I'm on pretty good terms with a lot of my bad guys."

"Yes, I know, because you treat them with respect." I pronounced the last two words "wit respeck."

"Uh-huh."

I shook my head. Then I glanced around the room and hitched my chair a few inches closer to Jack's.

"Time to be serious," I said softly.

He looked at me curiously. I crooked my forefinger at him and he leaned forward.

"Dalton Craig stole your gun," I whispered.

Anyone else greeted with news of that tenor would have reacted as if I'd slung a bucket of cold water in his face. Jack, long trained in the habit of professional impassivity, merely stared at me.

I told him what had happened Sunday night, including the part about how Harvey and John had had to drag me off Craig. Jack was silent when I finished. Silent for quite a little while. Then he looked away, to the left at the big windows that offered a panoramic view of Boston.

"Honey?" I said.

"Christ," he said. "Dalton must really hate me."

"He's sick, Jack. He's warped. There's something wrong with his brain."

Jack shook his head slightly. "I always knew he thought I was responsible for Diana's death."

"Oh, honey—"

He gave me a faint smile. "It's okay."

I sucked in both my lips and gazed down at my lap. Neither of us said anything for a few moments.

Jack was the first to speak again.

"I can buy Dalton and Parkes together on this," he said. "I just wish to hell I could figure out what Parkes was getting out of the deal. Besides maybe eventually some money if he decides to sue me."

I looked up sharply. "We were wondering that, too."

Jack ran his right hand back through his hair, a quick exasperated gesture. "It makes no goddamn sense, this whole—"

"Vendetta?" I suggested.

He nodded. "Yeah, good word."

I clasped my hands and pressed them against my chin, leaning my elbows on my knees. "Parkes isn't Iago, Jack. Somewhere there's a

motive for what he's doing. We just haven't found it." I lifted my
head. "Yet."

I was finishing breakfast the next morning when the doorbell rang.
Lucy barked and ran to the door. I rose and followed her.

"Yes?" I said into the intercom.

"It's me. Harvey."

I hit the release button for the downstairs door.

This morning Harvey was wearing a dark red warm-up suit.

"What do you have, a different color for each day of the week?"
I asked. "Do your underpants have 'Tuesday' written on them in
scroll?"

"Got any coffee?"

"Sure."

We went to the kitchen. Harvey sat at the table in Jack's chair. I
got a cup, filled it with coffee, and placed it in front of him. Then
I sat down across from him.

"What's up?" I said.

"I found out who Yolanda Sims worked for when her kid was
arrested."

I raised my eyebrows. "Parkes?"

Harvey shook his head.

"Well, who, then?" I said, a bit impatiently.

Harvey picked up his cup. "Otway Gilmore."

"Holy shit."

Harvey nodded. "That was pretty much my reaction."

"Holy shit," I repeated, more softly.

Harvey blew gently on the coffee to cool it.

"That means—" I began.

"Uh-huh."

I pushed my chair back from the table. "We gotta tell Sam."

"Good idea."

I went to the telephone table in the living room. As I dialed Sam's
number in the C.I.D., I noticed that my hands were shaking.

Sam answered on the third ring.

"Oh, Sam, I'm so glad I caught you," I said, the words tripping over each other on the way out of my mouth.

"Hey, hey, take it easy, doll," he said. "What's up?"

I told him.

"Now ain't that interesting?" he said. "My, my, that *is* interesting. I got some news for you, too."

"What's that?"

"We don't have Dalton Craig to kick around no more."

"Huh?"

"Somebody shot him twice in the back of the head last night."

28

JOANNE DEMARCO, Sam, Harvey, John, and I sat in a table in a Greek luncheonette on Cambridge Street between Third and Sciarappa in east Cambridge. Flaherty was telling us what little he knew about the murder of Dalton Craig. The body had been found in the front seat of Craig's black Trans Am. The car itself had been left in the parking lot of Shoppers World in Framingham. It was not clear whether Craig had driven to the shopping center himself or been driven there. In whatever condition.

The killing had all the earmarks of a gangland slaying.

Somehow, none of us believed it was that. Not exactly.

John, in his characteristic judicious fashion, remarked that it seemed fairly clear that Parkes had killed Craig, or had him killed.

"No shit, Sherlock," Harvey said.

"Boys, boys," Joanne said.

"John's right," I said. "Craig probably told Parkes what happened Sunday night. And Parkes probably figured, 'Well, this clown has become a distinct liability.' So . . ." I raised my right hand, forefinger extended and thumb raised, then lowered the latter as if it were the hammer of a gun.

"How're the Framingham police treating this, Sam—you have any idea?" Harvey asked.

Sam shrugged. "I told you all I know."

"Well," I said. "At least they can't pin this one on Jack."

"Yeah, but they may try to pin it on us," Joanne said.

John and Sam lit cigarettes.

Harvey cleared his throat. "I wonder," he said, "if Mrs. Craig has told the police about what happened on her front lawn Sunday night."

"Wouldn't be a bit surprised," Sam said.

I looked at Harvey, my eyes wide. "Harvey, you *didn't* tell her your name or that you were a reporter from the *Herald*, did you?"

"No. But she can describe me."

"That bartender can describe all of us."

"Uh-huh."

"We should also consider," Joanne said, very carefully, "that maybe Dalton told his wife what went on when he got home Sunday night. Assuming he *went* home."

John nodded. "And told her our names and affiliations. Which she could in turn tell the cops."

"Well," Harvey said. "If the Framingham and state police come looking for us, we'll know she did, won't we?"

"They haven't yet," I said.

"Give them a chance," Sam said.

John's face was impassive. I noticed, though, that as soon as he put out his first cigarette, he lit a second. Same for Sam.

"Doesn't do us an awful lot of good to worry about it, does it?" I asked.

Joanne was tapping her can of diet soda very gently and very rhythmically on the Formica tabletop. "No," she agreed. There were two small creases in the skin between her eyebrows that she was too young to have acquired naturally.

"No matter what happens," Harvey said, "I'm still not sorry about what we did Sunday night."

I smiled at him. "Me, neither." I glanced around the table and saw approbation on the faces of the other three.

God, they were so good.

"Maybe," I said, "we should start thinking along more constructive lines. Such as the Yolanda Sims–Otway Gilmore connection. That Harvey here so brilliantly uncovered."

Harvey rolled his eyes.

"Yeah, how'd you do that, Harv?" John asked.

"Fuck you—you think I'm giving away professional secrets to the competition?"

Joanne sighed.

"Gilmore and Sims," I said. "Sims and Gilmore."

John ground out his cigarette. "Not to leap to conclusions," he said. "But the connection you"—he nodded at me—"speak of does suggest that Gilmore may on some level be involved in this, um, conspiracy against Jack."

"Well put," Harvey said.

Sam leaned back against the vinyl booth cushions. "What's the level?"

I rubbed my forehead, hard. "Yes. Gilmore's involvement makes even less sense than Parkes's does."

Joanne drank some soda. In front of me was a Styrofoam cup full of fast-cooling coffee. On the grayish-brown surface of the liquid the cream was breaking up into islets. I drank it anyway.

"Anybody here heard anything at *all* recently about Gilmore?" I asked.

Harvey shook his head.

I looked at John.

He shrugged. "Only what I told you a few weeks ago about him buying up that land in East Cambridge to build some kind of super-mall. And that development he's doing on the waterfront."

I thought for a moment. "Yeah," I said. "I remember you saying that. Sort of. Gilmore's in partnership with somebody on the water-front deal, isn't he?"

"On the East Cambridge thing, too. Guy named Arthur Barrow." John lit a third cigarette. "He's a partner in an investment capital firm. Barrow, Showalter, and Stevens."

I had just taken another mouthful of awful coffee. I ejected it back into the cup.

Sam said, "*What? Repeat that.*"

John looked startled. "Barrow, Showalter, and Stevens."

I coughed raspily. Sam looked at me.

"What's up?" John said, glancing from me to Sam and back again.

I wiped my mouth with the palm of my right hand. "John, re-member the woman who got murdered on Trowbridge Street here in town about a month ago?"

He nodded. "Sure." He frowned. "Patricia Something?"

"Paula," I said. "Paula Young."

"Unsolved murder," Harvey said.

"Mmm," Joanne said.

"I know that," John said. "What about her?"

"She was an auditor," I said. "Her last job before she died was doing the books for Barrow, Showalter, and Stevens."

There was silence around the table.

"What does that mean?" John said finally.

I raised my eyebrows at Sam.

He rubbed the side of his face very slowly, massaging his jowl.

"I got some information right after she died. Paula was bugged about something at work," he said. "Bugged enough so that one other person noticed it."

"Yeah, who?" Harvey said.

"Her sister."

"Paula had visited the sister two weeks before she—Paula, I mean—died," I explained.

Harvey nodded. He was watching not me, but Sam.

"Were you able to find out what was bothering her?" he asked.

Sam shook his head. "The sister didn't know."

"Did it have something to do with this Barrow, Showalter, and . . . whatever?" Joanne said.

Sam gave her a steady look. "Who knows?"

"You checked with them? About her?"

Sam smiled. "Everything was fine and dandy."

"So they said."

"So they said."

Joanne and Sam grinned at each other in that kind of bleak and black-humored way that cops do.

Harvey made a noise that was halfway between a grunt and a sigh. "Christ, this thing is getting more and fucking more complicated each minute."

"Yup." I peered at my coffee. It had broken down into yet smaller particles of its components. I pushed the cup away from me.

"You know," John said, "it could be mere coincidence that Paula Young worked for someone closely connected with Otway Gilmore and also got murdered. In the same time frame that Jack got into all *his* shit."

"Do you really think so, John?" I asked. I wasn't being snide, just genuinely curious.

John poked at the inside of his left cheek with his tongue, as if prodding a canker. "At this point," he said. "No."

We batted Paula Young and Otway Gilmore and Yolanda Sims around for another fifteen minutes. There were no hits, no runs, and, insofar as the errors were concerned, no way to tell. The discussion ended because Sam and Joanne and John and Harvey had to get back to work. I had to get back to . . . what? We broke, with promises all around to keep in touch. I refused three offers of a ride back to my place. I wanted to walk. And to think.

The Framingham and state police weren't camped on my doorstep when I got there. Which was nice for more than the obvious reason. Halfway home, I'd gotten the germ of an idea. I wanted the time to cultivate it.

29

THE CONTACT visit area of the jail was quite crowded. Did that have something to do with the fact that the holiday season was bearing down on us? And people felt it incumbent on them to pay special heed to the incarcerated as well as to the sick and the elderly?

God, imagine spending Thanksgiving in the slam. On the other hand, a lot of people had to do just that. Not Jack, though. Never him. We would get him out well before then.

I was astonished at the number of very young children present. I wondered how it felt to visit your daddy or your brother or your uncle behind bars. Most of the kids, by the look of them, didn't seem to mind. Too young to notice, or to care if they did? Perhaps, God help them, they were used to such a circumstance.

Ironically, all the commotion in the visiting area gave Jack and me an additional measure of privacy. Even if we'd discussed his case at the tops of our lungs, no one would have overheard us.

"I'll bet," Jack murmured, "we could fuck in here unnoticed."

"Don't tempt me," I said. "I'm here on serious business."

"Oh? What's that?"

"Somebody shot Dalton Craig to death."

This time, Jack did react, to the extent that the skin on his face seemed to tighten. "Jesus Christ," he said.

"And," I said, "Yolanda Sims worked for Otway Gilmore at the time you arrested Joey Sims."

He stared at me.

"Also," I added, "Paula Young—that name ring a bell? Her last work assignment was for a firm whose senior partner is tied to Gilmore."

"Wait a minute, wait a minute," Jack said. "Start from the top and go from there slowly."

I did as he asked.

When I'd finished, he rose from his chair and paced toward the big window. I followed him through the preholiday throng. We stood side by side before the expanse of plate glass.

Jack said softly, "What the hell is going on?"

"I was hoping you could tell me. Do you want to hear my ideas?"

He nodded.

"Okay. The first has to do with Paula Young. Remember how her apartment and three others on Trowbridge Street got ripped off and trashed? After she died?"

"Sure."

"All right, what I'm thinking is, suppose Paula, in the course of auditing Barrow, Showalter, and Stevens's books, stumbled on some information suggesting that Barrow and Gilmore were involved in a crooked business deal. They found out, had her killed, and arranged to make her murder look like a random street crime."

Jack said, "Uh," and shrugged. Then he added. "What's that got to do with the breaks on Trowbridge Street?"

I knew he'd already figured it out; he just wanted to hear me say it.

"Paula's apartment got torn up by somebody who figured she might have made copies of whatever documents she uncovered that related to the deal. Maybe she even stole the originals. Whatever. Anyway, the burglar was looking for them in her place. That's why it got ransacked. He probably stole her jewelry and stuff just to make it look like a regular burglary."

"And the other three breaks?"

"Covers. To make it appear as if the one burglary was part of a series."

Jack nodded. "Okay. Say you're right. How does that tie into my situation?"

"I've been thinking about that, too."

Jack smiled faintly.

"Go on," he said.

I leaned my forehead against the window. "Gilmore's the prime mover behind all your trouble. Parkes is just fronting for him."

"But why?"

I beat a fist softly on the windowsill. "That's what I've been racking my brains trying to figure out. And"—I looked up at Jack—"the only thing I can come up with is that it has something to do with a case you were working on before all the bad stuff started to happen."

Jack frowned. "Which one?"

"*I don't know.*"

"Okay, okay," he said. "Let's think. When did Dalton go on television?"

"End of September."

"Right. And we can assume that Parkes didn't come up with the idea of getting me in trouble the day before that."

"No, it would have been in his mind for a while, anyway. Maybe even a few months."

"Okay. So that means that if they wanted to get me in trouble over a case I was working on, it would have been one I was investigating last summer or late last spring."

"Uh-huh." I nodded. "Now all we have to do is figure out which one."

Jack looked at me. "Out of several dozen."

I was silent for a moment. "Well, surely there are some we can eliminate right off the bat."

"Like the closed ones."

"And the relatively small-time ones."

"Plus things like barroom stabbings."

"Probably the minor drug stuff."

"So where does that leave us?"

"It leaves us here," I said. "We're looking for a case that you were"—I started ticking the items off on my fingers—"number one, the principal investigator on; number two, that was a big case; number three, that was a long-running case; and number four, was open for a long time and still is open. Which of your cases fits all those criteria?"

Jack gave me a funny look. "The Edward Hassler murder. The car-bombing."

"My God," I said. "It does."

We stared unseeingly out the window.

"Holy God," Jack said, in a whisper.

"What?"

"What happened just before Yolanda Sims accused me of raping her? Like about four days before?"

I shook my head. "Gee, I don't . . ."

"I'll tell you." He turned to face me. "I got put on special assignment, remember? To investigate nothing but the Hassler murder."

"That's right."

"And then what happened after that?"

"You got suspended for five days. Obviously, Gilmore and Parkes must have assumed the rape charge would be enough to get you kicked out of the police department permanently." I drummed my fingers on the sill. "But it wasn't, was it? You went back to work after five days. Back to work on the Hassler case."

"And following that?"

"Yolanda got murdered and you got arrested and thrown in jail."

"Where I couldn't investigate Hassler anymore."

"That's it! That's right!" I hugged him. "We got it."

He held me for a moment and then let me go, very slowly. He was scowling.

"What's the matter?" I said.

He shook his head. "It still doesn't make sense. I mean, why me? Granted I may have been the head investigator, but there were plenty of other people working on Hassler at one time or another."

"Jack, you have a piece of knowledge about that case that no other detective has. Whatever it is, what's more, is the key to the puzzle.

And Gilmore knows you have it. Or at the very least, is afraid you have it."

"Yeah, but what the hell is it?"

"Jack, it's something you know, but you don't *know* you know it. If you know what I mean."

He nodded.

"Shit," I said. "Now what?"

Jack looked thoughtful. "Sam working on Hassler now?"

"Uh-huh."

"Okay, then he has all my files and notes."

"Right. And he's been having zero luck with it."

"I'm going to do something I never thought I'd do. Something that could really get me kicked out of the police department."

"Oh, honey," I said wearily, "does that matter, at this point?"

"No, I guess it doesn't."

"All that matters is getting you out of *here*."

"We'll see about that," Jack said. "Now. Here's what I want you to do. Tell Sam that I want him to give you the Hassler file. Then, you go through it and find out if there's anything there you pick up on."

I stared at him. "Are you *serious*?"

"Absolutely. Don't worry, you won't get in trouble."

"Jesus. You think I care about that? Whether *I* get in trouble?"

"No," he said. "I don't."

"And"—I shook my head—"my God, I don't care how high Sam's opinion might be of me, he's not going to give me that stuff. The file on an open case? No way."

"Ask him. He will." Jack's voice was calm, certain.

I looked away, shaking my head, and then back up at him. "You can be *that* sure?"

"Yup."

"But the rules . . ."

"Fuck the rules."

I took a deep breath, then let it out slowly. "If you say so. I'll talk to him as soon as . . . as I leave here."

Jack smiled at me. "If there *is* anything in the file, you'll find it." I moved up next to him. He put his arm around me. Together, we gazed out the window at the Boston skyline as the sunlight danced off the Statehouse dome.

John Ouellette was standing on my front steps when I got home. He had a manila folder in his right hand and was tapping it against his leg. He looked tired, his round face flushed with cold.

"How long have you been here?" I said.

"Long enough. You just come from seeing Jack?"

"Yes. And I have something to tell you."

"And I have something to show you."

"Well, come inside," I said, unlocking the door. "Jack Frost must be nipping at your nose."

"Yeah, that and a few other parts."

I smiled. "You can dunk it in some Scotch."

He followed me upstairs.

When we were in the living room, I said, "Sit down, be comfortable, say hello to the dog. You want rocks in your booze?"

"Please." He was shivering a little.

I poured him a hefty slug of Balvenie over ice and myself a little tot of applejack. When I handed him the drink, he said, "Jesus, do I need this."

"Rough day?" I asked.

He shrugged.

I took a sip of applejack. "So," I said. "Who first?"

"Hmmm?" He was busy sucking up single malt.

"Do you want to hear my story, or show me whatever it is you have in that folder?"

John set his glass down carefully on the arm of the chair. "Me first." He reached for the folder and flipped it open. From it he removed a five-by-seven black-and-white photograph. He rose, somewhat heavily, and walked toward me. When he was about three feet away from where I sat, he held the photograph up against his chest.

"Who's this?" he asked.

I leaned forward slightly, squinting. Then I frowned. "It looks like Jack."

John smiled thinly. "Take a closer look." He held the photograph out to me. I took it, and he returned to his chair.

The picture was a grainy, full-length shot of a tall, lean man in jeans and a windbreaker walking down what appeared to be a driveway lined with junipers. I didn't recognize the jacket the man was wearing as one that belonged to Jack. Still, the man seemed to be him. I held the photograph closer to the light. No. This man's sideburns were longer, his face was a bit too thin and bony, the forehead just a shade narrower than Jack's. The haircut, too, was slightly different. And the mouth wasn't quite . . . Also, the nose had a bump in the bridge. Jack's didn't.

This wasn't Jack.

I dropped the photograph into my lap and looked up at John. He was still smiling.

"Who *is* this?" I said.

He bolted the last of his drink. "I think he's the guy who shot Yolanda Sims."

I sat as if calcified. "What's he called?"

"Duchesne. Walter Duchesne."

I thought a moment. The name meant nothing to me. I shrugged. "Who is he?"

"A cheap, very small-time hood. A leg-breaker, basically."

"And now maybe a hired gun."

"That, too."

I picked up the photograph and stared at it again. Duchesne was by no means Jack's identical twin, but I could see how someone who didn't know either man could mistake one for the other at a glance. Or at night, from a slight distance. Like the distance between Mrs. George Watson's window and Yolanda Sims's front steps. I set the photograph on the coffee table. "Where did you get this?"

"From our morgue. Four, five years ago we did a 'Spotlight' series on organized crime in Boston outside of the Mafia. There was a

paragraph or so in one of the articles about Duchesne. I only came on the photo by accident. We never ran it with the article."

"What mob does Duchesne work for?"

John snorted. "He's like you, a free-lancer. Hangs out on the fringes of things. He's who you call if you want one of your competitor's warehouses burned down or the guy who runs the floating crap game threatened. He's been a suspect in a couple of murders. Everybody knows he did them, they just can't prove it."

I looked at John. "He sounds a lot like Phillie Joyce."

"Yes."

"So if Parkes could hire Joyce, he could hire Duchesne, couldn't he?" I finished my applejack. "Can we connect the two of them?"

John smiled. "We'll find a way."

30

SAM DROPPED the Hassler file off at my house at eight the next morning. It wasn't even a file, really, just a cardboard box half-filled with investigation report forms, a couple of spiral-bound notebooks, an autopsy report, a forensic report (the results of the tests conducted on the fragments of Hassler's car), and last year's annual report for Hassler's biotech company.

I wondered how Sam felt, deep inside, about handing this stuff over to me. When I'd conveyed Jack's request to him, I'd been careful how I phrased it. God forbid he should think that either Jack or I thought he was incapable of handling the case. But maybe he was relieved to be rid of it, even temporarily—he had, by his own admission been getting nowhere fast.

I took the box into the kitchen and dumped its contents onto the table. Then I sat down with a fresh cup of coffee and began to read.

There wasn't much in the investigation reports that I didn't know. There also wasn't anything I could remotely connect with Otway Gilmore, Albert Parkes, Dalton Craig, Yolanda Sims, or Wally Duchesne.

The forensic reports offered a meticulous description of the kind of device that had been used to blow Hassler's car, and Hassler, into smithereens. It was a kind of interesting document, in its way. There was nothing fancy about the bomb—it was just a detonator attached to a couple of sticks of dynamite, then placed under the hood of the

car and connected to the ignition system. Fast, simple, effective. When you turned the key . . .

The autopsy report, despite—or maybe because of—its clinical language, was nauseating. I read through it with my teeth clenched. Some of the language I didn't understand, which was just as well. I have a pretty strong stomach, but reading about ruptured internal organs, shattered bones, and burned flesh was enough to make even me queasy. But at any rate, the report did seem to confirm that Hassler had not been stabbed, shot, bludgeoned, or poisoned prior to being blown to bits. Nor had he appeared to be suffering from any chronic or life-threatening diseases. Given how little of him had been left to test, I wondered how the pathologist could be absolutely sure.

I put down the autopsy with relief, and turned to the annual report.

Hassler's company—according to the balance sheets—was in good financial shape. The message to shareholders talked about the breakthroughs that had been made by research and development. Particularly promising strides had come in the area of vaccines.

I let the report fall shut. Hassler's business was apparently as healthy as Hassler. There was no reason, then, for him to have committed suicide. Nobody thought he had.

I turned to the spiral-bound notebooks. These contained the notes from the interviews Jack had conducted with Hassler's wife, his relatives, coworkers, friends, business associates, neighbors, and acquaintances.

I opened the first notebook and Jack's small, even, legible handwriting leaped off the page at me.

The first interview I read was the first one Jack had conducted with Hassler's wife, Claire. What I found in it was pretty much what I expected. Mrs. Hassler couldn't think of anyone who'd want to harm her husband. No, he had no enemies. No, he hadn't had any business deals that turned sour. No, there weren't any labor problems at his company. No, he hadn't fired anyone recently. No, he hadn't received any threatening mail. Certainly he had never been involved in any extralegal activities.

The interview notes were copious; Jack was fanatic about col-

lecting details accurately—even those seemingly irrelevant ones. What I was looking for, of course, was one of those superficially insignificant bits of information. I hoped I'd recognize it when I found it. But Hassler was as clean as the proverbial whistle. Nice for him but not helpful to me in my role of detective. In the meantime, I was grateful that Jack's script was so clear.

At eleven-thirty, I made more coffee and let Lucy out for her midday backyard patrol. I stood on the deck while she thrashed around in the bushes. The sky was leaden and I thought I could smell snow. I shivered and went inside. After a few moments, Lucy followed me.

The last notebook contained re-interviews with Mrs. Hassler and several of Hassler's colleagues. These seemed to have more the flavor of general conversation than of a specific question-and-answer session. A lot of what I read had to do with the biotech industry, and the various products Hassler's firm had been working on at the time of his death. Mrs. Hassler talked about her and her husband's finances. She mentioned, in passing, that she'd recently sold a parcel of riverfront land in East Cambridge that she and her husband had owned jointly. She'd taken the profit and put it in trust for her children. The lot had been purchased by the FSX Corporation for commercial development.

I closed the notebook and tossed it disconsolately across the table. No wonder Sam was discouraged. Come to think of it, Jack hadn't been any too thrilled about the progress of the Hassler case, either.

But, damnit, he must have been on to something.

I went to the living room for my own notebook and began leafing through it dispiritedly. There was a lot of stuff in there about Otway Gilmore and Albert Parkes, and various peoples' impressions of them. Lots about the Stephen Larrain murder case and that awful business about Merton Holmes, the man who'd committed suicide after Gilmore had driven him out of business. Some notes about Gilmore's ownership of the Bay State Plaza. A reference to his and Arthur Barrow's purchase of land in East Cambridge on which to build some kind of giant shopping mall.

Shopping mall.

East Cambridge.

I jumped off the couch and ran to the kitchen. I grabbed Interview Notebook Number Four and flung it open at the last page.

The blue ink on the white lined paper stood out like an engraving on parchment:

> C.H. sold parcel land 1st. St. Camb. to FSX
> corp. 7/28 purpose of commerc. dev.

The interview was dated October 17.

A week before Yolanda Sims had accused Jack of raping her.

I dropped the notebook on the table, raced back to the living room, grabbed the phone, and called the *Globe*. John Ouellette was out on assignment. Shit. I dialed the *Herald*.

"Are any of your business reporters in the office now, Harvey?" I asked when I got through to him.

"Lemme check." I heard a *clunk* as he put the receiver on his desk, and then a hum of background noise. I thought I heard someone yell something about Ted Kennedy and there was a hoot of distant laughter. Somebody turned on a radio. Party time in Herald Square. Whistle while you work.

Harvey came back on the line. "Yeah, Jill McMenamin's in, and Paul Wriston, Kathy Davis."

"Fine," I said. "Do me a giant favor and ask if any of them know who owns, or is the principal in, an outfit called FSX."

"Sure," he replied. "This mean what I think it does?"

"Uh-huh."

"Did I get that right? F-S-X? Just those letters?"

"Yes."

"Okay. Call you back in ten minutes."

I leaned back on the couch and gulped my coffee as if it were going to be rationed immediately. Lucy ambled into the room and rubbed her nose against my knees. Her tail was wagging frantically; she must have sensed the tension I was feeling. After what seemed an hour, the phone rang.

"FSX is a real estate development company," Harvey said. "Specializing in developing commercial properties. Office and retail space, hotels, cinemas."

"I see."

"I have here a recent FSX press release announcing plans for the construction of a trilevel shopping mall between First Street and the Cambridge Parkway. Ground-breaking to take place the end of next March."

"Go on."

"The principals for FSX are Otway Gilmore and Arthur Barrow."

"Uh-huh."

"Liz—"

"Harvey," I said. "I'm going to hang up now, so I can round up Sam and Joanne and John. Be at my house tonight at six. I'll do dinner."

"Liz—"

"Tonight. Six. And, Harvey?"

"What?"

"Thanks."

"It hangs together," John said. "And it makes sense. And I believe it. But there's nothing in it we can fucking prove."

"Would you mind going through it again, Liz?" Joanne asked.

"Sure. Can I do it in short form?"

She smiled and nodded.

"Okay. What I think—what I'm sure of—is that Otway Gilmore and Arthur Barrow approached Edward Hassler about buying the land Hassler and his wife co-owned in East Cambridge. Probably they made a good offer. But Hassler, for whatever reason, didn't want to sell. Maybe he had plans for the land himself, or maybe he just thought Gilmore was a sleaze and didn't want to do business with him. That could be it. By all accounts, Hassler was a decent, upright guy. And, as we all know, Gilmore is a—"

"Bag of shit," Sam interrupted.

"That sums it up nicely. So, anyway, Gilmore probably upped the

offer, and Hassler turned him down again. So Gilmore did what he
did with Merton Holmes. Only he took a more direct approach."

"Who?" Joanne asked.

"Merton Holmes," I explained, "was a developer on the South
Shore. Gilmore wanted to buy land from him. Holmes refused to
sell." I took a deep breath. "To make a long story short, Gilmore
made life hell for Holmes thereafter."

"Don't get mad, get even," Harvey said.

"Precisely. Anyway, Holmes ended up committing suicide."

Joanne inhaled audibly.

"And," I concluded, "Gilmore bought Holmes's property from the
grieving widow. Which is exactly what he did with Claire Hassler.
Only with Mrs. Hassler, he didn't have to wait for probate."

"Evil," Joanne said softly.

Harvey shook his head slowly. "What a thing to do, though," he
said. "Murder some guy just because he didn't want to do business
with you."

"It's an old story for Gilmore," I said crisply. "Besides, he caused
the death of an eighteen-month-old girl in a fire in one of his rattrap
apartment buildings, and he had Stephen Larrain shot because Larrain wrote nasty things about him in the newspaper." I shrugged.
"Why should he balk at murdering two other people?"

"Three," Sam said.

I looked at him.

"Paula Young."

"Of course." I bit my lower lip. "Forgive me for having left her
out, even momentarily."

"Sometimes it's hard to keep an accurate tally," Harvey said.

"Yes. I guess."

There was a brief silence around the kitchen table. We picked at
the remains of our dinner—not sandwiches or pizza this time, but
chicken breasts and au gratin potatoes, broccoli and salad.

Harvey cleared his throat. "So Paula Young had to die because she
found out something about how Gilmore and Barrow had Hassler
murdered."

I nodded.

John frowned. "That wouldn't have been in the books she was auditing."

"No," I said. "It was probably only a detail she stumbled on that gave her a funny feeling. Or maybe a letter from Gilmore to Barrow, or Barrow to Gilmore, or she overheard a conversation she shouldn't have, or she found a tape. A note. Who knows?"

"If it was in written form or something on a tape, it was stupid of Barrow not to have destroyed it," Joanne said.

"On his and Gilmore's level of arrogance," I replied, "you sometimes forget things like that. Remember the insider-trading scandal on Wall Street a couple of years ago? Some of those guys never bothered to cover their tracks. None of them thought they'd be caught or even discovered, either. Most of them were genuinely puzzled and offended when they had the cuffs put on them. I think their feelings were hurt."

When we were settled in the living room with coffee, I said, "Now what? Even the cops among us agree we have nothing to take to the police."

John rested his head against the back of the rocking chair and closed his eyes. Joanne looked at the cup and saucer she had sitting on her knee. Sam was petting Lucy and murmuring to her what a nice dog she was.

"We could," Harvey said, "force a confrontation."

I raised my eyebrows.

"With whom?" John asked, his eyes still closed. "Otway Gilmore? You suggesting we kidnap him outside his house like we did Dalton Craig?"

"We couldn't get within a mile of Gilmore," I said. "He's too well protected."

"No shit," John replied.

"I don't think that's true of Albert Parkes, though."

John opened his eyes.

"I bet we could brace *him*," I said.

31

"GOD, I hope it doesn't snow," Joanne said, peering anxiously through the windshield at the sky.

"It sure looks like it," I said. I pried up the plastic lid on a Styrofoam cup of coffee. On the seat between us was a bag of ham-and-cheese croissants. Breakfast.

It was seven-thirty A.M., and Joanne and I were sitting in her car on Greenwood Street in Melrose, parked a few hundred feet up from a great, white-frame ark of a house. It wasn't Noah who lived in the ark, though, but Albert Parkes.

I had his photograph in my lap.

"Want a croissant?" I asked Joanne. She nodded and I passed her the bag.

"I've never been on an extended stakeout before," I said. "Suppose I gotta go to the bathroom?"

Joanne smiled. "There's an empty milk carton in the backseat. Use that. Or your coffee cup."

"Maybe I'll just hold it," I said.

She laughed and ate some more of her croissant.

At five minutes to eight, a silver Cadillac Seville backed out of the ark's driveway and cruised up the street past us.

"That's him," I said.

Joanne started the car, pulled it out of the parking place, and cut a sharp U-turn in the middle of Greenwood Street.

"The fox and the hounds," I said.

"Woof."

We followed the Seville through Melrose and onto the Fellsway, past Spot Pond, and from there onto Route 93. The rush-hour traffic was horrendous. Just twenty years ago, 93 was a cowpath.

"You don't have a driver's license, do you?" Joanne asked.

"Nope."

"Why not?"

I shrugged. "None of the high schools and private schools I went to had driver-ed programs. Then I went to an urban college, and didn't have the time. After that, I went to graduate school in Scotland. I do know how to drive, though."

"Oh. Well, ever think of getting a license?"

"Naw, what for? I can't afford a car. Anyway, I hate them. I'd rather have a pilot's license. I like flying. There's a lot fewer idiots zoning around up there than there are down here."

A blue Volvo swerved in front of us. Joanne hit the brakes.

"You're probably right," she said.

We kept the Seville in sight all the way into Boston and then lost it in the madhouse of the expressway.

"Shit," Joanne said.

"Never mind. We're right near where his business is. Let's just keep going."

The offices for Parkes Construction were on a street off Haymarket Square. Of course, there was nowhere for us to stop.

"Drop me," I said. "I'll check and see if he's gotten in."

It took me maybe a second to hop out of Joanne's car. Even so, there was a blast of horns from the traffic behind us, enraged at this unconscionable delay. Boston drivers were even more hysterical than Roman ones. Another good reason not to get a license.

The first floor of the office building was a small arcade with a coffee shop, newsstand, flower shop, art gallery, a shop that sold Celtics and Patriots and Red Sox souvenirs, and a jewelry store. Only the newsstand and coffee shop were open. I bought a copy of the *Times* and sat down on a bench opposite the elevator bank. The

arcade was fairly crowded. Good. I wouldn't have trouble being unobtrusive. Not that Parkes knew what I looked like, anyway.

Unless Craig had told him. A pleasant thought, but one that I couldn't do much about. I dismissed it.

Five minutes later, Parkes came through the revolving entrance door and went to the elevator bank. He and ten other people squeezed onto the next upbound car. I left the building. Joanne was standing outside, looking at the display in the jewelry-store window.

"I picked him up again," she said. "He put the Caddie in the parking garage over there. I got a place on the same level as his."

"Oh, good. Well, he's gone up to his office."

We went back inside the building, to the coffee shop. There was one very recently vacated table for two. We grabbed it. The shop was mobbed. The waitress probably wouldn't get to us for a while, which was perfectly okay. We had a lot of time to burn.

"Steel yourself for an incredibly boring day," Joanne said.

I smiled. "I can handle it. Anyway, we have to do this, right? Keep tabs on the son-of-a-bitch?"

She nodded.

"So," I said. "It'll be my pleasure."

The waitress, who was shooting around like a character in a silent movie shown at high speed, eventually reached our table. We ordered orange juice, toast, and coffee, none of which either of us wanted but what we figured would cover the rent for the shop space we were occupying.

"Nice of you to blow your day off doing this, Jo," I said.

She looked at me as if I'd said something offensive or stupid. "Liz, forget it."

The waitress slapped a platter of toast down on the table between us. Somehow the cook had managed to make it burned and underdone simultaneously.

I sipped my orange juice. "I wonder . . ."

Joanne shook her head at the toast. "What?"

"Oh, just that . . . if we hadn't found out what we know now, and Sam had kept working on the Hassler case, do you think eventually—"

"What happened to Jack would have happened to him?"

"Yeah."

"Jesus." Joanne whistled softly. "Maybe." She chewed absently on a corner of her toast. "Hard to believe, though."

"That Gilmore would think he could keep on setting up and knocking down any cop who got in his way?"

She nodded.

"I don't find it hard to believe at all," I said.

Joanne was right; it was an incredibly boring day. But we had to know where Parkes was at all times. If he took a cab to the airport and got on a plane to New York or Los Angeles it would put a crimp in the plans we had for later. And Joanne and I were the only two of the five of us who had an entire day to invest in bird-dogging the bastard. Still, the procedure became monumentally tedious.

As far as we could tell, Parkes didn't even leave his office building for lunch.

We took a lot of walks around the area, separately, with strictly defined time limits for each. The furthest afield either of us went was to the ladies' room in Quincy Market. We took turns nosing around in the produce. One of us was always right near Parkes's building, and we didn't stay anywhere long enough to attract attention. Over a late afternoon snack at the arcade lunch counter, Joanne told me some of the little tricks she had for altering her appearance during a stakeout, such as putting on a hat, taking off a pair of sunglasses, changing a jacket. Minor stuff, but it could mean the difference between somebody noticing you or not.

At six-thirty, Joanne was sitting in the arcade lobby reading the *Herald* and I was looking in the windows of the souvenir shop. Parkes emerged from the elevator and left the building. We sauntered after him. He went directly to the parking garage.

I felt something tiny and cold kiss my cheek. I glanced up at one of the streetlamps. In the halo of light I could see an occasional snowflake.

Parkes took an elevator to the third level of the parking garage.

Joanne and I sprinted up the stairs. We were just getting into her car as he was backing the Seville out of its place.

As we drove out into the night, I said, "I hope this doesn't turn into our first major blizzard."

"Why not?" Joanne said. "It'll just increase the excitement."

Instead of heading toward the expressway entrance ramp, the Seville made a hook in a direction that would take it to the Boston continuation of Cambridge Street.

"My radio's in the glove compartment," Joanne said. "Could you get it out?"

I fumbled a black, boxy-looking object out of the glove compartment. The standard Cambridge Police Department radio was a Motorola, much different in shape and size.

"What the hell's this?" I asked.

"I have a college friend who joined the FBI. She's here in the Boston office." Joanne nodded at the radio. "I borrowed two of those from her. Sam has the other."

I handed her the radio. "Did you get the recorder I have in my purse from the same source?"

"Uh-huh. We don't have any equipment that matches it."

"Tell your friend I owe her one."

Joanne smiled. She pressed the button on the side of the radio and held it up to her mouth. "Forty-eight to fifty-two," she said.

There was a second of faint, crackly static and then Sam's voice replied, "This is thirty-two, same's my age. How you doing, babe?"

"I think we have a slight change in plans," Joanne said.

"Yeah?"

"He's apparently not heading directly home. We're behind him now, on Cambridge Street in Boston."

"Okay. Update your location."

"Ten-four," Joanne said. She set the radio on the seat beside her.

We followed Parkes onto the Longfellow Bridge across the Charles. The snow was coming down softly and gently but quite steadily now. Fortunately the traffic was moderate and it wasn't too hard to keep the Seville in view.

Joanne picked up her radio. "Forty-eight to thirty-two. Heading west on Main Street now. You almost ready to move?"

"We'll be behind you. Keep in touch."

"Okay. We're on Mass. Ave now, going through Central."

"Gotcha. We're rolling now."

Joanne dropped the radio into her lap. She leaned forward slightly and squinted at the windshield. Snowflakes flurried and danced in the headlights. "I hope this lets up."

"Gee," I said, "weren't you the one who was saying a blizzard would just make things more fun?"

"Yeah, but I haven't put the snow tires on this shitbox, yet." She passed her radio over to me. "Why don't you take care of the communications and I'll concentrate on driving."

"Well . . ." I hesitated. "Sure." I hefted the radio, then pressed the side button. "Uh, Liz to thirty-two," I said, feeling suddenly like a bit of a horse's ass, or a kid playing astronaut.

Thirty-two sounded amused. "What's happening, doll?"

"We just went through Harvard Square. Now we're going north on Mass. Ave."

"We're with you."

I couldn't bring myself to say "ten-four."

Joanne was keeping a careful two cars behind the Seville. We rolled past Cambridge Common and the Harvard Law School.

"Where the hell do you think we're going?" I asked.

"Not too goddamn far, I hope," Joanne replied.

"Be funny if we ended up in the Berkshires."

"Hilarious."

I picked up the radio. "Hi, thirty-two. We're just going through Porter Square."

"Gotcha."

Parkes drove as far on Mass. Ave as the Arlington–Cambridge line and turned left.

"Hey, thirty-two," I said. "We just got on Route Two."

"Maybe we *are* on our way to the Berkshires," Joanne mumbled. "Too bad I didn't bring my skis."

For the next twenty-five minutes, we stayed on Route 2, passing through Belmont, Lexington, Lincoln, and Concord. Joanne didn't speak, but I could sense how antsy she was getting. Me, too.

The Seville's right directional signal began to flash.

"Thirty-two," I said into the radio, "we're getting off at Acton. First exit."

"Yup."

"Okay, now we're just making a left at the end of the exit. I don't know what street we're on. There's no sign."

"Left at the top of the exit," thirty-two repeated.

"Uh-huh. Keep you posted."

We went another half mile before the Seville made a right turn onto a narrow, twisty street with woods on either side. Presently we came to a large white roadside sign that read, "Le Marsouin. Cuisine Française. Two hundred yards ahead."

"Maybe he's meeting his mistress for an intimate dinner," Joanne remarked.

Parkes turned in at the entrance to the drive that led up to the restaurant. Joanne slowed and pulled over onto the shoulder.

"Don't want to follow him right in," she explained. "Might look suspicious."

I'd figured that out already.

Five minutes later, we pulled into the parking lot. It was only about a fifth full. The Seville was in the right rear corner of the lot. Joanne parked about fifty feet away from it.

"I'll go in," I said. "Get the lay of the land."

She nodded.

"Thank God I'm not wearing jeans," I said. What I had on, under my jacket, was a pair of brown wool slacks, a tweed blazer, and silk blouse. Neat but not gaudy. At least the maître d' of this joint wouldn't hold his nose at the sight of me.

"Just let me check this gizmo and see if it works," I added, reaching into my handbag.

The gizmo was a miniature tape recorder that purported to pick up the sound of a pin dropping at fifty paces, or fulfill some such

similarly extravagant claim. I punched the record button and whispered, "You better do what you claim to, sucker." I pressed "rewind" and then "play." My voice came back to me loud and clear.

A black Lincoln Continental limousine slid past us and up to the restaurant door. I put the tape recorder back into my purse.

"Holy shit," Joanne said.

Startled, I glanced at her. "What?"

She pointed. "Look who's getting out of the limo."

I peered through the windshield.

The restaurant entrance was brightly lit, enough to make anyone passing through it eminently visible even through the gauzy curtain of snow.

Had the visibility been far lower, however, there would have been no mistaking the identity of the man emerging from the Lincoln.

It was Otway Gilmore.

32

THE LIMOUSINE glided away from the restaurant door and into a parking place on the side of the lot opposite us.

"Son of a gun," Joanne said. "Business meeting." She took the radio from me and held it up to her mouth. "Forty-eight to thirty-two."

"Thirty-two," Sam replied. "We're getting onto the Acton exit now."

"Uh-huh," Joanne said. "We have here a dramatic new development."

I raised my left hand to her, got out of the car, and headed toward the restaurant entrance.

A blond young man in a dark suit intercepted me in the restaurant foyer. I gave him a brilliant smile.

"I'm meeting friends here at seven-thirty," I said.

"Do you have a reservation?"

I changed my smile from brilliant to blank. "Oh, I'm not sure if they made one. May I glance in the dining room and see if they've arrived?"

The young man smiled. "Of course."

I walked past him and thrust my head through the dining-room archway. Perhaps four out of thirty tables were occupied. None by Parkes or Gilmore, though. I returned to the foyer and looked ruefully at the maître d'.

"Perhaps you'd care to wait in the bar," he said.

"Good idea," I replied. "But I need to get something from my car first." I went back out into the snow.

Joanne was leaning back, her hands behind her head. She rolled down the window when I tapped on it.

"They're either in the kitchen or the bar," I said. "I'm betting on the bar. Anyway, I'm going back in."

She nodded.

As I returned to the restaurant, I saw Sam's LTD pull into the lot and draw up next to Joanne's Chevy.

The cocktail lounge was dim and cozy, done in French farmhouse style, with a working fireplace at the far end. To the right ran a mahogany bar. To the left were tables with easy chairs grouped around them. Given that *marsouin* meant "porpoise," I'd have expected a nautical motif.

The only people there, other than the bartender and the waitress, were Gilmore and Parkes. They had a table near the fireplace. I took one about ten feet away, so they wouldn't feel eavesdropped upon.

Whatever they were talking about, I wanted them to continue doing so. My gizmo would pick up the conversation, even if I couldn't. Or so Joanne's pal at the FBI claimed.

The waitress put a ceramic bowl of dry-roasted peanuts in front of me, lit the candle in the center of the table, and took my order for a vodka martini.

I slid the tape recorder out of my purse, placed it in my lap, and pressed the "record" button. Then I ate two peanuts and glanced around the room, as if doing a casual inventory.

Gilmore and Parkes were seated so that their profiles were turned toward me. Parkes was hunched forward slightly over the table, talking quite intensely but inaudibly (to me) to Gilmore. Gilmore sat relaxed, smiling faintly, occasionally nodding, a small glass of something in his right hand.

You could easily tell the employer from the employee.

Gilmore in the flesh projected the same aura of physical power as his photographic image did—if anything, even more so. Had I

known nothing about him, I would still have pegged him as the kind of tall man who used his height to intimidate, no doubt with considerable success. He was well-built, with a broad-shouldered, lean, athletic frame.

For someone who had the means to live like the most Babylonian of voluptuaries, he had the look of an ascetic, or at least of someone whose appetites were carefully controlled and regulated. Perhaps this was only the effect of a rather austere set of features—the high, almost Slavic cheekbones, the long narrow jaw, and the black eyebrows that contrasted so sharply with the bald head.

Well, Gilmore was supposed to have a certain magnetism.

Parkes, on the other hand, looked like an animate sack of potatoes. Portly to begin with, he seemed to have gained about twenty-five pounds since the photograph I had of him had been taken. And he'd lost a little more hair. What was left was raked straight back and plastered to his scalp. His nose, even in the dim light and at a distance of ten feet, was red and large-pored. The flesh around his eyes was puffy.

The waitress brought me my drink. I sipped it and ate another peanut, as quietly as possible so that the recorder wouldn't pick up any crunching or slurping sounds.

Harvey Searle came into the bar. I waved to him. He came over to my table and sat down in the chair to the right of me. I leaned sideways and kissed him lightly on the mouth, so that anyone looking at us would think I was just a lady meeting her date.

"Try not to talk much," I breathed into his ear. "I'm recording their conversation."

He nodded.

The waitress came to the table. Harvey ordered a draft Michelob. I gave him a fatuous smile and put my hand on his arm. He rolled his eyes.

Gilmore was now speaking to Parkes. Parkes was nodding very seriously.

The waitress delivered Harvey his beer.

I drank some of my martini and tried to dissolve a few more

peanuts on my tongue. Two more people, not together, drifted into the lounge and took seats at the bar. I gave Harvey a sappy leer. Given the propensity of some loving couples virtually to copulate in public, I was sure I wasn't overdoing it.

At ten after eight, Parkes summoned the waitress for the check.

I raised my eyebrows at Harvey. He took a ten-dollar bill from his wallet and put it on the table. I clicked off the tape recorder and slipped it into my bag. Then Harvey and I rose and strolled arm in arm out of the bar.

Once outside the restaurant door, we broke free of each other and raced across the parking lot. The snow was still falling, neither more lightly nor more heavily than it had been before. The trees looked as if they had a sugar glaze. The asphalt lot was slippery underfoot.

Sam's car was still alongside Joanne's. John sat in the front seat with Sam. I gave them a grin and a thumbs-up sign. Harvey and I got into Joanne's car.

"What've you got?" she asked.

I reached into my purse for the tape recorder. "Whatever Gilmore and Parkes spent the last thirty-five minutes discussing."

The Lincoln limo pulled up in front of Le Marsouin. Gilmore came out of the restaurant and climbed into the rear seat. Parkes hurried off toward his own car.

Joanne started the Chevy.

The Lincoln wheeled out of the parking lot and down the drive, trailed by the Seville. Joanne let about fifteen seconds pass before she followed them.

At the base of the drive, the Lincoln and Seville turned left.

"I think we're going back to Route Two," Joanne said.

"And from there to where?" Harvey asked.

"Maybe the tape'll tell us," I said. I pushed the "rewind" button.

The gizmo lived up to its promise. The first thing we heard sounded like windows shattering. It was the Le Marsouin bartender putting away glasses. I lowered the volume.

The first part of the recording had to do with Gilmore's planned purchase of a tract of land in Shirley, for the purpose of industrial

development. The town management was apparently favorable to the proposition. Tax rates were low. The land was the ideal site for a major office park. Mention was made of leaseback agreements, something I only dimly understood.

Suddenly my voice came on the tape, breathily enjoining Harvey to keep still. Then his voice could be heard, ordering beer from the waitress. I shut the recorder off for a moment so he and Joanne and I could finish laughing. A good tension reliever.

The next speaker on the tape was Parkes. It wasn't difficult to distinguish his voice from Gilmore's. Both men spoke the way they looked, Gilmore's diction clipped and polished, Parkes's coarse and slurry, at least by comparison.

PARKES: Our other business is going along okay.

GILMORE: So far.

PARKES: Looks good to me. We don't have to listen to no more shit from the Sims broad. And Craig won't give us no more trouble.

GILMORE: We had to use the material at hand. Sims and Craig served their purpose. We don't have to worry about them anymore.

PARKES: Or pay them, neither.

GILMORE: The least of my concerns. If I have to deal with . . . undesirable people, I terminate the association as fast as I can.

PARKES: Yeah, that Craig had a few screws loose, huh? A fuckin' banana.

GILMORE: True. But he was helpful at the time. But thanks to you, he's not a problem anymore, Albert. Is he?

There was a pause in the conversation, and some clinking and tinkling noises. Ice cubes in glasses. Then Parkes's voice came over the tape again.

PARKES: The cop's in jail, and he's not gonna be out for a long time. If he ever gets out.

GILMORE: Well, we can hope he doesn't.

PARKES: How much did you slip that judge—Sanger? That the guy's name? How much did you give him?

Whatever Gilmore's response was, the tape hadn't picked it up.

PARKES: The fuckin' cop's gonna rot in there. I hope he dies in jail, the prick.

GILMORE: We may have to make sure of that.

PARKES: Yeah? How do we do that?

GILMORE: It shouldn't be too difficult to arrange for some sort of tragic accident. In the jail. With the right inducement, you can arrange almost anything. Who would know that better than you, Albert?

I felt as if I'd swallowed a ten-pound block of dry ice.

Gilmore's mechanical voice continued, placidly malevolent. "I have to admit, though, Lingemann's not quite the bumbling jackass some of those other investigators obviously were. Well, he's not a problem anymore, either. Shall we pay up and get out of here? Then I'll show you the site in Shirley."

The recorder went silent except for the faint hum of blank tape unreeling.

"Got you, you son-of-a-bitch," I said.

33

JOANNE BANGED her fist on the steering wheel. Her face radiated a kind of grim exultation. I turned to look at Harvey. He was grinning.

"Not bad," he said. "Not fucking bad at all."

"I'll say it's not. Want to hear it again?"

"Absolutely."

I rewound the tape. I was about to play it back when Joanne said sharply, "They're getting off." She snatched up the radio. "Thirty-two, we're taking the next exit. Shirley."

"Right," Sam said laconically. "Keep in touch."

"This is going to be tricky," Joanne said, mostly to herself.

"Yeah," Harvey said. "What the hell does Gilmore want to show Parkes an industrial site for at night in a blizzard?"

"I know, there's something very odd there."

"That's what we're going to find out," I said. "Besides, those two are going to try to have Jack killed. You think I'm going to let them out of my sight?"

Joanne looked tense.

"Relax," I said. I felt as if I had steel wires running through me. "I don't think it'll occur to either Gilmore or Parkes that they're being tailed. Why should it?"

She nodded, and sighed.

The Lincoln, followed by the Seville, turned left at the end of the

exit ramp. There was one car between us and them. Sam and John were maybe a mile or so behind us. They'd catch up.

The road we turned onto was only sparsely lit by streetlamps. The woods on either side were thick.

"Forest primeval," Harvey remarked. "Isn't there a prison somewhere around here?"

"Uh-huh," I said. "MCI Shirley. I'm taking it as a good omen."

A mile and a half beyond the exit the Lincoln and Seville slowed and made another left. A billboard-sized sign just off the verge of the road read: "For Sale. Three Hundred Acres. Industrial/Commercial Use."

"This must be it," Joanne said. She drove past the opening in the trees into which the Lincoln and Seville had turned and pulled over onto the shoulder. She picked up the radio. "Forty-eight to thirty-two."

"Yeah, forty-eight," Sam answered.

Joanne described where we were. "We'll be waiting," she said.

I buttoned the strap of my handbag beneath my right epaulet. There. At least I wouldn't have to worry about dropping it and shattering the recorder.

Three minutes later, Sam's LTD drew up behind us. He and John got out of the car and crunched their way over through the snow.

John looked at me with raised eyebrows. "Wait'll you hear what I got on tape," I said, patting my handbag.

"I wish I knew what the hell was going on," he said.

"You'll find out, John. Very shortly."

The five of us walked along the entrance to the access road up to the industrial site. It wasn't actually a road so much as a dirt track. It had rises in it like a toned-down and miniaturized roller coaster.

About five hundred feet in, and around a bend, we could detect a faint glow.

Frowning, I moved up next to Joanne. "What's that? They got a campfire going or something?"

She shrugged. "Probably got the car headlights on. How do you inspect a building site in the pitch dark?"

I nodded.

We went around another curve and the illumination grew stronger.

Joanne slid her right hand into her coat pocket. So, I noticed, did Sam.

As we started up another rise, there was a choked, bubbly scream from the illumined area. I froze. We heard two gunshots, the second following the first so quickly it was almost a single sound.

Joanne and Sam glanced at each other and, simultaneously, broke into a run.

"God almighty," Harvey said. He and John took off after the other two.

I snapped myself out of paralysis and followed them reflexively.

Just beyond the rise was a clearing maybe fifty feet across. In it were parked, at right angles to each other, the Lincoln and the Seville. The Seville pointed away from us. The Lincoln's low beams were on. In the twin cones of light stood two figures. A third lay on the ground before them.

"Police," Sam yelled.

One of the two standing figures swung toward us. There was another shot.

Sam made a staggering half-step forward and then fell face-first to the ground.

I could hear myself screaming, and through the screaming, another shot, this one from barely ten feet away. One of the standing figures dropped. The other spun around and vanished into the woods.

Joanne fired twice more into the trees. Then she turned and gave me a wild, anguished look.

Harvey and John were crouched down beside Sam. As I watched, Joanne stumbled toward them. "In the thigh," I heard John say. He ripped the tie from under his collar and began binding it around the top of Sam's right leg.

I felt the rage boil up and begin pouring through my veins like lava.

I ran across the clearing to the two bodies in front of the Lincoln. The one nearest me was Parkes. His left temple was shattered and pulpy. I gagged and looked at the other body. A large man in a black suit, white shirt, and black tie. Gilmore's chauffeur. There was blood on the man's shirt front and snow collecting in his open eyes.

The gun he'd used on Parkes and Sam lay a foot or so away from him, where it had fallen from his hand like a discarded toy. I snatched it up and crashed into the woods after the fleeing figure.

After Otway Gilmore.

"Gilmore," I screamed. "Give it up. We've got you, you son-of-a-bitch."

The only answer was the gentle, steady hiss of the snow in trees. I blundered on through the underbrush.

Christ, suppose Gilmore was armed, too?

I heard a faint thrashing noise from somewhere ahead of me and to the right.

"Gilmore," I yelled. "This is my first and last warning. I'm going to shoot."

The gun in my hand was a thirty-eight. A lot like the one that had been stolen from Jack's apartment. In theory, I knew how it operated. I raised it and fired it in the direction from which the thrashing had come. Then I hurled myself behind a thick-trunked oak, trembling and waiting for a return salvo to drill the tree.

There was none. Maybe the noise I'd shot at had been an animal, and I'd plinked a raccoon or a deer or a fox. I waited another moment, and then stepped out from behind the tree.

I heard faint voices calling to me. Harvey and Joanne. And then I heard the thrashing sound again, this time from a greater distance. I ran toward it, yelling over my shoulder, "I'm okay." I stumbled over a log or a branch and nearly fell. I straightened and went crashing through a stand of birches, slim and ethereal in the snow.

Ahead of me was a boulder-studded slope. I scrambled up it virtually on all fours. As I reached the top I heard the thrashing again.

"Okay, Gilmore," I yelled. "Here it comes." I fired the thirty-

eight. There was a final frantic little rustle and then silence. I leaned against the trunk of a very tall pine, panting.

I looked at the gun in my hand. Gilmore's chauffeur had fired three shots. I'd fired two.

That meant, if the gun had been carrying a full load, there was only one round left in the cylinder.

One round.

"Gilmore," I screamed.

Silence.

The far slope of the ridge I was standing on was much gentler, barely forming a twenty-degree angle. I ran down to the base. What seemed to be a rudimentary path meandered off into the trees to my right. I started along it, my footfalls cushioned by the thin blanket of snow.

Were Harvey and Joanne somewhere behind me? Where was John?

And what had happened to Sam? I closed my mind against the thought that he might be . . . could a thigh wound be fatal? Of course, if the bullet had severed an artery.

The muscles in the hinges of my jaw got that funny stiff sensation they always did when I was fighting nausea.

The snow had tapered off to just the occasional fugitive flurry. I felt as if I were shrink-wrapped in darkness.

The path took a sudden downward turn. For several feet I skidded helplessly.

I heard the thrashing noise again.

I grasped the trunk of a birch to steady myself. Then I wiped my mouth with the back of my gun hand and yelled, "Gilmore?"

No answer. I let go of the tree and fumbled along the path. Some tiny unidentifiable creature skittered frantically over the snow in front of me, and I drew a quick, sharp breath. The animal disappeared into the scrub.

The woodland world had been turned upside down tonight.

I came to a fork in the path, nearly running into the trunk of the

maple tree that bisected it. I stopped and squinted first to the left and
then to the right tine of the fork. The left side was somewhat wider.
I knelt at the entrance to it. I thought I could discern very faint
footprints in the snow. I followed them.

The blackness around me seemed—I thought—to recede. I looked
up at the branches overhanging the path. Through them I could see
that the clouds had broken. In one of the clear patches I could make
out a star. Or maybe it was a planet.

"Gilmore!" I shouted.

"Over here," said a dry, clipped voice.

I gasped and spun in a complete circle, pivoting on my right heel.
I fanned the gun at the trees.

A noise that sounded like a laugh filtered through the wood. It
seemed to be coming from somewhere farther down the path. I
advanced a few steps, cautiously.

I had no idea how far and only the vaguest sense of how long I'd
run.

"Here," the voice repeated.

I cocked my head. The speaker was very definitely somewhere in
front of me, perhaps a little to the side.

I crept along the path. Another twenty feet and it swerved again to
the left and angled slightly downward.

"I'm coming," I said. "Get ready."

Again, I heard that slight laugh. I raised the gun in my hand,
holding it straight out before me.

The path emptied into a small clearing. As I neared it, the moon
came out from behind a cloud and threw the landscape into stark
chiaroscuro relief. I paused at the end of the path and looked out and
around me.

"Careful where you walk," the voice said. "We're on the edge of
a quarry. A deep one."

I jerked my head to the right. Fifteen feet from where I stood the
tree line ended abruptly. Beyond that was a darkness my eyes couldn't
penetrate. I turned my head and squinted into the clearing before

me. Just ten feet away, on a low flat rock beneath an elm tree, sat Otway Gilmore.

I walked toward him, my gun arm stiff and straight. He watched me approach with the faintest of smiles.

"I can't run anymore," he said. "My leg's gone."

I gestured with the gun. "Did I hit it?"

He shook his head. "I caught my foot in a tree root. The ankle is . . . well, it's not functioning."

"Too bad," I said. "Not that you're hurt, but that I didn't do it."

He lifted his right leg a few inches. The foot seemed to flop nervelessly from the end of it. At the very least, he had a bad sprain. More likely a break and some ripped tendons. He had to be in considerable pain.

Good. But not nearly good enough.

It would be very unwise of me to take Gilmore's word that he was disabled. "If you move, I'll shoot you," I said. I crouched down before him. He was wearing neither topcoat nor jacket. The fine wool of his suit was damp with melted snow. With my free hand I reached under his suitcoat and felt his arms and front and sides. I bent forward a little further and ran the hand down his back. Then I patted his legs. I dug in his pockets. He sat perfectly still as I searched him, almost as if he were unaware of what I was doing.

No knife. No gun.

I settled back on my heels and grinned at him.

"Finally we meet," I said.

He gave me that sparse ironic smile. "You know it doesn't do for a police officer to shoot an unarmed person."

"Guess what," I said. "I'm not a cop."

He looked at me curiously.

"This is a purely private enterprise," I said. I moved the gun a little closer to his face. "What is it with guys like you, Gilmore? Don't you ever stop?"

"Stop what?"

"Murdering people, you son-of-a-bitch," I said. "You want a

list? Okay, here it is. Stephen Larrain. Merton Holmes. Edward
Hassler. Paula Young. Yolanda Sims. Dalton Craig. Albert Parkes.
Not that the last three are any great loss." I took a deep breath.
"Plus you also slaughtered an eighteen-month-old girl. Your first
victim, I believe. Did killing a baby make it easier to knock off the
seven adults?"

He shook his head as if bewildered.

"Did it, asshole?" I leaned forward and prodded the barrel of the
gun against the tip of his nose. "Your tame gorilla also shot another
good friend of mine tonight. Maybe he's dead, too."

Gilmore arched his eyebrows and shrugged. "If you feel that way,
why *don't* you shoot me?"

I looked at him consideringly. Then I shook my head. "No. I was
going to a few minutes ago. It would have given me great pleasure.
Still would. But killing you would put me on your level, God forbid.
So I'll leave you to the courts."

He sighed. "What am I guilty of? These people you mentioned
. . . Didn't Merton Holmes commit suicide? Paula Young—wasn't
she killed by a mugger? Dalton Craig, I understand from the papers,
was the victim of a gangland slaying. Stephen Larrain . . . didn't
someone break into his house and shoot him?"

"Yes, and you know damn well who, too. A free-lance crud named
Phillie Joyce, at your orders. Parkes was the middleman."

Gilmore went on, ignoring me. "I have no idea how poor Mr.
Hassler came to his end."

"Oh, bullshit."

"And I have no idea what baby you're speaking of. That I'm
supposed to have slaughtered. To use your word."

"She died in a fire in one of your roach holes."

Gilmore shrugged. "Careless, irresponsible tenants." He gave me
another oblique smile. "And as for this Yolanda person—wasn't she
shot to death by some police officer? Lindman? Something like that?
Sordid situation from what I understand."

It was all I could do to keep from squeezing the trigger then and
there. The gun was shaking in my hand.

"You're forgetting about Parkes," I said. "Five people just saw that go down, Gilmore. Five eyewitnesses."

"I didn't shoot Albert. My chauffeur did. In self-defense. Albert threatened me. Richard overreacted. An unfortunate accident."

"You're an inventive liar," I said. "I'll give you that."

"On the contrary, I'm telling the complete truth."

I nodded. "With the kind of legal talent you can afford to hire, you'll probably get the courts to believe you are."

"So does that mean you'll change your mind about shooting me?"

"Nope. There're enough killers on the loose already."

"So what now?"

"I guess we'll wait here until my friends find us."

"Why don't you put the gun away, then? As long as you're not going to use it."

I smiled. "Nah. I don't trust you even if you can't walk."

Gilmore seemed to shiver.

"Chilly?" I asked, without sympathy.

He didn't answer me.

"How's your foot?"

Still no response.

"Gee, you're a tough bastard, aren't you?"

He looked at me then. "In my business, you have to be."

"Cutthroat wheeling and dealing." I nodded. "Emphasis on cut-throat."

"Real estate's a cutthroat business," he replied calmly.

I was getting cramped, crouched the way I was. I shifted my position a little. Then I squinted at my watch. Nine-thirty.

"Could be a little while till my friends get here," I said. "By the way, one of them *is* a cop."

"Good. I can have you arrested for assault with a deadly weapon."

I laughed, caught between disbelief in and something like admiration for his chutzpah. "Oh, sure."

"You think I'm joking?"

"You really do have balls," I said. "I have to give you credit. But I suppose that's the secret of your success. And you *are* successful—

there's no doubt about that." I frowned thoughtfully. "I know it's a vulgar question, but about how much are you worth?"

"About seven hundred million."

I clicked my tongue. "Imagine."

"I don't have to."

"All that money must give you a tremendous sense of power. More than any politician."

"Politicians are a dime a dozen."

I nodded. "Judges too. *They* can be bought."

He shot me a narrow look. "What do you mean by that?"

"Oh, nothing. A lot of judges are politicians, that's all."

"Yes."

Aware that my comment about judges had startled him, I wondered if an abrupt change of subject might have a similar effect. "Why did you warn me about the quarry? You could have let me run right over the edge."

He smiled. "And miss this scintillating conversation? Besides, you're no threat to me."

"Then why'd you run?"

"Wouldn't you? If someone was firing a gun in your direction?"

"I suppose I would," I conceded. "Take cover, anyway."

"Well, there you are."

"Right. Well, you certainly are a larger-than-life character. Nothing dime-a-dozen about you. I bet the Harvard Business School will do a case study on you one of these days." I gestured with the gun. "I mean, on how you built a seven-hundred-million-dollar real estate empire out of—what was it? A gravel-hauling business?"

"Mm-hmm."

"Amazing," I said. "By the way, I understand you're constructing a mall in East Cambridge. You and Arthur Barrow. One of the biggest in the Northeast."

"Mm-hmm."

"Part of it on the land you bought from Edward Hassler's widow."

"Oh, is there something illegal about buying land and building on it?"

"There is if you murder one of the owners. I bet Hassler himself didn't want to sell you the land, did he? So you had him eliminated."

"Ah," Gilmore said, in amused tones. "Is that how you figure it?"

With my free hand, I scratched my head. "I suppose poor Paula Young accidentally stumbled over some information that shed light on your involvement—and Barrow's—with the Hassler killing. So you had her knocked off, and then hired someone to ransack her apartment looking for a copy of whatever the incriminating stuff was."

Gilmore sat listening, smiling slightly. Perhaps it was the bad lighting, but his lips appeared to be turning blue. Well, dressed as he was, he had to be freezing. And his ankle had to be giving him agony, despite his massive control.

"Can I go back for a moment to Yolanda Sims?" I asked. Without waiting for his permission, I continued. "What I figure is, you got Parkes to hire Wally Duchesne to kill her. I assume you picked Duchesne 'cause he could be mistaken for the cop they charged with the murder. His name's Lingemann, by the way, not Lindman. As you damn well know."

"Your imagination's running away with you, dear."

"Not really. Let me go on. I guess Dalton Craig must have gotten greedy, and that's why you disposed of him. And Sims?" I shrugged. "You knocked her off primarily to get Lingemann out of the picture, but I bet she was becoming a pain in the ass, too. It's hard to do business with *undesirable* people, huh?"

I thought I saw Gilmore stiffen.

"No matter how you look at it," I said, "killing Sims and Craig was an economical move. Cost-effective. By the way, did Wally Duchesne do Craig as well as Sims? I bet he did."

"This," Gilmore said, "is a fantasy."

If only he'd known I was extrapolating from the tape of him and Parkes. "Let me ask you something else. Did it give you a twinge tonight when your chauffeur shot Parkes? I mean, you and he go back a long way. The guy went to prison for you. I know you made

him rich in return, but . . ." I shook my head slowly. "I guess Parkes
was getting greedy, too. Or was it just that he knew too much about
you?"

Gilmore smiled. "This is quite a villainous picture you're painting
of me."

"I think it's a very accurate portrait," I said. "But let's not get off
the subject. There was one thing that puzzled me for a little while.
I couldn't figure out why the hell you just didn't kill Lieutenant
Lingemann right off instead of rigging up the whole charade with
Dalton Craig and Yolanda Sims. Then I realized that you were
probably shrewd enough to know that when a cop gets murdered, the
investigation never stops. And it *could* have led back to you, eventually."

"Oh, really," Gilmore said. He sounded bored.

"But now," I continued, "I don't think it's so much that you were
being shrewd. I think you were being arrogant. I think you liked
pulling all those strings. It was like a really elaborate business deal.
Like setting up a competitor and knocking him down. A hostile
takeover. Somebody once told me you had an ego the size of Rhode
Island. I bet it got a big charge out of getting Lingemann arrested and
thrown in jail. Plus making all the other players dance to your tune.
And then getting rid of them when they'd served their purposes.
People with your kind of money just assume that everything else
exists for their amusement, their benefit, don't they?" I gestured
again with the gun. "Don't they?"

"This was amusing at first," Gilmore said. "Now it's only tire-
some. When will the help you say is coming get here?"

"Soon enough." I grinned at him. "And since it *will* be soon, I
have a parting comment for you."

"I'm not interested in hearing it."

"You're dumb, Gilmore."

He was silent and motionless, ignoring me.

"Yeah, you are," I said. "I guess you figured that if you got
Lingemann into jail and off the Hassler case, nobody else would
connect you and FSX to Hassler. Well, guess what, dummy? *I* did.

The cop your chauffeur shot tonight did. So did the cop who'll be along in about two minutes. So did two newspaper reporters. You think we'll keep it a secret?"

Gilmore looked straight at me then. "You can prove nothing."

"That's *your* fantasy, buddy."

He raised his eyes, as if appealing to the heavens.

"You got a tip-off from someone in the DA's office that Lingemann was going to work exclusively on the Hassler case," I said. "And then, after you set up Lingemann's arrest, you bribed the judge to make sure he didn't get out on bail."

Gilmore sighed.

"I know I'm trying your patience," I said. "But bear with me. Your patience isn't the only thing that's going to be tried. Because guess what, asshole?"

I rose, reached into my purse, and with my free hand hauled out the tape recorder. "See this? Know what's on it? The entire conversation you had with Parkes back in that French restaurant in Acton. Lots of good stuff there. I especially like the part where you tell Parkes how you're going to have Lieutenant Lingemann killed in jail. Nice. It'll make great listening for the honest people in the DA's office. The vast majority of them *are* honest, you know. But trust you to find the resident sleaze. Just like you knew a corruptible judge. Oh, yeah, that's on the tape, too. How you paid off Judge Sanger to make sure Lieutenant Lingemann didn't get any bail."

Gilmore's face was blank. I squatted down in front of him. "You know, Gilmore, you may be a legendary tycoon and a hell of a smart operator and a resourceful multiple murderer, but you have one fundamental thing in common with every other two-bit moronic slimeball dirtbag of a killer who ever came down the pike. You talk too goddamn much. Sooner or later all of you cockroaches have to shoot off your mouths and—"

He launched himself off the rock on his good leg and came at me. I fell back onto the snowy ground with him on top of me. The gun flew out of my hand to God knew where. He was a big man, taller

and even heavier than Jack. His weight made my ribs compress and the air go out of my lungs.

"I'll kill *you* now," he said through his teeth. "*Give me that tape.*"

My left hand held the recorder. He grabbed my wrist and banged it on the ground.

With my right hand, I grabbed his ear and yanked as hard as I could. Then I clawed my nails down the side of his face. He jerked his head back, and I bucked like someone undergoing electroshock.

There was probably more adrenaline than blood boiling through my system.

He let go of my wrist and backhanded me across the mouth. My vision went blurry. I squirmed my legs out from beneath his and rammed the heel of my hand up against his chin. We rolled onto our sides. He grabbed my arm and twisted it. I put my knee into his groin. He flopped over onto his back, and I straddled his chest.

My lip had been cut when he backhanded me, and I could feel the blood running down my chin. I pounded my right fist into his nose, and felt something yield squashily.

I flung the tape recorder into the bushes behind me, praying that the leather casing around it would protect the tape inside the machine from serious damage.

Gilmore grabbed my right wrist and gave it a tremendous pull, not so much dragging me as hurling me off him. I landed on the base of my spine.

Why hadn't I shot him when I'd had the chance?

He had a knee on either side of me and his hands were grappling at my throat. I pulled my chin down. Blood from his nose dripped onto my face. I grabbed both his ears and thrust my knee up again between his legs. His hands still at my neck, he lifted my head and knocked it against the ground.

Then I did something that even today, when I think about it, turns my stomach.

I jabbed a thumb into his eye.

He screamed and let go of my neck and toppled sideways. I rolled away from him and lay with my face pressed into the crook of my

arm, my breath sobbing in and out of me. Then I pushed myself to my knees, my head swaying back and forth like that of a wounded animal.

I looked over at Gilmore. He was standing five feet away, trying to remain upright on his one good leg. The other would bend, and he'd try to straighten it, and it would give yet again. His hands were clamped over his eyes.

I got to my feet, slowly and unsteadily. "Gilmore," I said. I took a lurching step toward him. He swayed an equivalent step backward.

And kept going.

Careful where you walk. We're on the edge of a quarry. A deep one.

"Gilmore," I screamed.

For an instant he hovered on the brink, arms outflung as if to beat winglike the chill air. Then the blackness swallowed him.

A second later, I heard a thud like someone dropping a meal sack on concrete.

I slumped to the ground and put my face in my hands. The woods seemed to close around me. I could taste my own blood. Or maybe Gilmore's. I turned and spat violently.

There was a furious crashing in the bushes behind me. Then I felt a hand on my shoulder. I looked up blearily.

Joanne knelt beside me. "Jesus Christ, what happened?" she said.

I shook my head. "Gilmore's dead."

"What?"

I pointed to the lip of the quarry. "We were fighting. He went over."

Joanne stared at me for a moment. Then she rose, and walked carefully to the rim of the quarry.

I heard some more rustling, and Harvey pushed his way through the brambles into the clearing.

"Liz, you okay?"

"Yeah, I'm fine." I was stabbing my thumb repeatedly into the snow, trying to cleanse it of the blood and whatever from Gilmore's eye.

"What . . . ?"

"Gilmore tried to get the tape recorder away from me. We struggled. He tried to strangle me. I put a thumb in his eye. He fell in that pit. He's dead."

Harvey looked from me to Joanne and back again. I scooped up some snow and scrubbed my face with it, hard. The cold stung my cut and puffed lip. Then I felt the back of my head. There was a bump there. I'd probably gotten it when Gilmore had banged my head against the ground.

Harvey went to the quarry edge and stood alongside Joanne. I got up and plodded over to where I thought the tape recorder had landed. On the way, I found the gun. The tape recorder was caked with snow. I wiped it off on my coat and shoved it into my bag. Thank God I'd secured the purse strap underneath my epaulet. Otherwise it would have been long gone.

Joanne and Harvey came back to me. Harvey put his arm around me.

"Self-defense," Joanne said. "We saw the whole thing. Didn't we, Harv?"

He nodded.

"Thanks," I said.

"You know, Liz, if Gilmore had lived to be arrested and charged and tried, he might have beaten it."

"I know." I raised my head. "How's Sam? Is—he's all right? Is he?"

"John took him to Emerson Hospital in Concord," Joanne said. "Other than that, we don't know."

"I never killed anyone before," I said. I was suddenly so exhausted I could barely speak.

"Me neither," Joanne said softly.

We looked at each other.

I shivered.

"Come on," Harvey said. "Let's go." He used his arm to turn me around, away from the quarry.

We crossed the clearing silently.

"Watch it here," Harvey said, at the entrance to the path. "Kind of slippery." He pushed some brambles aside.

"Wait a minute, wait a minute," I said.

I knelt and brushed the snow from the ground in front of me. Then I scratched at the earth until I had a handful of dirt. I stood and walked to the edge of the quarry. I flung the dirt down where Gilmore's body had disappeared.

"Rot in hell, you bastard," I said.

34

"GLAD to be back?" I asked.

Jack shoved some papers into a manila folder, slapped it shut, and sent it scooting sideways across the desk. "Glad to be back."

"Even if you have to spend half the day arranging vacation schedules?"

"Even so."

I reached across the desk and patted his hand. "Well, it's good to see you restored to your proper place."

We both smiled.

It was a month to the day after Gilmore's death. The cut on my lip had long since healed. Most of the less visible damage hadn't.

"I think there's some fresh coffee," Jack said. "Want a cup?"

"Sure."

He got up and left the office. I put my feet on the corner of the desk, leaned back in my chair, and looked out of the window. I found myself thinking, as I often did, about the events of the last four weeks.

The tape had gone to the district attorney's office. Of course, I'd thought its contents would get Jack released in five minutes. That didn't happen. What did happen was that they went looking for Wally Duchesne. They didn't find him. That didn't surprise me. Guys like Duchesne always disappeared.

They had a little better luck when they went to talk to Arthur

Barrow. At first he denied all knowledge of anything to do with the murders of Hassler, Young, Sims, and Craig. But they kept bracing him and he finally caved. And once he started talking, they couldn't shut him up. What he said confirmed and supplemented everything I'd gotten on the tape from Gilmore and Parkes. According to Barrow, it had been Duchesne who'd killed Craig as well as Sims, because—as I'd figured—Craig had been agitating for more money than Gilmore was willing to give him. Craig had also been the one to coach Yolanda Sims in how to bring a convincing-sounding rape charge against Jack. He would know.

Gilmore's chauffeur had done the bludgeon job on Paula Young and the trashing of her apartment and the three others on Trowbridge Street. He'd also planted the explosive in Edward Hassler's car.

The chauffeur, Richard Warner, was an interesting case. Forty-five years old, he was a Vietnam vet and a former Golden Gloves champ, heavyweight division. In 1975, he'd been arrested for, charged with, tried for, and convicted of attempted murder, and had ended up serving seven years in Attica. After his release, he'd drifted north to Boston, and in 1983 had been hired by one of Gilmore's companies as a trucker. Gilmore had hired him as chauffeur/bodyguard in 1984.

In the army, he'd been a specialist in demolitions.

Naturally, Barrow claimed to have found out all this stuff after the fact. Also naturally, he'd been shocked and horrified. When they asked him why, if he'd been so appalled, he hadn't gone straight to the police, he had no response.

He also claimed not to have any idea why Gilmore had had Warner kill Paula Young.

He was arrested and charged with four counts of being an accessory after the fact to murder.

They showed a photograph of Wally Duchesne to Mrs. George Watson. She identified it as being of the man she'd seen going into Yolanda Sim's house.

So, finally, they set Jack loose.

I suggested we take a vacation. He wanted to go back to work. He went back to work.

I myself was in no legal trouble whatsoever. Everyone agreed that a woman being strangled is entitled to fight off her attacker. If he falls off a cliff afterward, that's not her fault.

I did have to testify before a grand jury, though. But the way the prosecutor phrased his questions, my only possible answers made me sound like Mother Teresa.

Harvey and John were having a splendid time writing their stories. I read them every day. I had the feeling I was witnessing a duel for the next Pulitzer. Maybe they could split it. They both deserved it.

Joanne was back plugging away in narcotics. The difference was, nobody was giving her any shit anymore. She'd dropped a bad guy, with a single bullet in the dark.

Sam was still in the hospital, bitching because they wanted to keep him there another week. He'd nearly died.

Judge Milton Sanger was being investigated on charges of accepting bribes.

There was a special task force assiduously looking for the leak in the DA's office. Since there were more than three hundred people working out of the office, figuring out who'd been on Gilmore's payroll would probably take a while.

There was a warrant out on Wally Duchesne.

Jack came back into the office with the coffee. He handed me mine. I smiled.

"We doing anything tonight?" he asked.

"Well, that singer who sounds like Sarah Vaughan is at Ryle's. You want to go?"

He nodded. "Sounds good. Should we eat there, too?" He sat down behind his desk and began shuffling through the huge pile of papers on the blotter.

There was a light tap on the door. We both looked up. In the entrance to the office stood a slender woman of medium height, with curly brown hair and a pale, lightly freckled face. Her eyes were large and blue. She was perhaps in her early or mid-forties, and attractive.

She also looked familiar. I peered at her a little harder. And then I recognized her.

"Lieutenant Lingemann?"

Jack stood up and smiled. "Yes?"

"May I speak with you?"

He waved her into the office. I rose so she could have the visitor's chair.

"I'll step outside," I offered.

"No," the woman said. "Stay."

I looked at Jack. He gave the merest hint of a shrug, and I went over to stand by the filing cabinet. The woman sat down in the chair I'd just vacated.

"I'm Linda Crosbie," the woman said. "Head of the Citizens' Committee Against Police Repression."

"I know," said Jack.

Linda Crosbie's already large eyes grew larger.

"Not because I've been keeping tabs on you," Jack said. His tone was serious, but he had the expression of someone trying not to laugh. "But I *have* heard of you. And I've seen you on the TV news."

"Yes," Crosbie said. "You would have." She fiddled with the clasp on her shoulder bag. I leaned against the filing cabinet.

"This is difficult," Crosbie said.

Jack said nothing.

She lifted her head and looked at him directly, steadily.

"I want to apologize," she said.

The repressed amusement was gone from Jack's face.

"I shouldn't have been so quick"—she raised her hand and then let it drop—"I shouldn't have been so quick to accept Yolanda Sims's story."

Jack inclined his head slightly.

Crosbie took a deep breath. "I was wrong. I'm sorry."

"I see."

She exhaled softly. "I'm afraid I've caused you a great deal of trouble and embarrassment."

Jack made a dismissive gesture. "Well, it's over. Anyway"—he

grinned, suddenly and surprisingly—"you turned out to be the least of my worries."

Crosbie looked startled. Then she shook her head slowly. "You're being very nice about this."

Jack shrugged, more obviously this time. "It's over," he repeated. She smiled.

"Thanks for coming by," he said.

Crosbie stood. So did Jack. She hesitated a moment, and then held out her hand. He took it, and they shook hands across his desk.

"And, Lieutenant?" she said, rising and going to the door.

"Yes?"

"This doesn't mean my committee and I won't continue to keep an eye on what goes on in this department."

"Your privilege," Jack said.

She nodded, and left.

I pushed myself off the filing cabinet. "I wonder how she'll feel if she ever gets mugged, or her house gets broken into."

Jack laughed. "Drink your coffee," he said. "It's getting cold."

"Actually," I said, "it took guts for her to come here."

"Yeah."

"And you," I said. "You were particularly saintly in dealing with her. 'It's over.' God!"

"Well, what was I supposed to do? Beat her up?"

I shook my head and resumed the visitor's chair. He started riffling through some more papers. I finished my coffee and tossed the cup into the wastebasket. Then I put my elbow on the edge of the desk and my chin in my hand.

I must have sighed without knowing it, because Jack said, "What's the matter?"

I raised my chin, startled. "Huh?"

"What're you moaning and groaning about?"

"Oh, nothing. It's just . . ."

"Yes?"

"Oh, I wish there were a better resolution to the Paula Young business, that's all."

Jack gave me an odd look. "We know who killed her. And why."

"I know, I know. I just wish that piece of evidence or whatever would turn up—something by which we could link Barrow and Gilmore."

"I'm sure they destroyed it."

"If they hadn't, Barrow could be charged with conspiracy to commit murder. Or even murder. Couldn't he?"

Jack smiled. "He's in pretty deep shit as it is."

"Yeah. I guess."

Jack got up, walked around the desk, and put his hand on my shoulder. "Be happy with what we have. I sure as hell am." He stroked my hair. "You solved a string of very bad crimes. You got me out of jail. Nobody else. Just you."

"Well, I had help. But you know why I did it."

"Yes. I do."

I sighed again.

After a moment, Jack said, "I know what's bothering you. I've always known."

I was silent.

"I've been through it, too, you know."

I nodded.

He sat down on the desk, facing me, and took both my hands in his. "It doesn't seem like it now," he said, "but you will come to terms with it eventually. It'll take a while, but you will."

"I'm okay."

"Got that right." He gave my hands a final squeeze and released them.

I rose. "I should be getting along." I hugged him. "See you later. It's nice to be able to say that, isn't it?"

He laughed. "It is."

I left his office and went down the old cast-iron stairs. It was ten to four and the shift was changing. A lot of the younger night officers

just coming on were former students of mine in the police academy. They'd always been very friendly, but now there was a slight difference in the way they treated me. It was as if I were more . . . one of them than just a well-liked outsider.

I hadn't lied to Jack about being okay. I was. I was fine. Jack was free and nothing else mattered.

But I couldn't imagine the day when I wouldn't wake up remembering that because I loved one man, I killed another.

ABOUT THE AUTHOR

SUSAN KELLY's first Liz Connors novel, *The Gemini Man*, was nominated by the World Mystery Convention for an Anthony Award for best first novel of 1985 and was one of the top-ten books in the National Mystery Readers Poll for the same year. Kelly has a Ph.D. from the University of Edinburgh and has taught at Tufts University and the Harvard Business School. She has been a consultant to the Massachusetts Criminal Justice Training Council and a lecturer in arrest/incident and criminal-investigation report writing at the Cambridge (Massachusetts) Police Academy. She lives in Cambridge, Massachusetts.